continued . . .

BLOOD ORANGE BREWING

Tea Shop Mystery #7

LAURA CHILDS

BERKLEY PRIME CRIME, NEW YORK

THE BERKLEY PUBLISHING GROUP
Published by the Penguin Group
Penguin Group (USA) Inc.
375 Hudson Street, New York, New York 10014, USA
Penguin Group (Canada), 90 Eglinton Avenue East, Suite 700, Toronto, Ontario M4P 2Y3, Canada
(a division of Pearson Penguin Canada Inc.)
Penguin Books Ltd., 80 Strand, London WC2R 0RL, England
Penguin Group Ireland, 25 St. Stephen's Green, Dublin 2, Ireland (a division of Penguin Books Ltd.)
Penguin Group (Australia), 250 Camberwell Road, Camberwell, Victoria 3124, Australia
(a division of Pearson Australia Group Pty. Ltd.)
Penguin Books India Pvt. Ltd., 11 Community Centre, Panchsheel Park, New Delhi—110 017, India
Penguin Group (NZ), 67 Apollo Drive, Mairangi Bay, Auckland 1310, New Zealand
(a division of Pearson New Zealand Ltd.)
Penguin Books (South Africa) (Pty.) Ltd., 24 Sturdee Avenue, Rosebank, Johannesburg 2196,
South Africa

Penguin Books Ltd., Registered Offices: 80 Strand, London WC2R 0RL, England

This is a work of fiction. Names, characters, places, and incidents either are the product of the author's imagination or are used fictitiously, and any resemblance to actual persons, living or dead, business establishments, events, or locales is entirely coincidental. The publisher does not have any control over and does not assume any responsibility for author or third-party websites or their content.

PUBLISHER'S NOTE: The recipes contained in this book are to be followed exactly as written. The publisher is not responsible for your specific health or allergy needs that may require medical supervision. The publisher is not responsible for any adverse reactions to the recipes contained in this book.

BLOOD ORANGE BREWING

A Berkley Prime Crime Book / published by arrangement with the author

PRINTING HISTORY
Berkley Prime Crime hardcover edition / April 2006
Berkley Prime Crime mass-market edition / March 2007

Copyright © 2006 by Gerry Schmitt & Associates, Inc.
Cover art by Stephanie Henderson.
Cover design by Lesley Worrell.

ISBN: 978-0-425-21057-4

BERKLEY® PRIME CRIME
Berkley Prime Crime Books are published by The Berkley Publishing Group,
a division of Penguin Group (USA) Inc.,
375 Hudson Street, New York, New York 10014.
The name BERKLEY PRIME CRIME and the BERKLEY PRIME CRIME design
are trademarks belonging to Penguin Group (USA) Inc.

PRINTED IN THE UNITED STATES OF AMERICA

10   9   8   7   6   5   4

This book is dedicated to Jennie and Elmo.

ACKNOWLEDGMENTS

My thanks to some very special people: my agent, Sam Pinkus; my editor, Samantha Mandor; my husband, Bob; my sister, Jennie; and Lillian in North Charleston for all her help. My heartfelt thanks also goes to all the "tea ladies," those hard-working tea shop owners, tea retailers, and tea publishers—entrepreneurs all—who continue to help foster the gentle art of tea.

The poem "Tea," from which Drayton freely quotes, was written by Robert Ford and appears in the book *Tea Poetry*, a compilation of tea poems by Pearl Dexter, Olde English Tea Company, Inc.

1

"Fascinating," declared Theodosia Browning as her quizzical blue eyes roved about the hexagon shaped room. Packed with antique medical instruments, colorful jars, and old anatomical charts, the tucked-away alcove must have been the old surgical suite back when this Victorian-style Charleston home had been a hospital almost a century and a half ago, Theodosia decided. Its builder and owner had made a fortune in early pharmaceuticals and patent drugs. *Because, lord, have mercy,* she told herself, *this is what medical facilities were like in the 1860s.*

"This place totally gives me the creeps," whispered Haley Parker. She was awed by the strange surroundings and strobelike effect of the candles and somewhat freaked out by the cloudy specimen jars in which floated bits and fragments of unrecognizable objects.

"Think about it, Haley," said Theodosia, studying a long, tubelike stethoscope carved from elephant ivory. "If you had a serious medical problem like a ruptured appendix or a broken leg, you'd be grateful for whatever medical know-how was available. Even if it was the 1860s variety."

Haley gave a resolute shake of her head. "Not me," she said. "I'd rather rely on herbs and natural remedies. Things you could find in the forest to knock back inflammation or infection."

Theodosia nodded and her lush auburn hair casually brushed her shoulders. Thick, bordering on bountiful, it framed her oval face and gave her a pre-Raphaelite look. Theodosia's hair was inherited from a grandmother who'd bragged about breaking combs, and her fair skin was also a by-product of her English-Irish ancestors.

Theodosia understood where Haley was coming from. Ever since she'd opened the Indigo Tea Shop in Charleston's historic district, she, too, had been fascinated by the curative powers of various teas, tisanes, and herbs. For example, a simple brew of chamomile tea went a long way to alleviate anxiety and insomnia. While meadowsweet tea was often the perfect antidote to a nasty headache.

"We'd better get back," suggested Haley. "Here we are, playing explorer in this old house just as Delaine's fancy Candlelight Concert is about to get under way. Can't you just hear Drayton fussing and muttering because we're not there to help him?"

"You're probably right," agreed Theodosia. "Although Drayton always does a masterful job even if we're not around to chatter at him." She cast a final inquiring glance at a surgical set that glinted hypnotically from its purple velvet case on a narrow sideboard. "But this room with its antique medical instruments really *is* quite remarkable."

Negotiating their way through the library, dining room, and center hallway where throngs of well-heeled guests mingled and chatted, Theodosia and Haley finally made their way to the small side parlor near the front of the old house. There, Drayton Conneley, professional tea taster and Indigo Tea Shop right-hand man, was fretting away in his own inimitable style. Bone china cups were getting a final fastidious wipe, candles were being carefully positioned in silver candelabras, and floral bouquets were being arranged just so. Drayton had even discovered a narrow back passageway to the old kitchen. So most of the food and tea that would be served here tonight had been stashed back there where it could be prepped and staged.

"Theodosia," came Drayton's pleading tone as he noted her approach. "Where have you been? Your presence is *needed.*" He glanced at Haley. "Yours, too, Miss Parker. If you don't mind."

"Pop a chill pill, Drayton," joked Haley as she shook back her long mane of stick-straight hair and subtly repositioned a sugar bowl on his elegantly set table. "We're not going to be serving guests for at least another hour. Besides, we're supposed to have a little fun tonight."

Drayton lifted his grizzled head and leveled a steady gaze at Haley. In his mid-sixties, clad in a tweed jacket and omnipresent bow tie, Drayton was the picture of discombobulated decorum. "Why do you taunt me like this?" he asked as one eyebrow pulled itself into a furry arc. "Have I wronged you in some way? Has my efficiency offended you?" Drayton slid the sugar bowl back into its original position and gave her a knowing smile.

"It's just good sport, Drayton," said Haley. "Just sport."

Even though they were the best of friends, Haley loved nothing better than to chide Drayton about his fastidiousness and over-the-top work ethic. But, truth be known, once Haley assumed dominion in her small but well-provisioned kitchen at the Indigo Tea Shop, she herself turned into a virtual martinet. Tasked with baking the lemon cream scones, cranberry muffins, almond trifle cakes, and all the other sumptuous goodies that the Indigo Tea Shop served up daily to its delighted customers, Haley herself was hard-working, sharply focused, and, some might even say, slightly dictatorial when it came to food preparation and service.

Theodosia beamed as the two of them stood shoulder to shoulder, arguing in their easy, bantering way. She was no stranger to this magical friction of personalities that added creativity, vigor, and chutzpah to the mix. A few years ago, when Theodosia's dream morphed into the reality of opening the Indigo Tea Shop on Charleston's historic Church Street, Drayton and Haley had both been at the top of her "to hire" list.

Drayton Conneley had been working as catering manager at one of Charleston's finer hotels, but Theodosia knew his courtly manners and eloquent bearing would appeal to her customers. Plus, Drayton had grown up on a tea plantation in China, worked in the tea industry, and attended the great tea auctions in Amsterdam. So his wealth of knowledge made him a natural for master-minding tea blends and conducting tea tastings.

Haley Parker had been and still was attending college

part-time, but her prodigious baking skills and youthful enthusiasm made her a prime candidate.

Luckily for Theodosia, she never had to twist any arms to get them on board. And smart cookies that they were, Drayton and Haley had also seen the handwriting on the wall. They understood that the gentle art of tea was big and getting bigger, growing into a marvelous, daily ritual that was happily engulfing the country. Because whatever it was in today's society that drove people to distraction—the hustlebustle 24/7 pace of modern life, stress-filled jobs, multiple responsibilities—women (and plenty of men, too) were finding respite and solace in tea rooms.

A tea shop, especially Theodosia's Indigo Tea Shop, was a place that just naturally granted patrons the permission to slow down. To sit at one of the little wooden tables impeccably set with sterling silver and bone china. To appreciate the way the sunlight filtered through the old leaded-glass windows, breathe in the aroma of fresh tea and engage in relaxing conversation. And, of course, there was the major diversion of partaking in a languid three-course, four-course, or even six-course tea menu. A menu that began with fruit or cream scones accompanied by billowing poufs of Devonshire cream and strawberry jam. Then segued into three-tiered trays laden with cucumber sandwiches, smoked salmon pinwheels, individual cheese and mushroom quiches, and other mouth-watering savories. Of course, an Indigo Tea Shop grand finale always included sinfully rich desserts such as chocolate truffles, raspberry cobbler, apricot tortes, or miniature almond cakes.

"Delaine's going to be thrilled," said Theodosia, gazing at Drayton's gleaming table. He'd brought along a large, formal sterling silver tea server that tilted on a fulcrum to pour out a steady stream of fresh-brewed tea. Positioned in the middle of a large table covered by a hand-embroidered linen tablecloth, the server was flanked by heroically tall bouquets of roses and lilies. And once candles were lit and crystal bowls and pitchers filled with sugar cubes, pouring cream, slices of lemon, and Devonshire cream, the effect would be one of sparkling elegance. Old world but so very inviting, too.

"Did I hear my name mentioned?" drawled a soft voice.

"Delaine," said Drayton. "Speak of the devil."

Delaine Dish, proprietor of Cotton Duck Clothing and the instigator of tonight's Candlelight Concert, came slithering up to the table. "Devil?" she said, a mischievous grin lighting her lovely, heart-shaped face. "Is that what you think I am, really?"

"Dear lady," replied Drayton, extending his arms in a theatrical manner. "In reality you are a much-loved savior and delirious workaholic. If it were not for you this poor house that has been so generously donated to the Heritage Society would still be sitting empty, looking forlorn and utterly abandoned."

"It *was* wonderful of you to volunteer to head up the Restoration Committee," added Theodosia. Delaine might be a social butterfly with a flippant manner and a penchant for attractive bachelors, but she was also a whiz at taking charge of committees and raising stupendous amounts of money for worthwhile causes.

Delaine cocked her head and gazed around. "This house is *still* in a miserable state of disrepair," she told them. "But I am making it my mission in life to raise enough funds to at least have this main floor restored to its former grandeur. Once that happens we shall open the house for tours and begin to charge a small admission fee. Of course, it's too late to include it in this autumn's Lamplighter Tour, but maybe next year." Delaine smiled and held up a carefully manicured index finger to punctuate her sentence. "By that time the Augustus Chait House should be able to sustain itself as a tourist attraction and going concern."

Theodosia grinned. All in all, Delaine had come up with a fairly workable business plan.

"You're going to have to twist the arms of a lot of high-powered business people just to get this main floor in shape," said Drayton.

Delaine threw him a Cheshire cat smile. "Look around." She waved an imperious arm at the crowd that was milling about, sipping flutes of champagne. "See those people? Feel that buzz of excitement? Those aren't just *business* people out there," she drawled. "Those are captains of industry as well as important Southern politicos. We've got doctors, attorneys, giants from the computer industry, even television executives here tonight."

Drayton peered owlishly over the top of his half-glasses. "Well, when you put it that way . . ." he began.

"You see that fellow over there?" snapped Delaine. "The one in the cashmere jacket?"

Theodosia, Drayton, and Haley followed Delaine's triumphant gaze toward a tall, good-looking ginger-haired man who was holding court with two attractive women. Broad-shouldered yet sleek, the man had a well-bred, almost patrician air about him. Like he might be a wealthy plantation owner or someone to the manor born.

"That's Clive Bonham," bragged Delaine. "*Congressman* Clive Bonham."

"Ah, yes," said Drayton. "As it so happens, we're going to

be catering a tea for the congressman this week. A *political* tea, I believe." Curling his lip slightly, Drayton pronounced the word political as though he were referring to a piece of slightly overripened fish.

"And standing over there," Delaine continued, pointing to a dark-haired man who sported a pencil mustache and what looked like a perpetual sun tan, "is Jock Rowley, the real estate developer."

"Good heavens," said Drayton. "Not the same Jock Rowley who put up those awful time-share condos on the Isle of Palms!"

"Why are you always so all-fired opposed to progress?" demanded Delaine. "Nothing gets accomplished without progress. Haven't you ever heard the phrase, *You've got to break a few eggs to make an omelet?*"

"None of us are opposed to progress," said Theodosia, stepping in. "But when quaint beach houses are torn down to make way for ticky-tack, Monopoly-board structures, and access to all those picturesque little creeks and inlets is denied, it's rather upsetting."

"To us and the environment," said Drayton unhappily. "So, you see, it's really not an omelet at all. More like scrambled eggs."

"Mmm," said Delaine as a middle-aged man in a preppy-looking navy blazer approached her with a slightly tentative air.

"Delaine?" asked the man, extending his hand.

"Oh, my goodness!" exclaimed Delaine as she clasped the man's hand and pumped it. "Look who's here! Corky Chait, our illustrious donor! Come, come," she urged him. "You must meet everyone." And she made hasty introductions to Theodosia, Drayton, and Haley.

"Corky and I have met before," Drayton told the group once the handshakes were completed and Delaine had distributed a sufficient amount of air kisses. "We served on a youth orchestra committee together."

"Indeed, we did," said Corky, smiling and showing a heroic array of teeth. "Back when I was still flying for Transcon Airlines. Although Drayton displayed a far better understanding than I of how to help foster the arts."

"It's so generous of you to donate this house to the Heritage Society," Theodosia told Corky. "I've been a member of the Heritage Society for almost five years now and, I must say, this has to be the most magnificent donation they've ever received." As Corky graciously demurred, Theodosia was imbued with a feeling of warmth. Here was a person who was both social and civic-minded. He probably could have sold this old house and realized a very tidy profit. Instead, he made a generous donation that would be appreciated for generations to come.

Delaine seemed to read Theodosia's thoughts: "A house is such a living, tangible memorial," she told Corky. "Although the city of Charleston has always done a masterful job in preserving historic homes, your donation of this grand old Victorian helps assure the integrity of our historic district." Though Delaine's words had the ring of a canned chamber of commerce speech, Corky still looked pleased.

"Thank you," he said. "But to be completely honest, the bequest had already been written into my grandfather's will. He was the one who selected the Heritage Society as beneficiary."

"Your grandfather passed away recently?" asked Theodosia.

"Two months ago," answered Corky. "Jedediah lived to the ripe old age of ninety-six. A truly amazing man."

"You have our sympathy," murmured Theodosia.

"Thank you," said Corky. "But realize, my wife and I probably would have donated the house *anyway*. We really had
no use for it. And the Heritage Society is *such* a worthwhile
cause."

"Theodosia," said Drayton, "you know Corky's wife,
Claudia, don't you? She owns Le Nest, that lovely little shop
over on Society Street. In fact, this is one of her tablecloths
that we're using tonight." He gestured at his tea table.

"Of course," said Theodosia. "I've stopped by Le Nest two
or three times since it opened." She threw Corky a questioning glance. "Is Claudia here tonight?"

Corky shook his head. "Unfortunately, Claudia had to su-
pervise a newly arrived shipment at our warehouse. She's just
back from a nonstop buying trip which has pretty much led
to a complete overhaul in her merchandise mix at Le Nest.
Before, her focus was on Porthault and Pratesi sheets along
with European toiletries and French-milled soaps. Now she's
carrying handmade European linens, trousseau sets, antique
fabrics, brocade and lace table linens, and French herbs. Oh,
and tea towels. You should see her collection of tea towels!"

"Are you serious?" squealed Theodosia. "Tea towels are
an absolute passion of mine!"

"Then you'd better stop by," said Corky, as a small knot
of people pressed up behind him, obviously eager to chat. "I
know she just received some new ones from Les Olivades."
He began to edge away. "Talk to you all later? After the
concert?"

"Count on it," said Drayton. "We'll be right here serving
tea and our special scones."

They all murmured their good-byes and then Corky
moved on to chat with another group of well-wishers.

"Nice fellow," said Drayton. "What does he do now?"

"Corky imports exotic woods from South America," said Delaine. "I believe he sells mostly to high-end builders. As you know, so many home owners today want special cabinetry or exotic inlaid flooring or wine tasting rooms."

"I didn't know that," said Drayton, who also lived in a Civil War–era dwelling, though his home was extremely small and austere compared to the one they were in this evening.

Posturing grandly, Delaine turned to Theodosia. "You haven't said boo about my dress, honey." Then, before Theodosia had a chance to make any comment at all concerning Delaine's reddish-orange, form-hugging cocktail dress, Delaine went on: "Isn't it smashing? Chiffon cut on the bias. And such a vibrant color. I do love vibrant colors."

"It's beautiful," murmured Theodosia, who was wearing a silver shift with matching stilettos, also from Delaine's shop.

"I'd call it blood orange, just like the tea we'll be serving this evening," Drayton told her.

Delaine let out a high tinkling laugh. "Blood orange, gunpowder green, golden tips, red raspberry . . . your teas always sound like such wonderful colors. *Fashion* colors."

"I suppose that's the beauty of tea," agreed Drayton. "With each sip, tiny explosions of taste and color delight the senses and intrigue the palette. The smoky flavor of gunpowder tea, the sweet fruitiness from Assam golden tips, the rich, ripe flavors from teas and infusions containing bits of raspberry or peaches. Oh, I could go on . . ."

"Please don't," said Delaine. She touched a hand to a matching silk rose that was pinned just below her left shoulder. "And did you notice? I had this flower made to match.

Flower pins are still so popular. I've been selling *gazillions* of them at Cotton Duck." Delaine's boutique was one of the premier clothing shops in Charleston.

"They sell them at Bow Geste, too," volunteered Haley. Located just down the street from the Indigo Tea Shop, Bow Geste was a hat and accessory shop.

Rolling her eyes, Delaine looked decidedly peeved. "Yes," she said. "But those are undoubtedly *commercially* made. Whereas this particular flower was pleated by hand. A true work of art."

"Speaking of works of art," said Theodosia, eager to change the subject and move on, "I can't wait to see the marvelous tea towels Claudia has in her store."

Delaine focused bright eyes on Theodosia "What did you call them, dear? *Tea* towels? I suppose that sort of thing is interesting if you're an old-fashioned gal who like to fuss over towels and napkins. Or enjoys little convent-stitched items."

"You don't have to be old-fashioned to love fine linens," said Haley a trifle defensively. She'd been fairly quiet until now.

"You know what I mean," said Delaine in a breezy tone. "It's wonderful to have a beautifully turned out table, but all that *washing and ironing* of linens. Makes me wilt just thinking about it!" Delaine whirled on her stiletto heels. "Oh, good heavens! There's that society photographer. I was so hoping he'd show up."

"*So what's the* drill tonight?" asked Haley, once Delaine had rushed off.

Drayton glanced across the hallway where four dozen or so folding chairs had been set up in the large library. The chairs all faced the far end of the room where an oversized fireplace with a dazzling black granite mantle served as focal point. Timothy Neville, the octogenarian director of the Heritage Society, had set up music stands and chairs in front of that great fireplace for his string quartet, which would be playing shortly. Timothy's group, of which he was the violinist, was scheduled to play for approximately forty minutes. Then Delaine would give a short speech and invite all the guests to partake of tea and refreshments. And once everyone was relaxed and sipping tea, Delaine planned to work the room, making her appeal for donations to help complete much-needed renovations on the house.

"To be honest," said Drayton, glancing around, "we're fairly well set. While the concert is in progress I'll putter around in the kitchen. You know, heat water for tea, set out the scones and tea sandwiches on trays. Then, once Timothy strikes his final chord and Delaine chats for a few moments, you two can jump up and help me serve. Oh, and I'll be sure to pull these pocket doors closed so I won't disrupt the concert."

"I can help you in the kitchen," volunteered Haley. "I don't mind."

"Don't be silly," said Drayton. "Enjoy the concert. Go out and mingle with Delaine's captains of industry."

"Can I get a quick shot of you three?" asked the photographer who suddenly loomed in front of them. Clutching a small but expensive-looking digital camera and wearing a khaki photojournalist vest, the photographer also had two traditional Nikons slung casually about his neck.

"Why not?" said Theodosia, as she, Drayton, and Haley edged closer to each other from their vantage point behind the tea table.

"Good," said the photographer, a brusque-looking man with slicked back hair and olive skin. "Closer, please. Smile. Perfect!" he declared with enthusiasm as he clicked off a few shots then bounded off to stalk his next quarry.

"Who was *that*?" asked Drayton, somewhat taken aback.

"Are you kidding?" said Haley. "That's Bill Glass, our own local paparazzi. You know who he is, don't you? Besides being a self-professed society photographer, he also publishes that little weekly tabloid, *Shooting Star.*"

"Good heavens," sniffed Drayton. "That awful rag? It's nothing more than a local scandal sheet."

"Call me wacky, but I get a kick out of reading *Shooting Star,*" said Haley, with a lopsided grin. "It's like Charleston's own little mini *Enquirer.* Besides, it's fun to read local gossip."

"Only when you aren't the subject of it," responded Drayton in an arch tone.

"This is great," said Haley as she sipped daintily from a glass of champagne. "Mingling with the upper crust."

"They're just people, Haley," said Theodosia. They had stepped away from Drayton's tea table and helped themselves to glasses of Perrier-Jouët champagne from the bar that was set up in the hallway. "Don't let Delaine turn your head with her talk of upper classes and bigwigs. These people have the same challenges and problems in their lives as we do." Haley was still young, early twenties, and easily impressionable. She was also more than a little cowed by wealth and privilege. Or at least by Delaine's *impression* of what represented wealth and privilege.

"This is some place, huh?" said Haley looking around the

Augustus Chait House. "Do you ever wish you lived in a house like this?"

Theodosia gazed at the high ceilings, the wainscoting, and the elaborate chandeliers. "Sometimes I do," she told Haley. Theodosia had to admit that even though this house needed considerable sprucing up, it was still quite glorious. Plus, Delaine had helped set the stage by raiding the storeroom at the Heritage Society. She'd had several pieces of Hepplewhite furniture trucked in as well as two large eighteenth-century landscape paintings. And various pieces of chinoiserie had been artfully positioned to help enliven the place.

"I just love living in Charleston," said Haley, taking another sip of champagne. "I don't think there's another city quite as beautiful. Except maybe Paris and I haven't been *there* yet."

Theodosia nodded in silent agreement. When it came to mansions, row houses, and carriage houses, Charleston was unsurpassed. The historic district alone boasted block after block of magnificent edifices. Throw in the enormous live oak trees dripping with Spanish moss, the cobblestone streets, and its catbird location at the confluence of the Ashley and Cooper Rivers with the Atlantic Ocean surging into the harbor, and you had to admit, Charleston was beyond spectacular. Highly atmospheric, very romantic, bordering on ethereal.

Back when Theodosia had been dating Jory Davis, a local attorney, she'd allowed herself to imagine that they might get married one day and buy a big old house in the historic district. Maybe one close to the Battery, where you could almost feel the sea spray off the harbor when the wind was just right. Now, of course, Jory was in New York working twelve hours a day at his law firm. And she was still cozily ensconced in her apartment above the Indigo Tea Shop with her beloved dog, Earl Grey, as roommate.

"*I was just* telling Pookie about our tea offerings," Drayton said to Theodosia as she rejoined him at the tea table. In her late fifties, Pookie Wilkes was a dynamo of a woman and one of their tea shop regulars. She headed up the Meeting Street Tea Club and was married to Duke Wilkes, a prominent retired executive who was thirty years her senior and who Delaine would probably accost later in hopes of garnering a generous donation.

Theodosia nodded as Pookie flashed her a winning smile. "So glad you could make it tonight," she told Pookie.

"We wouldn't have missed this for the world," said Pookie in her upbeat, positive manner. "Restoring this old house was a grand idea. And Duke and I are happy to help any way we can." She grabbed Theodosia's arm and gave it a friendly squeeze, then turned her attention back to Drayton. "Now hurry up and tell me about those teas, Drayton."

"We're serving two of our custom Indigo Tea Shop blends this evening," began Drayton. "The first one is Blood Orange Evening. It's basically a rich black tea flavored with bits of Sicilian blood oranges, hibiscus flowers, and rose hips."

"So it's what exactly?" asked Pookie. "An herbal tea?"

"No, no," said Drayton. "There *are* blood orange herbal teas on the market, but this particular tea features plenty of strong camellia sinesis."

"And what's your other tea?" asked Pookie, always intrigued by anything to do with tea.

"Another house blend we've dubbed Carolina Plum,"

said Drayton. "A black Ceylonese tea flavored with plum, vanilla, and a hint of cinnamon."

"They both sound delicious as well as dramatic." Pookie was enthused. "I can't wait to try them."

"They're wonderful," agreed Theodosia as she fussed with the flower bouquets. She was trying to make something that was already perfect into something even more perfect and knew she wasn't having much luck. Better leave well enough alone, she decided.

Pookie nudged Theodosia with an elbow. "Look at Duke," she said, her voice dropping to a low, warm whisper. The three of them gazed across the room, where Duke Wilkes, Pookie's husband, was holding court. Attired in a bright blue blazer with various pins and ribbons scattered boldly across his lapels, Duke was gesturing excitedly to a group of guests.

"He's such a crazy old coot," Pookie said lovingly. "Always wearing his ribbons and decorations."

Even though Duke Wilkes often bragged that he was the last living Confederate soldier, Theodosia knew that Duke had proudly served in World War II, fighting hand-to-hand during the Battle of the Bulge with Patton's Third Army. Duke's warped sense of time and great love of history were just a few of his strange though endearing qualities.

"Is Duke still active in the Fair Housing League and People's Law Office?" asked Drayton.

Pookie nodded. "And the Heritage Society and Wildlife Conservation Society," she added as the first high warning note from Timothy's violin sounded, signaling all the guest to take their seats. "He's busier now than when he was working sixty hours a week heading up Victory Capital!"

"Come on," said Theodosia, gently grasping Pookie's arm.

"Let's go sit down." And they slipped across the hallway to find seats in the back row just as Drayton quietly pulled the pocket doors closed on the small parlor.

Timothy Neville and his string quartet outdid themselves. Then again, all four of them were card-carrying members of the Charleston Symphony. Professional musicians who could perform Beethoven's Quartet in C-sharp Minor with great skill and aplomb.

Theodosia quickly found herself lost among the notes, focused on the grandeur and majesty of Beethoven's composition. In the flickering candlelight, the warm music pouring over her, all cares and distractions seemed to simply slide away.

And then, all too soon, the music ended. As the string quartet's final, mellow notes hung in the air, a burst of delighted applause filled the room. Then the four tuxedo-clad musicians were on their feet, taking their bows, and Delaine was fluttering to the front of the room, a colorful moth among the strobe of the candles.

"Lovely, lovely," an exuberant Delaine told the musicians. Then she whirled to face her audience. "And my thanks to all of *you* for coming here tonight. As you can see, there's much work ahead of us if this grande dame home is to be properly restored. . . ." Delaine gestured theatrically as she moved slowly toward the front parlor. "But I just *know* in my heart of hearts that your generosity will help us see this project through to completion. Which is why I'd like to spend a moment with each and every one of you. But first . . ."

Delaine beamed at her guests as she paused dramatically, ready to invite them all to partake of tea and dessert. But as she slid the pocket doors open to reveal the parlor, someone was standing in that darkened space, silhouetted by blazing candles and sparkling silver and teacups.

Drayton? thought Theodosia immediately, then checked herself. *No. Someone smaller, thinner.*

And as Theodosia continued to peer into that dim light, she saw that the person wasn't really standing at all. His posture was more slumped, as though he were leaning back against the tea table.

And in the flickering light from the candelabras, whoever it was seemed to weave and teeter precariously.

Sitting next to her, Pookie let out a sharp gasp.

Good heavens! Theodosia thought suddenly. *Could that be Duke Wilkes up there?* And on the heels of that thought: *What on earth is Duke up to? Has he been drinking? Or is he . . . ?*

But in that split second, Theodosia knew something was horribly wrong.

Jumping up, trembling with fright, Pookie stared straight ahead at the wavering figure. "Duke?" came Pookie's high, strangled cry. And with her heartfelt plea, the crowd fell silent, every eye in the house suddenly focused directly on the strange scene that was being played out before them.

"It *is* Duke," came Pookie's hoarse voice. And now Theodosia could see that Pookie was right. Old Duke Wilkes was clearly in distress. Was definitely in trouble.

Staring straight ahead, a ghostly gray pallor on his face, Duke continued to waver drunkenly. Then a low moan escaped Duke's lips and he seemed to give a final, strangled, pleading gasp for air.

Delaine, who'd been standing there the whole time, horrified, unsure what to do, slowly stretched out an arm.

Seeming to acknowledge her gesture of help, Duke's head turned robotically. He stared at her, gave one final, gargled cry, and then a terrible fine spray of blood filled the air.

Startled and completely unnerved, Delaine uttered a piercing scream and jumped backwards. And in that same split second, Duke Wilkes, Civil War reenactor, retired CEO, and political and social activist, toppled face forward and hit the worn cypress floorboards with a bone-crunching *thwack!*

Screams filled the air as guests sprang to their feet, turning over chairs in the ensuing pandemonium. A circle of horrified onlookers began to close in around Duke, each one seeming to grapple for a cell phone, the better to summon an ambulance. And then a horrified Theodosia was pulling Pookie through the crowd to stand in the middle of what had become a rugby-like scrum.

Was he . . . is he . . . dead? wondered Theodosia. Her eyes took in Duke's thin white hair and pale pink parchment skin. And . . . finally . . . the nasty glint from a jagged piece of metal protruding from the right side of Duke's scrawny neck even as his ruined carotid artery pulsed and pumped a final glut of blood.

2

❧

Maraschino cherry scones and apple muffins emerged from the oven looking golden-brown and smelling delicious. The steamy, malty scent of Assam tea and the light, fruitiness of Ceylon Breakfast tea hung redolent in the air. A fire crackled in the little stone fireplace as customers sipped tea and eagerly slathered white mounds of Devonshire cream and spoonfuls of jam on their scones. All in all, the atmosphere in the Indigo Tea Shop this Monday morning should have been sheer heaven. But it wasn't.

As Haley moved woodenly from table to table, pouring refills and delivering seconds on fresh-baked goods, Theodosia and Drayton huddled together at the little table nearest the kitchen, pondering the terrible events of the previous evening.

"It was nothing short of bizarre," said Drayton, shaking his grizzled head for the umpteenth time. "Poor Duke."

"Poor Pookie," said Theodosia. "Did you see the look on her face when the ambulance came and the EMTs carried him out?"

"She was devastated, poor soul," said Drayton. "Absolutely devastated. And of course there was nothing anyone could do to revive him. Duke was already gone."

"I heard the two of them were absolutely inseparable," said Haley, coming over to their table to pour an extra splash of Assam into Drayton's cup.

"They were a perfect match," said Drayton. He bent his head forward, cupped a hand at the back of his neck and massaged nervously. "Oh, dear, such an awful thing."

"You're feeling guilty about this," said Theodosia, peering at him. "I know you. I know how your mind works"

Drayton raised his head slowly to meet her gaze. His eyes blazed passionately. "Of course I am!" he declared. "There I was, stumping about in the kitchen, barely twenty feet from the proverbial scene of the crime, and I neither heard nor saw a thing!" He shook his head sadly. "Not a single, niggling clue that might give the police a jump start on solving this hideous crime."

"A crime that wasn't your fault," said Haley. "Besides, why would you have heard anything, Drayton? Water was boiling, tea kettles were chirping, you were busy working. You were totally focused . . . *in the zone,* as they say."

"Plus Timothy's string quartet was playing that marvelous Beethoven Quartet," said Theodosia. "So Haley's right."

"Of course, I'm right," said Haley, jumping in again.

"Still, some maniac managed to sneak in and murder Duke Wilkes," was Drayton's bitter comment. "If only I'd gone back into the parlor, if only I'd been more vigilant . . ."

"It's hard to be vigilant when you don't *know* something's going to happen," said Theodosia. "It's similar to the dilemma of homeland security. You can't take precautions when you have no idea which direction your enemies are coming from." She felt great sympathy for Drayton who had been a member of the same Civil War reenactment group as old Duke.

"A penetrating neck wound is what the police called it," said Drayton. "But from what, I wonder? Some kind of knife?"

"Maybe one of the surgical instruments from that old operating room?" suggested Haley.

Drayton shook his head. "I don't think so. I overheard one of the investigators talking. Apparently nothing was missing."

"Detective Tidwell talked to you last night, didn't he?" Haley asked Drayton.

"Afraid so," said Drayton in an acerbic tone. "And I must say, Tidwell was none too pleasant."

"Burt Tidwell was in work mode," said Theodosia. "And please realize, Tidwell was there to glean the most he could from the crime scene, not shmooze around making friends." Detective Burt Tidwell was the Chief of Detectives in the Charleston Police Department's Robbery-Homicide Division. He was aggressive, boorish, and totally brilliant. As they'd found out when they had previous dealings with him.

"Still," said Drayton. "Tidwell's manners could use some serious polishing."

"I agree with Drayton," said Haley. "Detective Burt Tidwell can be a condescending bully."

"He's also helped us out on more than one occasion," murmured Theodosia. But she wasn't about to change anyone's mind today. She didn't harbor glowing feelings for the rather brusque and brash Tidwell. But she did have serious respect for the man. He could be an absolute genius at sleuthing out clues, maddening though he was. And as for sullenly sniffing about the crime scene? She knew that was simply Tidwell's modus operandi. Head down, hackles up, and woe to anyone who crossed his path.

"Tidwell and that other detective . . . Detective Henderson? They were busy interviewing a lot of other folks, too," said Haley. "Unfortunately, no one . . ." Haley's voice trailed off.

"No one else heard or saw anything either," said Drayton, finishing her thought. "I know, I know, please don't remind me."

The three of them gazed morosely at each other for a few moments.

"It's kind of a locked room murder mystery, isn't it?" said Theodosia finally. She set her bone china tea cup down and it made a tiny *clink.*

Drayton knit his brows together. "Pardon?"

"Like in an Agatha Christie mystery," explained Theodosia. "Agatha Christie is pretty much the acknowledged master at penning locked room mysteries."

"Ah," said Drayton, comprehension dawning. "You mean like her *Ten Little Indians.* Or . . . let's see . . . Ellery Queen's *Chinese Orange Mystery.*"

"Exactly," said Theodosia.

"When you put it that way," said Haley, eyes narrowing, "you're saying the murderer was right there among us. That it could have been almost anyone."

"That's right," said Theodosia.

"So . . . you made mention of this to Tidwell last

night?" asked Drayton, gazing speculatively at Theodosia.

"I tried to," she admitted. Unfortunately, Tidwell hadn't really given her the time of day.

"Of course, someone could have snuck in, too," said Drayton. "After all, lights were off and candles were flickering. There's a front door and a back door. . . ." He shrugged. "What did Tidwell say?"

"Burt Tidwell was his usual maddening closed-mouthed self," said Theodosia. "Not caring to share any of his lofty theories with me. But from what little I could wrangle from him, he seemed fairly confident that the suspect, or unsub as he prefers to call the murderer, was one of the guests at the Candlelight Concert."

Haley shivered. "That's fairly creepy."

"Pray tell, what exactly is an unsub?" asked Drayton.

"Unknown subject of an investigation," replied Theodosia. "It's lingo that apparently started within the FBI, but is pretty much used by all police departments now." She paused. "You know Tidwell used to be an FBI agent. An SAIC. Special agent in charge."

"That's right," said Drayton.

"Delaine must be upset that her cadre of carefully chosen guests has suddenly come under suspicion," said Haley.

"Delaine was completely hysterical last night," said Theodosia. "Almost more so than Pookie."

"Delaine did get sprayed with blood," allowed Drayton.

"It was all over her face and dress," said Haley. "She looked so scared and stunned I actually felt sorry for her."

Drayton lifted an eyebrow until it quivered and stared pointedly at Haley. "You of all people felt compassion for our dear Miss Dish?"

Haley shrugged. "Well, sort of," she mumbled.

"So what do we know about the murder weapon?" asked Haley.

"Not much at all," said Theodosia. "From what little I saw, it looked like a knife blade. But one that had broken off."

"Broken off," murmured Drayton. "Why would it . . . ?"

Theodosia hesitated. "Violent struggle?"

Haley suddenly stared at Theodosia with big eyes. "If there was a struggle, how come nobody heard anything? Did the murderer slip past everyone and find his way back into the audience? And how exactly did Duke end up in the parlor?"

"I haven't got a clue," said Theodosia. "But remember, the concert went on for a good thirty minutes. And even though the lights were dim, people *were* moving around. Late arrivals, folks departing early. Even Delaine was tiptoeing around, I think."

"And you were working in the kitchen the whole time?" Haley asked Drayton.

"Pretty much," Drayton replied.

"Most of the time?" asked Theodosia. "Or the whole time?"

Drayton frowned, then wrinkled his nose. "I went into the parlor just once," he said. "To fill the creamers. Otherwise I was occupied in the kitchen." He took a final sip of tea, shook out a clean hanky, and daubed at his lips. "And on that happy note I think we'd all better get busy. Some of our early morning customers are probably ready for a refill or will be wanting their check." Pushing back his chair, Drayton rose to his feet. "And it won't be long before our luncheon customers start arriving. We have reservations for the three big tables and there are always plenty of drop-ins."

"Right," said Haley, glancing at her large-faced silver Timex and jumping up, too. "It's time I head back to my kitchen. I've got orange muffins coming out of the oven in exactly four minutes."

"We'll noodle this around later," agreed Theodosia, as the bell over the front door tinkled and more customers pushed their way in.

"Welcome," cried Drayton, tugging at his vest, the very picture of friendliness and decorum as he hustled over to greet their new arrivals. "I have a table for you right here by the fireplace. Very cozy, yes? Now, may I start you off with a cup of Sessa Estate Assam? Very smooth and rich. Or I can brew a lovely pot of tea from our collection of more than one hundred teas. Allow me to recommend . . ."

Theodosia dashed to the counter to deal with a couple takeout orders, then grabbed fresh pots of tea and made the rounds of the tables herself, refilling cups, and bidding good morning to some of their regular customers.

Ten minutes later she stuck her head in Haley's tiny kitchen. "Is Miss Dimple coming in today?" Theodosia asked.

Squiggles of creamy white frosting oozed from Haley's pastry bag as she topped her fresh-baked orange muffins. "She'll be here at eleven to help us set up and serve," said Haley. "Plus I think she wants to meet with you after lunch to review the monthly P-and-L statement."

"Right," said Theodosia. There were the financials to deal with. In fact, there were *always* business details to take care of. Financial statements, vendor orders to place, Internet orders to fill, meetings with her CPA firm. Still, she hung in the doorway, savoring the sights and smells that Haley's handiwork had produced. "We're still doing the cucumber soup and the shrimp salad sandwiches?" she asked.

"Absolutely," said Haley. "Plus I'm doing pineapple cream cheese tea sandwiches and baking spiced tea bread and almond cookies since we've got guests from the Featherbed House coming in at three o'clock." She hesitated. "They specifically requested a five-course tea."

"Gotcha," said Theodosia, as the nearby wall telephone shrilled in her ear. "I'll grab this in my office," she told Haley as she scurried into the back room. "Let you get lunch going."

"Indigo Tea Shop," said Theodosia as she slipped behind her desk, inwardly cringing at the mess of brochures and tea catalogs spread out on top of it. "Theodosia speaking."

"Is Drayton there?" came an impatient sounding male voice.

Is this someone from the police? wondered Theodosia. *Calling about last night?*

"Drayton's busy right now," said Theodosia. "Could I have him return your call?" She paused. "Or perhaps I can help you?"

"Ah . . . this is Greg Killman, Congressman Clive Bonham's aide? I just wanted to confirm the arrangements I made with Drayton concerning the congressman's tea."

"The tea," said Theodosia, her eyes darting to her calendar. "We have it scheduled for tomorrow afternoon. Tuesday." She picked up a yellow pencil, tapped at the calendar. "Your reservation is still for twenty-five guests?"

"Actually," said Greg Killman, his voice suddenly warm and a trifle wheedling, "we've added a few additional names. It's going to be closer to forty guests now. Can you handle that? Is that a problem?"

"No," said Theodosia slowly. "But it's good you called instead of just surprising us."

"Glad to hear you're a resilient bunch," said Greg Killman. "Especially in light of last night's disaster." Killman hesitated. "This may sound a trifle harsh, but as the election draws closer our campaign must push boldly forward."

"Of course," said Theodosia. "I understand completely." *What is he talking about?* she wondered.

"Excellent," said Killman. "Glad to see we're on the same page. Oh . . . and the event tomorrow? The congressman is counting on over-the-top elegance, okay? Just do whatever it is you people do to impress the ladies. Bone china, candelabras, fancy food, whatever it takes. As I told Drayton before, cost is no object."

Sitting at her desk, Theodosia rolled her eyes. Whenever someone told her cost was no object it usually meant cost was a major consideration.

But Greg Killman continued to wax poetic. "I'm sure I don't have to tell you, Miss Browning, that our guest list will feature some extremely prominent women. The congressman is seeking wholehearted endorsement from these women as well as from their highly influential husbands. So he wants to make a *very* favorable impression."

"Of course he does," said Theodosia. "Which is why, as always, we shall put forth our very best effort."

"Excellent," said Killman. "I'd appreciate it if you could work up an amended cost estimate, then call Congressman Bonham's office and leave that information with one of the secretaries. Anything else, call me on my cell phone." He gave Theodosia his number, then rang off hurriedly.

Goodness, she thought, as she leaned back in her chair and twiddled her pen. *This is one of those catering gigs I never would have seen coming in a million years.* Still, it had popped up at an opportune moment. Business was good, but it could always be better. And having Congressman Bonham and his female constituency as their guests offered a fine opportunity to showcase the Indigo Tea Shop to a group of well-heeled business women.

Theodosia bent forward intently and began to scribble notes.

3

❧

"*Can you manage* all these soup bowls, Miss Dimple?" asked Haley as she ladled cucumber soup into a dozen celadon green bowls then placed them hastily on a large silver tray.

"Not a problem," replied Miss Dimple. "And thanks for asking me in again. You know I just adore working here." A broad grin lit Miss Dimple's round face with its plump apple cheeks. "And the extra money helps keep Sampson and Delilah rolling in catnip."

"Hey," said Haley, plopping tiny mounds of sour cream atop each bowl of soup. "Love those cats. And we love having *you*."

Technically, Miss Dimple was their bookkeeper, a past-retirement-age sweetheart who had worked for years in the Peregrine Building next door. When the building's owner passed away and Miss Dimple was faced with the bleak prospect of finally being out of a job, it was Theodosia who'd suggested Miss Dimple turn to freelance bookkeeping. After all, she'd been collecting rent and balancing the books for the owner of the Peregrine Building for almost forty years.

Now Miss Dimple handled the books for several retailers up and down Church Street as well as the Indigo Tea Shop. And her sweet nature and enthusiasm made her a natural to bring in as an assistant to Drayton and Haley. Besides, Miss Dimple knew almost everyone in the neighborhood and adored working in the tea shop a couple days a week.

"We sure could use you tomorrow afternoon, too, if you can make it," Haley told her, as she topped each daub of sour cream with a pinch of chives. "Theodosia just told me this big catering thing we're doing has expanded by thirty percent."

"The food or the guests?" asked Miss Dimple.

"Both, I suppose," responded Haley.

Miss Dimple gave Haley a sideways glance. "How are you folks holding up after last night? Such a nasty thing," she said shaking her head. "Poor old Duke's murder was the lead story on the ten o'clock news."

"We're terrible," barked Drayton, suddenly looming in the doorway. "In fact, we're all shocked beyond belief."

"We're sick at heart for Pookie," agreed Haley, picking up the tray and handing it to Miss Dimple. "She's pretty much a fixture here at the tea shop."

"Pookie's a proud, gracious lady from a fine old Southern family," said Miss Dimple, balancing the tray against one ample hip. "But don't underestimate her. She's also blessed with a tremendous amount of inner strength and grit. Pookie's the kind of woman who can don a broad-brimmed hat and white gloves and preside over a fancy tea, then dash out and shoot a passel of partridges with the men-folk. And celebrate by downing a shot of bourbon neat. Believe me, Pookie's made of pretty stern stuff. She's not going to rest easy until justice is served."

Lunch was a madhouse at the Indigo Tea Shop. Just before noon one of the red and yellow horse-drawn jitneys that plied the historic district clopped to a halt at the front door and disgorged a dozen hungry passengers. They trooped in, eager and grinning, mingled with the regulars and the folks who had reservations, and helped keep the tea shop hopping for a good two hours. Haley had to scrape the bottom of the bowl for the last serving of cucumber soup while Theodosia scrambled to put together another two dozen sandwiches. And Drayton was a whirling dervish, brewing pots of Formosan Lapsang, Chinese Keemun, and Japanese Matcha tea.

Once the rush was over and things had settled down to a dull roar, Theodosia and Drayton sat down for a quick bite.

"I can't believe there's even a sandwich left," said Theodosia, taking a welcome nibble of her shrimp salad sandwich.

Glancing at his watch, an old Piaget that seemed to run a perpetual twenty minutes slow, Drayton said, "What I can't believe is that we're going to do this all over again in an hour."

"That's right." Theodosia winced. "You're doing a five-course tea for those guests from the Featherbed House."

"We most certainly are," said Drayton. He took a sip of Japanese Matcha, breathed a contented sigh. "Goodness this is delicious. I simply adore that roasted flavor.

"Drayton," said Theodosia, a tentative note in her voice. "I got a phone call from Greg Killman earlier."

Drayton raised his eyebrows. "Congressman Bonham's aide? They're still coming tomorrow, aren't they?"

"They are, and they've added a few more names to the guest list."

Drayton paused, teacup in midair. "How many more?"

"Fifteen more guests."

"Fifteen!" said Drayton, setting his cup down without taking a sip. "Does Haley know about this?"

Theodosia nodded. "I mentioned it to her earlier."

"And what exactly is she doing about it?" demanded Drayton. "And why am I always the last one to know about these changes in program?"

"I imagine Haley's on the phone ordering additional groceries," said Theodosia. "And Drayton, I didn't leave you out of the loop on purpose. Everything was slightly chaotic so I just now got around to telling you. For that I apologize."

"Mmm," said Drayton, reaching for a cherry scone, somewhat mollified.

"The other thing is . . ." began Theodosia.

"What?" asked Drayton, back on full alert.

"Greg Killman asked that we pull out all the stops."

"Pull out all the stops," repeated Drayton, looking wary.

"His words were something to the effect that Congressman Clive Bonham wants to make a *very favorable impression* on his guests. Which means, I suppose, that they'd like us to break out the good china, pretty up the tables with candelabras, and maybe even add another course."

Drayton furrowed his brow. "I see trouble looming already."

"Why?" asked Theodosia, peering at him and knowing

that Drayton wasn't the most flexible character in the world. "What?"

"For one thing," said Drayton, "I've already ordered small, rather tidy-looking floral bouquets. If we're supposed to pull out all the stops, we need bigger, more bountiful arrangements, don't you think?"

"You'll get no argument from me," said Theodosia. "Can you call Hattie at Floradora and change the order? Or, rather, upgrade it?"

"I'll see what can be done," said Drayton briskly. "Now about the china. We should definitely use the Crown Ducal. And perhaps even the Pickard Palladium if we don't have enough place settings. Both have a nice creamy luster that will give our tables a real sparkle."

Theodosia relaxed. Now that his initial shock was over, Drayton was starting to get into the swing of things.

"And let's use those hand-dipped, cream-colored tapers," Drayton suggested. "I think they'd complement the china. Now about the menu. . . ." Drayton swiveled in his chair. "Haley," he shouted. "We need you!"

A few seconds later, Haley appeared, wiping her hands on a towel, looking placidly at Theodosia. "I see you told Drayton about our expanded guest list for tomorrow."

"Haley, my dear, we have additional planning to do," said Drayton. "Congressman Bonham requested a tea that is over-the-top elegant and we're going to do our best to deliver exactly that."

"I'm on it," said Haley. "In fact, I've already added a fruit compote to the menu.

"You think that's fancy enough?" asked Drayton.

Haley pursed her lips and stared at Drayton. "You're getting befuzzled," she told him.

"I'm not befuzzled," said Drayton in a somewhat petulant tone. "A special request has been made and I for one like to deliver on it. We had an absolute *flop* on our hands last night . . ."

"Not our fault," said Theodosia briskly. "Who could predict . . . ?"

Drayton held up a hand. "I know, I know. But it would be nice if tomorrow afternoon's tea was a raging success. Wouldn't that be nice?"

In the interest of harmony they all agreed it would be nice.

"Perhaps we could even offer a *choice* of luncheon entrees," suggested Drayton. "Say, poached trout and stuffed chicken breast?"

"I can do that," said Haley. "And prepare a nice white wine sauce that would work with either."

"Excellent," said Drayton. "And what about a showy dessert? Something we could serve in a tall parfait glass?"

"Let me shuffle through my recipe box," said Haley. "I've got a couple things that might work."

"And we'll need to put out the good silver," said Drayton. "Probably the Towle Old Master. And I'd love to drape the tables in creamy beige linens. In fact, I wonder if this isn't the perfect time to invest in some new linens?" He cast an anxious eye toward Theodosia. "That is, if it's remotely in the budget."

"Absolutely it's in the budget," said Theodosia. "We haven't made any new purchases for a while. And I have a terrific idea on where to find those new linens."

"Le Nest," said Drayton, perking up considerably. "I've been looking for an excuse to go there."

"Good," said Theodosia. "So have I."

"We'll zip over there . . . when?" asked Drayton. "Tomorrow morning? Will we have time?"

"We will if we go first thing," promised Theodosia. She sat back, let loose a long sigh. "This is shaping up to be a fairly busy week."

"You think so?" asked Haley, who was a bit of an adrenaline junkie. The busier she was, the happier she was.

Theodosia nodded. "We've got the tea for Congressman Bonham tomorrow, I'm supposed to do a tea demo at the Women's Expo on Thursday, and then on Friday Earl Grey has been tapped to participate in a service dog demo for the Ainsworth Kennel Club Show." She pushed her chair back and stood up. "And now, I've got to meet with Miss Dimple and go over last week's receipts. Where is she, Haley? Holed up in the back office?"

Haley, whose eyes were suddenly fixed on the front door, nodded. Then added under her breath: "Yes, but I think things just got a little more complicated." She slid her elbow over to connect with Theodosia's just as the door flew open and two people came blasting into the tea room.

Her head swiveling to see who these new arrivals were, Theodosia wasn't at all surprised to see Delaine Dish steamrolling toward her. But she was stunned beyond belief when she saw that Delaine had Pookie Wilkes in tow.

Drayton immediately hustled about, clearing dishes, brewing tea, and graciously seating Delaine and Pookie at the table with them. Now the four of them sat hunched around the small table, a plate of scones and fresh cups of tea before them, all looking rather sober and serious.

"Pookie," said Drayton in somber, drawn out tones, "you have our deepest sympathy."

"Thank you," murmured Pookie. Dressed in a black suit,

she looked tired and weary. But her head was held high and she seemed to be handling the stress of the previous evening. And her new role as widow.

"We are *so* sorry," said Theodosia. "If there's anything we can do. Anything at all."

"As a matter-of-fact," said Delaine, looking somewhat pleased at the opening Theodosia had just given her, "there is."

"Just tell us," said Drayton, still focusing his commiserating gaze upon Pookie.

"A heinous crime has been committed," said Delaine in her slow drawl. "And we have come here to enlist Theodosia's help."

"Pardon?" said Theodosia. *What exactly is this about?*

"Oh, Theo," said Delaine, reaching across the table to clasp her hand. "Pookie needs you. In fact, we're *all* counting on you."

"Of course," said Theodosia. "Anything you . . ." Her voice faltered. She wasn't quite sure what was being asked of her.

"You have certain talents, Theodosia," continued Delaine. "Certain . . . well, let me be blunt, dear . . . certain *investigatory* skills."

"Oh, dear," mumbled Drayton in a strangled tone.

But Delaine ignored him and plunged ahead. "I've been telling Pookie about some of the strange little mysteries you've unraveled."

"Oh, no," demurred Theodosia, waving a hand as if shooing away a gnat. "Those were nothing. A few lucky breaks."

Delaine held up a manicured index finger. "I beg to differ," she said, her manner strict and stern.

"What I need," said Pookie, leaning forward and fixing Theodosia with a baleful look, "is someone who's smart and on the inside."

"Inside of what?" asked Theodosia. *Now who's the befuzzled one?* she asked herself. *It's me, that's who.*

"Inside the community," said Pookie. "Inside the neighborhood, the historic district, and the Church Street folks." She pulled out a hanky and dabbed at her eyes. "Maybe even inside the Heritage Society, too."

"Surely," said Theodosia, "you don't suspect . . ."

"I have a rather ominous feeling about this," responded Pookie in a strangled tone. "I wouldn't be surprised if the murderer was someone close to Duke. Familiar with his politics, possibly upset by his actions." Her voice dropped to a hoarse whisper. "Duke was rather strident in many of his opinions," she told them. "He's butted heads with more than a few people, which is why I suspect it could be someone who's possibly . . . well, not exactly inner circle . . . but in our circle. If you know what I mean?"

"Your locked room theory," muttered Drayton. "It's come back to haunt you."

"Locked room?" asked Delaine, pouncing on the phrase like a fat goose feasting on a June bug. "Kindly explain."

Flustered now, Theodosia stumbled about, trying to clarify her words. "I was just telling Drayton and, uh, Haley, that I thought . . . well, more like suspected, that the murderer might have been there among us. Although I don't know how he, uh . . ."

"She thinks it was someone who was in attendance last night," finished Drayton. "Someone who, shall we say, walks among us."

"That's the exact feeling I have, too," said Pookie with

a slight shiver. "And while I have faith in the Charleston Homicide Department, I'd feel a darn side better if I knew you were snooping around, too."

"Theodosia's a whiz at snooping," Delaine insisted.

"Thank you, Delaine . . . I think," said Theodosia.

"So you'll help?" asked Delaine. Once pressure had been applied, Delaine was never one to let up.

"You don't seriously . . . ?" began Theodosia.

"I'm afraid we do," said Pookie. She turned to face Drayton with red-rimmed eyes. "Didn't you once tell me how Theodosia was helpful to Lizbeth Cantrell?

"I suppose I did," whispered Drayton, looking somewhat guilty.

"And when Captain Buchanan was killed," offered Delaine. "Theo was a veritable pit bull. Unraveling leads, pouncing on clues." She flashed a shy smile at Theodosia. "See, honey? You're *good* at this. Admit it."

"Uh huh," was Theodosia's circumspect reply. *What did Detective Tidwell tell me last time I poked my nose into an investigation? He told me in no uncertain terms to mind my own business. So now I'm going to get tangled up in another murder? No way. I can't. Not this time.*

As if reading Theodosia's innermost thoughts, Pookie gazed sadly into her teacup as tears rolled down her cheeks. "I understand if you don't want to get involved," she said in a hoarse whisper. "I understand completely."

And just like that, Theodosia felt utterly wretched. "Wait a minute," she said, holding a hand up, making a cautionary gesture. "Maybe I could just keep my eyes and ears open. Make a few discreet inquiries." *Whoa. Am I crazy? Yeah, I must be.*

"What could it hurt?" murmured Delaine, favoring Theodosia with a beatific smile.

"Bless you, Theodosia," said Pookie, her tears flowing freely now. "You're a dear heart and an absolute angel."

4

❧

"*Delaine,*" *said Theodosia*, after Drayton had called a taxi and sent Pookie on her sad way. "You still have the keys to the Augustus Chait House, don't you?"

Delaine shot her a vaguely suspicious look. "Yes," she said slowly. "I do."

"Let me borrow them, will you?"

Delaine set her teacup down abruptly. "Theodosia Browning," she hissed. "Whatever do you have in mind?"

Theodosia put a finger to her lips. "Shhh. I'd rather Drayton and Haley didn't hear this. Especially Drayton."

"That house is a *crime* scene," said Delaine. "Besides, you promised Pookie you'd make discreet inquiries, not go charging back into that house."

"You're the one who dragged poor Pookie down here and bragged to high heaven about what a great amateur detective

I am," argued Theodosia. "Don't you want me to make good on my promise?"

"Well . . . yes," was Delaine's faint reply.

"Then I think we should go have ourselves a look," said Theodosia. "What harm can it do? Surely the police have finished taking photos and have run all the forensic tests they needed to," said Theodosia. She thought about the blood spatter tests and shivered.

"I *suppose* so," conceded Delaine.

"And it would be completely aboveboard if you accompanied me," said Theodosia. "After all, you *are* chairman of the Restoration Committee. You do have full and complete access to the property, don't you?"

"I certainly do," said Delaine, straightening up in her chair. "And as much as I love Pookie, I still intend to press forward with my plans to make that home a viable historical site. One that will attract a fair amount of visitors."

Theodosia smiled at Delaine. She was a determined woman. Once Delaine made up her mind, there was no stopping her. She certainly wasn't going to let a little thing like a murder stand in her way.

"Since Pookie *did* ask me for help," said Theodosia, pressing, "and you were instrumental in getting me to agree, that house is the logical place for us to start."

"I suppose you're right," said Delaine, suddenly looking stricken. "I so *adore* Pookie. And she *is* one of my very best customers at Cotton Duck. Whenever new silk jackets and beaded evening bags come in I always give her first crack."

"That's so sweet of you," insisted Theodosia. She hesitated a moment. "Then what's the problem in going over for a quick look-see?"

"Probably nothing at all," said Delaine, as though the whole thing had been her wonderfully bright idea.

But once they were standing on the broad verandah of the Augustus Chait House, staring at the carved double doors that would grant them access, Delaine Dish experienced a sudden and profound change of heart.

"What if there's blood all over?" she moaned. "What if I pass out from fright?"

"You won't," Theodosia assured her as she reached for Delaine's hand and carefully pried the large brass key from it. She noted, with satisfaction, that the black and yellow crime scene tape, the tape that proclaimed POLICE LINE, DO NOT CROSS, now hung in desultory strands from the door frame. In other words, the tape was no longer strung directly across the door. So it was sort of, probably, *technically* okay to enter the house. She hoped it was, anyway.

Inserting the key in the lock, Theodosia gave a mighty twist. The heavy door swung open and, seconds later, the two of them were inside, paused in the dimly lit front hallway, listening to the monotonous ticktock of a clock somewhere.

"Sounds so empty," whispered Delaine.

"That's because it is," said Theodosia. *What is it about empty houses, anyway?* she wondered. *They all have that same lonely, echoey, dust mites twirling in the air feel to them. And yet . . . this one has something else, too. A weird low-level vibe.*

Theodosia crept down the main hallway, Delaine tottering after her.

To their right was the front parlor where the tea table had been set up. Now it was just a bare wooden table. All the teacups and serving pieces had been hastily packed into wicker baskets last night, then shoved into the back of Theodosia's Jeep.

Theodosia also noted that the Chinese rug that had softened the clatter in the parlor had also disappeared. Probably rolled up and carted off by the police so forensic experts could search it for trace evidence.

Theodosia continued farther down the long hallway, her hand batting at the wall, searching for a light switch. "Where's the light switch?" she asked Delaine. "Oh, here we go," she said as her fingered brushed the switch. But when she punched the buttons, nothing happened. "No lights," said Theodosia, turning back toward Delaine.

Delaine made a sour face. "There aren't any lights. The two front parlors and the kitchen have a sort of tacit working electricity, but that's it. Squirrels apparently got in the walls and gnawed most of the wiring. It's all going to have to be replaced. That's one of the reasons I came up with the idea for a candlelight concert."

"Great," muttered Theodosia, continuing down the dark corridor.

"Theo! Wait!" hissed Delaine. Her stiletto heels clacked against the wooden floor as she hurried to catch up.

"Better stay close, Delaine," said Theodosia as she ducked into the dark library where long purple velvet draperies blocked out the afternoon sunlight, then wandered through a grand archway into what had probably been a dining room.

With so many people milling about last night, Theodosia hadn't really had a chance to look around. Now she was surprised to see a fair amount of furniture and antiquities present in the old house.

Wandering up to a glass curio cabinet, Theodosia pulled open the door, reached in for a purple glass orb. "Mercury glass," she murmured. She turned, her eyes searching the darkness for Delaine. "Is this from the Heritage Society?" she asked as she balanced the shimmering object in her hand. Produced around the turn of the century, the maker had achieved a lustrous, jewel tone by flowing mercury between two layers of glass.

"It's one of the things we pulled out of their storage room," said Delaine. She was hunched up against the wall, rubbing her foot. "It's going to take a lot of money to bring this place up to snuff," she told Theodosia. "Just the tuck pointing on the exterior alone is going to cost a small fortune." She bent down, rubbed at her foot again.

Gently, Theodosia replaced the glass orb in the case and wandered out into the hallway. "Are you okay?" she asked.

"Not really," said Delaine. "It's awfully creepy in here. Plus these shoes are pinching my feet."

"I can't imagine why," said Theodosia, peering at the apple green high-heeled sandals Delaine was wearing. They were drop dead gorgeous but didn't look like they were a picnic to walk in. "You're wearing four inch stilettos that have the minimum amount of strap allowed by law to keep them on your feet. Why don't you get a pair of heels you can walk in? Toss those crazy things out."

"Are you serious?" Delaine scoffed at her. "These are *Jimmy Choo* shoes. You don't cast off a perfectly elegant pair of Jimmy Choos on account of a silly little blister or bunion."

"Okay," said Theodosia, "then you and your Choos stay put. I want to wander farther back and see what's there."

"Hurry back, Theo," said Delaine. "This place is just too dark and weird to be left alone in. Gives me the heebie jee-bies. In fact, I'm going to go back to the front parlor where the lights are working."

"Suit yourself," said Theodosia. "I'll probably be back in about sixty seconds," she promised as she hurried down the hallway, heading for the kitchen.

But nothing in the kitchen with its dim overhead lights seemed to offer up any sort of insightful clue either. Just tall cupboards, minimal counter space, a 1940s vintage stove, and a refrigerator of the same era that had an annoying buzz.

"Hmph," said Theodosia, flicking off the light and making her way back down the dark hallway. She could honestly say she was disappointed. Not that she'd expected a big fat clue to jump right out at her. But it would have been nice to find *something*.

Standing in the front hallway, Theodosia looked around. Where was Delaine?

"Delaine?" called Theodosia, purposely raising her voice. "Where are you?"

No answer. Just the hollow echo of her voice bouncing off the walls. Theodosia frowned, bit at her lip, and thought for a moment. *Did Delaine chicken out and make a run for it? Was she so freaked out that she took off without telling me?*

Standing in the near dark, Theodosia could sense her anxiety level rising. Her heart gave a little thud against the inside of her chest. "Delaine," she called again. Then fell silent, listening for . . .

Thunck, thunck!

Theodosia jumped. *What the . . . ?*

"Theodosia!" cried a muffled voice. "Help me!"

"Delaine?" yelled Theodosia, twirling around fast. "Where

are you?" There was no sign of Delaine. It was like she'd vanished into thin air!

Thunck, thunck.

"In here!" yelled Delaine. "*Inside* . . . but I . . . I can't get out!"

Theodosia rushed into the parlor and put a hand to the cypress-paneled wall. "In here?" she said, alarm filling her voice. *Delaine is on the other side of this wall?*

Then Delaine's terrified voice was calling back to her. Still muffled, but sounding a little closer. "I was leaning against the wall and something gave way. I'm in a narrow little passage and, oh, lordy, is it ever dark and nasty! I think it's some sort of *dungeon!*"

Nervous but also intrigued now, Theodosia began banging and pounding on the wall.

"Is that you making all that racket?" came Delaine's voice. It was amazing how Delaine had gone from being utterly terrified to sounding vaguely critical in about three seconds flat.

"Be quiet," snapped Theodosia. "There must be some sort of secret lever or button out here. I've got to play around and try to figure it out." Theodosia pressed, banged, and tried sliding various pieces of paneling, kind of like you would with a wooden puzzle, but to no avail.

After a good three or four minutes she called back to Delaine. "What exactly did you do, Delaine? What were you doing when the wall gave way?"

"I just *leaned* against it," wailed Delaine. "I wasn't *trying* to get imprisoned in here!"

"I know, I know," said Theodosia. "You just sort of bumbled your way in." She spun around and leaned against the paneling. Nothing. She balanced on the backs of her heels and pressed harder. Still nothing. Perturbed, Theodosia made a half-turn and butted the wall with her shoulder. And suddenly found herself tumbling *Alice in Wonderland*–style down the rabbit hole as the wall yawned open, then snapped shut behind her just as fast. Sprawled on the floor, landing hard on one shoulder, Theodosia's first impression was of darkness, dust, and the nasty, tickling sensation of spiderwebs brushing her face!

5

"I see you finally found the secret panel," said an accusing voice. Hands on hips, Delaine's shadowy figure stared down at Theodosia. "It's about time."

"Ouch," said Theodosia in reply, rubbing her upper arm and shoulder. "I wasn't counting on staging such a dramatic entrance. Or making such a hard landing," she added. *My shoulder,* she thought to herself. *I would have to land on my shoulder.*

"Now you know how I feel," said Delaine, sounding peeved. "And by the way, I was hoping you'd find the way *out* of here, not the way in."

"So was I," agreed Theodosia, still a little stunned from being catapulted from quasi-reality into this strange dark space.

"What are we supposed to do now?" asked Delaine. "Now that we're *really* stuck."

"Matches," said Theodosia, easing herself up and feeling around gingerly in the dark. "Do you have a book of matches?"

"Maybe," said Delaine. "Possibly."

Theodosia knew that Delaine still indulged in an occasional cigarette. So maybe, if they were really lucky, she'd have a book of matches on her.

"How are you doing?" Theodosia asked. She could hear Delaine rustling about in her pocketbook. "Find anything?"

"We're in luck." Delaine chortled. "I found some. Probably the ones I picked up at the Charleston Grill," she added, sounding pleased. "When I had cocktails last week with Osgood Whitley."

Theodosia felt around for Delaine's hand, finally connected. At a bizarre moment such as this, only Delaine would brag about which upscale restaurant she'd gotten the matches from. And who she'd had drinks with.

Sliding open the box of matches, Theodosia poked a tentative finger in and grasped a single, thin wooden match. She struck it against the side of the package. The match flared briefly then went out, leaving them in total darkness again. But that one small bit of light had been enough to illuminate the immediate area and give Theodosia her bearings.

"This way," said Theodosia, easing herself down a narrow passageway. "I think there's something down here." The match had winked out in just a few seconds time, but Theodosia had seen enough. This passageway *did* lead somewhere. "Come on," said Theodosia. "Ten more feet and I think we might be on to something."

They shuffled along slowly in darkness, Theodosia leading, Delaine right behind. Theodosia stopped, fumbled for a second match, then struck it and held it high. Both women blinked, surprised to find they'd ended up in a small eight-by-ten-foot room.

"There's a lantern over there!" squealed Delaine, just as the second match fizzled out. "Sitting on that little table!"

But Theodosia had already darted across the room and was striking a third match.

"I hope there's oil in this lamp," said Delaine as Theodosia touched the tiny flame to the trimmed wick and hoped for the best.

"Lucky, lucky, lucky," Theodosia muttered under her breath, a mantra she hoped would pay off for them.

There was a dim glow, a quick spark, and just when Theodosia was positive the light would burn out, the wick caught, splashing light up the walls of the room.

Definitely lucky, she decided.

"What is this place?" asked Delaine peering around.

"Best guess," said Theodosia. "And without trying to sound overly melodramatic . . . I think it's a secret room."

"Good heavens," exclaimed Delaine as understanding dawned. "I've heard tales about these places. But I've never actually been in one before."

"Nor have I," said Theodosia as she spun slowly around, scrutinizing the small space.

More than a dozen old homes in Charleston were reputed to have secret rooms, including Timothy Neville's grand old Italianate mansion on Archdale Street. Most of the rooms were originally constructed as a place to hide valuables as well as shelter family members during times of strife. And Charleston, an active participant in the Revolutionary War, the War of 1812, and the War Between the States, to say nothing of skirmishes with marauding Caribbean pirates, had certainly endured more than its share of strife.

"Not much in here though." Delaine sighed. "I was hoping there'd be some sort of door that would take us back out to the hallway."

Theodosia held the lamp up, but all it revealed were cedar-planked walls, empty wooden shelves, the table, and a simple wooden chair.

"Not exactly a luxury suite." Delaine sniffed.

"No," said Theodosia. "But someone's been in here. And quite recently, too."

"How on earth would you know that?" demanded Delaine.

Theodosia pointed at the table and chair. "No dust. Somebody sat here. Or waited here."

"Oh, lord," was Delaine's strangled reply. "Are you thinking what I'm thinking?"

"That somebody else knows about this secret room, too?" said Theodosia. "Oh, yeah."

Delaine looked horrified. "What if whoever murdered Duke Wilkes was hiding in here?"

"Maybe," said Theodosia. "Or maybe this is how they escaped."

"But there isn't an exit," said Delaine, frowning. The killer would have been trapped." She thought about her words for a second. "Now *we're* trapped!"

"There doesn't seem to be an *obvious* exit," said Theodosia, peering about. "Nothing that says X marks the spot. But maybe if we hunt around a little . . ."

"This is totally freaking me out," said Delaine, her voice taking on a shrill quality. "I never mentioned this before, Theodosia, but I'm a tad claustrophobic. I don't do well in teeny-tiny little spaces. In fact, I absolutely despise small spaces like telephone booths, elevators, MRI tubes. . . ."

"And sports cars?" asked Theodosia.

"No, I'm okay with those," countered Delaine.

"Just take a few deep breaths," advised Theodosia. "Try to relax."

But Delaine's discomfort seemed to escalate. She fidgeted, moaned, and, in general, seemed to be on the verge of a crying jag. Theodosia, on the other hand, was beginning to feel a slight rush of exhilaration. Even though she'd taken a nasty tumble, was still brushing cobwebs from her hair, and was seemingly trapped in a dusty, hidden room searching for heaven knows what, she felt amazingly at ease. Theodosia knew her anxiety level should be jacked up to fever pitch, her adrenaline spiked so high, her fight or flight response should kick on like a jet engine. But it wasn't. She was excited but alert. Experiencing nervous tension, yes, but in a good way. Maybe she was permanently jaded from all those Nancy Drew books she'd devoured as a girl. Or all the time she'd spent playing Clue, trying to ascertain if Professor Plum had clobbered Colonel Mustard with a candlestick in the library. Whatever the reason, Theodosia was feeling more than just a little intrigued.

"Come hold this light, will you?" asked Theodosia. "I need to do some serious investigating, thump some more walls."

But as Delaine moved toward the table, she uttered a sharp squeal. "Ouch!"

"What's wrong?" asked Theodosia.

"Darn these shoes. Now I stubbed my toe."

Theodosia was down on the floor in a heartbeat. "You hit something with your toe?"

"I guess," said Delaine, fanning herself. "Or maybe I just tripped. I'm afraid I'm feeling awfully light-headed."

"No, there's something here," said Theodosia, feeling around with her hands.

"What do you mean?" asked Delaine. "Like a loose floorboard?"

"Floorboards," said Theodosia. She set the lantern down on the dusty floor where it cast a dim glow. "I think there might be some sort of opening here," said Theodosia, brushing her hands along the floor. "You see right here, where the floorboards don't fit quite flush with the others? There's kind of a crack."

Now Delaine was down on her hands and knees. "You think this could be a way out?" A note of hope had crept into her voice.

"Maybe," said Theodosia, struggling to scrunch her fingertips into the space between the floorboards. "Help me, Delaine. Lets try to pry this up."

"It's too heavy, nothing's happening," complained Delaine. "And I am absolutely *ruining* my manicure."

"We need some sort of tool," said Theodosia. "Nail file, pocket knife, something."

"Do I look like a janitor?" asked Delaine. "Do you think I carry *tools* around with me?"

"Hand me that old house key," said Theodosia.

Delaine handed it over to her and Theodosia wedged it down between two boards. "Good. Now get over here next to me," instructed Theodosia. "And try to slip your fingers under this board while I pry it up. On my count now . . . one, two, three . . . pull!"

"My fingers are *killing* me!" complained Delaine.

"Harder!" shouted Theodosia, as slowly, a small square of flooring moved under their goading, then rocked back on rusted hinges. A musty smell filled the room.

Delaine stared in disbelief. "You were right! That is a trap door!"

"The question is," said Theodosia, snatching up the lantern and holding it high. "Where does this lead?" She peered down a narrow, harrowingly steep set of stairs that seemed more ladder than staircase.

"You don't intend to climb down there, do you?" asked Delaine tremulously.

"Absolutely not," said Theodosia as she stared down into the tantalizing hole. "*We're* going to climb down there."

"No way," said Delaine stubbornly, folding her arms across her chest.

"Way," said Theodosia, shoving the lantern into Delaine's hands. "You hold this while I climb down, then you can pass it down to me and shinny down yourself."

"Yuck," said Delaine, peering down into the gaping hole. "More cobwebs. And I would have to be wearing a pencil skirt!"

The steps were narrow and poorly spaced, but both Theodosia and Delaine successfully negotiated them.

"We're in the cellar," said Delaine, once they'd both planted their feet on a rough flagstone floor and swung the lantern around. "I didn't even consider the fact that there must be a cellar."

Theodosia wrinkled her nose at the musty, loamy smell. "It's a cellar all right."

"So there's got to be a way out, right?" asked Delaine. She stared at a teetering pile of wooden boxes. "I mean look at all this junk. It had to get down here somehow. It sure wasn't dropped through that miserable little hole in the floor."

"What is all this stuff?" asked Theodosia. She swung the lantern from side to side, then aimed it at a wooden chest that was propped up at a crazy angle against a wooden pillar. Only the chest looked more lozenge-shaped than rectangular. "And what's *that* thing?"

"Some kind of old armoire?" asked Delaine.

Theodosia shone the light closer to it. A quarter inch of dust had settled on top, like dirty felt. "Agh," she exclaimed. "It's a coffin, standing on end."

Delaine sprang back. "A coffin. Are you serious?"

They stood together in the flickering light, staring at what had to be an antique coffin. Finally, Theodosia took a tentative step forward and peered at it. The coffin appeared to have tarnished brass handles, elaborate carving, and, of all things, a small oval glass window.

"It's got a window," said Theodosia. She was suddenly feeling a little light-headed herself.

"Stop trying to *scare* me!" hissed Delaine. She was almost in tears.

"No, I'm serious," stammered Theodosia. "A lot of old coffins had glass windows built into them. I suppose for . . . uh . . . viewing purposes?" She held the light up to the coffin's window, then suddenly pulled it away.

"What?" asked Delaine in a quavering whisper.

"I thought I saw something," said Theodosia. Her bravery seemed to be slipping away as the seconds ticked by.

Delaine clutched at Theodosia's sleeve. "You're freaking me out," she said in a low, pleading voice. "Please, Theo, I'm scared enough as it is."

"I wasn't trying to scare you," said Theodosia. She wasn't thrilled that they'd stumbled upon this coffin. But she *had* caught a quick peak of something inside. *A little face? A wisp of fabric? Oh, lord.*

"Open it," whispered Delaine.

"Why don't you open it?" said Theodosia.

Delaine shook her head violently. "I can't."

Theodosia tentatively stuck her hand out. She flipped the latch and stepped back as the coffin creaked open.

"Oh, my lord!" screamed Delaine, clamping a hand to her mouth. "Babies! Dead babies!"

Shining the light on the tiny creatures inside, Theodosia breathed a sigh of relief. "They're dolls," she told Delaine. "Look at the faces. Little fabric faces. They're just dirty rag dolls in tattered dresses."

Delaine put a hand on her heart. "Heaven help me. I thought I was going to go insane!"

Theodosia put a shaking hand on Delaine's shoulder. "You're okay," she told her. "We're both okay. Let's just keep shuffling our way through this junk and I'm sure we'll find a way out."

"Okay, okay," jabbered Delaine as they eased past an old spinning wheel piled on top of an old bed frame.

"This is like a nightmare version of the Heritage Society down here," said Theodosia. "Antiques without any of the charm."

"Are my eyes playing tricks on me?" asked Delaine with a hopeful lilt to her voice. "Or is it suddenly a little lighter down here?"

Theodosia gave a look around. They'd wandered another twenty feet or so since they'd first encountered the old coffin. "It does feel like filtered light, doesn't it?" said Theodosia.

"Even though the windows are obviously boarded up, a little light still seems to be finding its way in."

"Thank heavens," proclaimed Delaine.

"Let's keep snooping," suggested Theodosia. "See if we can find the stairway or even a root cellar or coal chute. Something that might have a door that leads to the outside world."

Delaine's startled gasp brought Theodosia up short.

"Now what?" asked Theodosia.

Saucer-eyed, Delaine pointed toward an old work bench. "Look!" was Delaine's choked response.

Theodosia raised the lantern high above her head and followed Delaine's stricken gaze. There, in the spill of the light, lying atop an old leather strap, was a knife handle with just the nub of a short, broken blade.

"What is it?" asked Delaine in a strangled voice.

Heart thumping like a timpani drum, Theodosia peered at the nasty-looking instrument. "Some sort of broken knife," said Theodosia. "But an old one. Look at the handle. It looks like it was carved from bone or ivory."

"I don't want to look," said Delaine, plucking at Theodosia's sleeve. But she was hypnotized by the implement. "What's that dark stuff? Where the blade's broken off?" asked Delaine.

"Not sure," said Theodosia, staring at the jagged, inch-long blade that projected from the bone handle. "But it looks like dried blood."

The two women stared at each other.

"Are you thinking what I'm thinking?" asked Delaine.

"'Fraid so," said Theodosia. She dug inside her shoulder bag, came up with a pencil. Gently, she prodded at the instrument, lifting it slightly then turning it over. "Hmm, interesting," she murmured.

"I wish you wouldn't fool around with that!" said Delaine, glancing about nervously.

Theodosia dropped the pen back in her shoulder bag, then pulled out a plastic bag filled with small dog treats. Jerky treats she used in Earl Grey's training sessions. "Hold out your hand," she told Delaine.

After emptying the treats into Delaine's hand, Theodosia took the plastic bag and carefully, very carefully, slid it under the broken knife.

"You're going to take it?" cried Delaine.

Theodosia stared at her. "Yes. Of course."

"Aren't we disturbing the crime scene?"

Theodosia hesitated. "Maybe. But this could turn out to be a critical piece of evidence. And if it disappears before we're able to get the police back here, we're really out of luck."

"You mean the *murderer* could come back for it?" Delaine shuddered. She hadn't thought about that possibility.

"You never know," said Theodosia. She slid the rest of the baggy under the knife, then gathered it up, taking care not to touch the handle or the perilously dangerous bit of metal until the knife was inside the plastic bag. Then she carefully laid the whole thing inside her purse, atop her wallet and checkbook.

"Be careful," warned Delaine. "Don't go reaching in there fast. You'll lose a finger for sure."

"Not to worry," Theodosia assured her. "I'm absolutely paranoid about sharp objects."

"With good reason," said Delaine, clutching Theodosia's arm tightly. "Now we've got to get out of here!" Absentmindedly she put one of the jerky treats to her lips, nibbled gently.

"This way," said Theodosia. "It seems a little lighter over here."

They threaded their way past mounds of broken furniture, an old trunk, a tangle of empty picture frames, and some old carriage wheels.

"You see what I see?" asked Theodosia. This part of the cellar wasn't quite so dark and Theodosia could see a flight of stairs leading up.

"Hooray!" said Theodosia as the two women pounded up the stairs. But when they arrived the door at the top was locked!

"We're trapped!" cried Delaine. "Trapped like rats!"

"Speak for yourself," said Theodosia, as she led Delaine back down the staircase. "C'mon, let's keep moving."

A few steps more and Delaine stopped short, suddenly staring at the wall ahead of them. "I think there's another way out!" she exclaimed.

Peering through the dark, Theodosia could vaguely see the outline of a narrow, wooden door.

"Thank goodness." Delaine sighed, suddenly hopeful. "You know, Theo, this beef jerky isn't half bad." She popped two pieces in her mouth. "Rather tasty, in fact."

"Delaine," said Theodosia, stopping in her tracks.

"What?" came Delaine's nervous reply, eyes darting around.

"You're eating Earl Grey's dog treats."

"What?" exclaimed a horrified Delaine. "I ate dog treats? You let me eat *dog* treats?" Grimacing mightily, she made a strangled, choking sound and spit out the half-chewed treats. "You could have *told* me, Theodosia. You *know* I eat when I'm nervous.

A muffled *clunk* just ahead of them shushed them immediately.

"What was that?" whispered Delaine.

"Don't know," Theodosia whispered back. "But if I had to guess, I'd say someone's on the other side of that door!"

"Are you serious?" whispered Delaine. "Then we've got to get out of here!"

"I'm pretty sure that *is* the way out," Theodosia whispered back.

"So we're going to do *what?*" asked Delaine, as they tiptoed toward the door. "Just go charging through like the light brigade?"

"Have you got a better idea?" asked Theodosia. She reached out and grasped the handle. It was a flat metal loop, like the handle on an old barn door.

"Can you feel the handle?" asked Theodosia in a low voice.

Delaine reached a hand out and nodded.

"Then pull!" yelled Theodosia.

The door slid open with a mighty groan, and then they were scrambling up a dilapidated stone staircase that ran parallel to an old cement coal chute.

Looking up, Theodosia saw wisps of silver clouds swirling overhead and felt fresh, cool air caress her face.

And then, like an eclipse suddenly blotting out the sun, a large, dark shape loomed above them! And Delaine's piercing scream echoed off the cellar walls!

6

"You!" shrieked Theodosia. The large, bulbous shape of Detective Burt Tidwell had not only blotted out the sun, it had blocked their scrambling exit.

"What on earth?" bellowed Burt Tidwell. "Where did you two come from?" He had a crowbar clutched in one chubby hand.

"Down there!" screamed Delaine. "We were trapped!"

Puzzled, Tidwell scratched at his head. "My investigators told me the basement was locked, that it was virtually closed off."

"You never checked the *basement?*" cried Theodosia.

Tidwell frowned, supremely unaccustomed to being yelled at. "We were going to send a team back later this afternoon to take a look, but it wasn't a priority."

"Well, you might want to *make* it a priority," said

Theodosia. "Since the entire downstairs is complete with cobwebs and coffins and things that go bump in the night."

"Goodness," said Tidwell, peering down. "Sounds more like a ride at Disneyland."

"You were trying to gain entrance?" asked Theodosia, suddenly noticing the crowbar in his hand.

"More like poking around," said Tidwell, with a big cat growl. He leaned over to drop the crowbar and his suit coat flapped open revealing his stomach, which billowed out like a weather balloon. "I have a highly suspicious nature," he added.

Tidwell might look like a bit of a buffoon, Theodosia decided, but he was as predatory as they came. Smart and canny, Tidwell was a dogged investigator who could lull you into thinking he was oblivious.

"We were *trapped* down there!" said Delaine, obviously still reeling from her terrifying adventure. "And then we saw this old coffin and found . . ." Delaine stopped suddenly, snapping her mouth shut like a scaly-backed swamp turtle.

"What did you find?" asked Tidwell, lifting a furry brow to peer at her.

Delaine's eyes slid sideways toward Theodosia, not sure whether she should reveal their strange findings to Tidwell.

But Theodosia was well aware that evidence must rightly be turned over to the police. And she was fairly sure this was, indeed, evidence.

Theodosia unsnapped the top of her handbag and tilted it so Tidwell could see in. The bit of knife glinted in the late afternoon sun, looking dangerous and sinister.

Burt Tidwell was suddenly taken aback. "Where on earth did you find that?"

Theodosia pointed silently at the dark hole they'd just scrambled out of.

"Is that a fact?" said Tidwell. "So you two ladies have been scuttling about the basement all afternoon, disturbing what might possibly be part of my crime scene?"

"Not at all," countered Theodosia. "If anything, we've conducted ourselves as helpful, concerned citizens."

"We certainly have," said Delaine, brushing herself off and gaining strength from Theodosia's bravado. "In fact, we even have a theory on how the murderer made his escape." She paused dramatically. "The same way we did!"

The pupils in Tidwell's beady eyes constricted slightly, betraying his surprise.

"Pray tell what are you blathering about, Miss Dish?" he asked.

"The secret room," said Delaine again.

His face finally registering surprise, Tidwell rocked back on his heels. "You really did stumble onto something," he muttered. He shook his head, jowls sloshing slightly.

"Literally and figuratively," said Theodosia.

"Show me where you found the knife," said Tidwell.

"This way, please," replied Delaine, suddenly adopting a superior air.

The three of them trooped down the cement stairway into the dark, dank basement. They wound their way back past the carriage wheels, picture frames, and old trunk, finally ending up at the work bench.

"See," said Delaine proudly as she held up the flickering lantern. "This is where we found it."

Tidwell bent forward and gave an inquisitive look. "Um hm."

"Do you think it came from upstairs?" asked Theodosia. "From the upstairs medical office?"

Tidwell stared at her for a long moment. "Not really," he said finally. "We checked last night and all the surgical sets and whatnots appeared to be complete."

"You're positive?" asked Theodosia.

"When the house was donated to the Heritage Society it came with an inventory list," said Tidwell. "Obviously we checked that list."

"And nothing was missing," said Theodosia. Now it was her turn to take a long pause. "Duke Wilkes was stabbed with some kind of knife that broke off when it was jammed into him." She paused. "And now the business end of a knife has turned up down here. Do you believe in coincidences, Detective Tidwell?"

"Only when they don't happen too often," he replied.

"You're going to have to hand over the knife," Tidwell told Theodosia after they'd climbed back up the coal chute steps. "Let me take it from here. We'll run our standard forensic tests and such."

"It's not going to take a forensic test to determine if this is the missing half of the piece that went into Duke Wilkes neck," said Theodosia. "You can eyeball it. *I* could eyeball it and make the call."

"Please," protested Tidwell. "I require neither your theories nor your help. In fact, I'm specifically requesting that you do not snoop, meddle, or otherwise tamper with anything related to this house."

Theodosia just stared at him.

"It's a polite request," said Tidwell. "Made with your safety in mind."

"I hear you," said Theodosia.

"I don't care for that look on your face, Miss Browning," continued Tidwell. "It's a sly, meddling look."

"She always looks like that," interjected Delaine.

This time Theodosia and Tidwell both stared at Delaine.

"Is that a fact?" asked Tidwell. He sounded unconvinced.

"Yes, it is," replied Delaine. She gave Theodosia a quick wink once Tidwell had turned toward the burgundy Crown Victoria that he'd parked in the back alley. "He likes you," whispered Delaine.

"What Tidwell really likes are scones and muffins and brioche," Theodosia insisted. "Me . . . well, let's just say he'd prefer I remain on the sidelines, minding my own business. And every once in a while I'm allowed to politely serve him tea and goodies."

"Miss Browning," said Tidwell as he returned from his car carrying the bottom half of a small, flat box. "Slide that baggy of yours in here, will you?"

Theodosia popped open her purse again, ready to dump her strange find onto Tidwell's cardboard tray.

But just as she tilted her purse and the baggy containing the knife slid onto the tray, there was a rustle and a bright flash as a young man sprang from a nearby clump of camellias.

The three of them looked up in surprise as the man held up a digital camera and snapped a second picture.

"Gotcha again!" exclaimed the young man in a gonzo tone of voice. "Wonderful!"

Tidwell reared back in anger. "Hand over that camera!" he demanded in his best law officer's voice.

"Not on your life," said the young photographer, cupping his camera protectively and talking two giant steps backward. "My boss is gonna love the shots! Maybe even give me a bonus!"

"And your boss is . . . ?" demanded Tidwell.

"Bill Glass," said the photographer. Dressed in jeans, a ragged sweater, and a floppy cap, he looked more like a slacker skateboarder than a professional photographer. "I'm Gep Bartlet, his protégé."

"This photo is going to appear in *Shooting Star?*" asked Delaine, suddenly interested. "Do you think you could take a couple more shots?" She brushed at her skirt and poufed up her hair. "I'm not sure you caught us at the most flattering moment."

"No problem, lady," said Gep, stepping forward and snapping another four or five shots.

"Stop it this instant!" cried Tidwell. "You're infringing on official police business!"

"Wrong," said the photographer. "I'm a photojournalist whose artistic freedom is protected by the United States Constitution and its right of free speech." Gep squinted at the back of his camera, clicking back through the half-dozen or so digital shots he'd taken. "Hey," he said to Theodosia. "I got a perfect shot of you with that knife."

"This is rather exciting." Delaine chortled. "Now everyone will know Theodosia's hot on the trail of a killer!"

"I'm not hot on the trail of anything," protested Theodosia.

"She certainly isn't!" said an outraged Tidwell. His face seemed to be changing hue faster than the NBC peacock, going from Technicolor red to outraged blue.

"Nice try, guys." The photographer grinned. "But after last night's murder this photo is the perfect art to run with that story. Ha! This is the kind of stuff that sells like crazy on the magazine stands. Mr. Glass told me to hang around here and see what turns up. I guess he's got a real nose for news!"

"Which issue will these photos appear in?" asked Delaine.

"Next *Shooting Star* comes out Friday," said the photographer.

"I'm going to be in Friday's issue?" Theodosia gasped. *Gulp. This wasn't what I bargained for. Not at all!*

7

The sun had already gone down by the time Theodosia arrived at the Heritage Society. She had to talk to Timothy Neville about something and she was hoping he hadn't yet left his office and headed for home.

Earlier, when Theodosia had first seen the knife in that dank basement, she'd poked at it with her pen. And noticed a small, faded label on one side of the handle. The side that Tidwell hadn't really looked at carefully. The label was paper, yellowed with age, almost matching the bone color of the handle, with a couple numbers handwritten on it.

Theodosia had visited the Heritage Society's storage room with Drayton when she was helping him set up a Civil War memorabilia show. And she was reasonably sure she'd seen that label before. In fact, it looked decidedly like the old labels and coding system that had been used by the Heritage Society's registrar in its pre-computer era.

Scurrying across the patio, Theodosia glanced up. A Charleston autumn sky had moved in and sprawled across the city. Moody and dark, thick with swirling clouds riding on a sharp breeze that carried a salty hint of sea.

Theodosia reached for the wrought iron handle and pulled at the heavy wooden door. Locked.

Impatient, she stabbed at the doorbell several times and listened as it rang deep within the heavy walls of the Heritage Society. For added impetus, Theodosia wrapped sharply on the door with her knuckles. *Please hear me Timothy. Please let me in.*

She kept up her doorbell-pushing and knuckle-wrapping for almost two full minutes, her efforts paying off when she finally heard Timothy's raspy voice on the other side of the door.

"We're closed," came his muffled response. "Kindly return tomorrow."

"Timothy!" cried Theodosia. "It's me, Theodosia. Let me in!"

There was a click and a second click and then Timothy's face appeared as the door cracked open. "Theodosia?" he said, clearly surprised to see her. "What are *you* doing here so late?"

She gazed into Timothy's high-cheeked simian-looking face. "There's a problem."

"There's always a problem," replied Timothy, cocking his head slightly, giving the illusion of a curious magpie.

"This has to do with last night," Theodosia told him.

Timothy's shoulders sagged visibly beneath his handmade suit. He was obviously deeply disturbed by Duke Wilkes's death. And why shouldn't he be? Duke Wilkes had been a friend and patron of the Heritage Society.

"I don't need more of this tragedy coming down upon my head," Timothy declared. But he moved aside and gestured impatiently for Theodosia to step in.

"There's something we have to check on," Theodosia told Timothy as she followed him down the long hallway toward his office. Lights were turned low, the Aubusson carpet whispered underfoot, and various South Carolina patriarchs stared down from oil paintings hung on the wall.

"*Tempus fugit,*" said Timothy. They had arrived at his office and, judging from his jittery gestures and stance, he was obviously impatient to get going. "I'm meeting friends for dinner at Antonio's and I'm already late," he explained in a brusque tone.

"Please," Theodosia said. "Just give me two minutes."

Timothy glanced at his watch again. "Go," he told her.

Quickly, Theodosia related her misadventures of an hour earlier. Timothy frowned in disapproval as her words poured out, but refrained from actually voicing any criticism.

When Theodosia finished, Timothy grimaced and said. "So you found the other half of the murder weapon. Which the police will now follow through on as far as evidence goes. Good news, I'd say. Though nothing can blunt this terrible tragedy."

"Not good news," said Theodosia. "I think the knife we found came from your storage room. At least it had one of the Heritage Society's old labels stuck to it."

Timothy stared at her with hooded eyes. "You can't be serious."

"I'd feel a whole lot better if we checked," said Theodosia. She hesitated, letting Timothy digest this new information. "I'm sure you would, too."

"You want to look at the registrar's records," he said.

Timothy seemed to be having some trouble getting his arms around the idea.

"Could we do that? Please?"

Timothy frowned and shook his head. "We have antique knives in storage, yes, but I'm confident none of them are missing or even misplaced. In fact, they're rarely brought out of storage anymore. The Heritage Society's main focus for the past few years has been art and antiquities rather than weaponry. That's not to say we haven't had exhibits in the . . ."

"Indulge me," said Theodosia.

Timothy let out a deep sigh. The sigh of a man who was not easily swayed, who abhorred capitulation. "As you wish," he replied.

Theodosia had always thought of the Heritage Society as the perfect baronial manor. Built of limestone, with high, soaring ceilings crisscrossed with wooden beams and stone fireplaces scattered throughout, the building projected a certain romantic *Prisoner of Zenda* aura. A person could live here, she felt, and happily collect all the books they wanted. Space would never be a problem. There would always be another room, another wall, where one could add a new section of floor-to-ceiling bookcases.

"Down here," said Timothy, pausing at the top of a flight of steps. "The storage room is down here."

Theodosia followed him down the wide, wooden steps and then through a labyrinth of rooms. Finally they came to the registrar's office. With its worn wooden desks, metal file cabinets, and steno chairs, it looked like an office plucked from the fifties. Except for the computers and phone system. Those were new and seemingly up to-date.

Timothy snatched a key ring off a hook and led her to a door. "Everything is kept in here," he told her. "The truly valuable items such as paintings, jewelry, and historical documents are locked in a vault upstairs. But everything else, the furniture, larger sculptures, antique ceramics, and odd whatnots are all stored here."

"And the record book?" Theodosia asked as Timothy pushed open the door.

"In here, too," sighed Timothy.

The Heritage Society's storage room looked exactly like a museum storage room ought to look. It was large with a vaulted ceiling, floor-to-ceiling shelves piled high with a delightful mix of art and artifacts. There were Civil War–era saddles, shelves of Edgefield pottery, old rice planting implements, vases, crocks, and what appeared to be thousands of boxes and cartons.

Timothy turned to a page marked *weaponry* and studied it, a frown creasing his lined face.

"What?" asked Theodosia.

"We show twelve knives in our collection," mumbled Timothy. "Let's have a look."

They edged their way down a narrow corridor between wooden shelves that were stacked with old bungling boards, sweetgrass baskets, antique picture frames, and Civil War sabers.

Timothy's eyes searched out one of the lower shelves. "Should be here," he told Theodosia.

"Twelve you say," said Theodosia, as she helped him pull out boxes.

They searched through the first six boxes.

"So far so good," said Timothy. "Ten knives accounted for."

"So they're probably all here," said Theodosia. "Which really is good news." She lifted the lid on a final leather case and they both stared into the interior. A single knife with a carved bone handle rested on aged velvet.

They both let out disappointed sighs.

"There were supposed to be a *pair* of dirks," said Timothy finally.

"A dirk?" said Theodosia.

"It's a type of knife," said Timothy. "Used during the Civil War."

"Look," said Theodosia, "you can still see a slight depression in the velvet." Her excitement was suddenly tempered by the gravity of the situation. "Well, at least we know it *was* here."

Timothy's face seemed to collapse on itself. "Dear lord, no," he breathed.

Back upstairs in Timothy's office, the two of them stared morosely at each other across Timothy's ocean-sized desk. A single Tiffany lamp illuminated the room.

They'd decided not to move or further touch the cases containing the rest of the knives. That part of the storage room would undoubtedly be deemed a crime scene or whatever the police decided to call it.

"So you didn't even realize one was missing," said Theodosia.

"Are you kidding?" replied Timothy. "I didn't even know we had that many knives. Or, in this case, a dirk." He bent down, slid open a desk drawer, and pulled out a silver flask and two small crystal glasses. Pouring measured servings of amber liquid into each of the glasses, Timothy handed one to Theodosia. "Cognac," he told her. "*L'Esprit de Courvoisier.* One of Napoleon's favorites."

Putting the glass to her lips, Theodosia tipped it back gently, and took a tiny sip. Cognac trickled down her throat, tickling and warming her in a reassuring way.

"And the set the dirk was taken from has never been put on view?" asked Theodosia.

Timothy downed his brandy in one gulp and was already pouring himself a second shot. "Not to my knowledge. As you probably know, our displays tend to be highly thematic. Nautical charts and sea-faring implements, rice plantations, the early settlement of Charles Town, and early architecture are our staple themes. In all my years as executive director of the Heritage Society I can't recall a display of knives. Guns yes, knives no."

Theodosia decided to try a different approach. "Who has access to the storeroom?" she asked Timothy.

He suddenly looked glum. "We've pretty much had a laissez-faire attitude about accessing the downstairs store room. I mean, the key ring is hung on a nail and whoever needs to go in there, just grabs it and takes it."

"So that might be . . . who?" prompted Theodosia.

"Employees, volunteers, board members, donors . . . pretty much anyone who comes through here. I already explained that the really valuable things are kept in a vault up here on the main floor. But everything else, the larger pieces and odd whatnots . . ." Timothy's voice trailed off.

Theodosia thought about this. The Heritage Society probably had hundreds of people streaming through the building all the time. There were always board meetings, fund-raisers, special events, public showings. Timothy was right, access was wide open.

Timothy took another measured sip of brandy and his eyes sparkled. Theodosia knew he was probably just short of shedding actual tears and felt awful that she had brought this problem to his door.

"I feel just terrible about this," stammered Timothy. "Duke was a very good friend of mine." He hesitated, then cleared his throat. "Duke was a good friend to Charleston."

"I know he was," said Theodosia. She took another tiny sip of her brandy. "Does the Heritage Society keep a visitors' log?"

Timothy continued to look morose. "There's an appointment book, yes," he answered. "But, obviously, not everyone is recorded. Board members, docents, and volunteers all come and go. Museum visitors . . . well, we just collect their six dollars and give them a pamphlet for a self-guided tour of our three galleries. There's an optional guest book, but not everyone signs it. There's never really been a problem until, uh . . . now."

"The police will be knocking on your door first thing tomorrow," said Theodosia. She knew Tidwell would spot the label as soon as he had a chance to really eyeball the knife . . . the dirk. He might not realize it was the Heritage Society's label right off the bat, but he was a clever fellow. He'd soon put two and two together.

"Why wait till morning?" asked Timothy. "Better to call the police right now."

"You're probably right," said Theodosia, wondering what Burt Tidwell's reaction was going to be. Probably . . . anger. Anger that she hadn't been up front in telling him about the Heritage Society connection. Well, that was water over the dam now.

Timothy put a hand to his head and slid down in his leather chair. "Last night's episode was simply awful," he said in a mournful tone. "And now this." His thin shoulders slumped. "You know," he added as he reached for the phone, "everyone associated with the Heritage Society thought the absolute world of Duke."

"Well . . . not quite everyone," murmured Theodosia.

8

❦

Theodosia was relieved to finally be home. It had been a long day, a dreadfully strange day. Thankfully, Haley, who lived in the garden apartment across the alley, had left a note saying she'd fed Earl Grey then taken him out for a walk around six o'clock. So the pup had eaten, stretched his legs, and blown the carbon out of his system. Which meant she'd be able to relax for a while. Fix a little supper, kick back, and spend some quality time with the mixed-breed dog she'd dubbed her "Dalbrador."

"Hey, big guy," she told Earl Grey as she stood at the stove, stirring a pot of crab bisque. "Friday's the big day. Think we should try to squeeze in a practice session tonight?"

Laying on his braided rag rug, elegant head resting on his suedelike paws, Earl Grey gazed at her with complete and unabashed love. He had been Theodosia's constant companion for three years and never a day went by that they didn't share a special moment together.

Theodosia had found Earl Grey as a pup, shivering and cowering in the back alley, soaked to the skin from a cold, hard spring rain. She'd brought him in, rubbed him down with soft towels, then fed him a couple leftover tea sandwiches. And when the rescued dog had gazed up at her, his limpid brown eyes filled with love and gratitude, Theodosia knew instantly that this was the dog for her. No pedigree was necessary. No AKC accreditation required. The only thing that mattered was the bond between them.

Of course, Earl Grey also proved to be a rather brilliant fellow. He took to obedience training like a duck to water, then went on to earn his Canine Good Citizen award. Six months of training with Big Paw Service Dogs of Charleston and Earl Grey also became an accredited Therapy Dog. Now when Earl Grey donned his spiffy blue vest and roamed the halls of the O'Doud Senior Home, he was a working dog on official business. He did playful "meet and greets" that cheered the residents and played a little "fetch." Even a few Alzheimer's patients, patients who no longer responded to their own family members, extended their gnarled hands to cup and stroke Earl Grey's velvety head when he gently poked his muzzle into their lap. Just that small connection, the veil of isolation momentarily lifting, never failed to touch Theodosia's heart.

After brewing a cup of Lapsang souchong, one of her favorite smoky-flavored Chinese teas, Theodosia poured her crab bisque into a blue and white Japanese bowl, then added a thin slice of lemon for garnish. She arranged everything on a small silver tray, added a napkin and a ramekin spoon, then carried it into the living room.

Sipping a few spoonfuls of soup, savoring the rich, melded flavors of the crab, onions, cream, and sherry, Theodosia settled back against the oversized cushions of her sofa. Although she often dreamt of owning a larger house, this little apartment above the Indigo Tea Shop served as a perfect refuge.

It had started out as shabby chic with lots of chintz and prints. Over the last year and a half, however, her apartment had veered toward old world elegance. Wallpaper had been stripped away and walls painted wonderful deep, rich shades. Oil paintings with ornate, gilded frames now graced the walls. Elegant Aubusson carpets covered hardwood floors. It was dramatic, it was restful, it was home.

And the perfect place to ponder a myriad of questions.

Like who murdered Duke Wilkes?

Theodosia supposed it could have been anyone who'd been at the Candlelight Concert last night.

Anyone. Last night's roster had offered up a veritable Who's Who of Charleston business people. Lots of executives and heads of companies. But which one of them had it in for Duke?

Theodosia pondered that for a minute. Duke Wilkes was retired now, but he still sat on the board of directors of Victory Capital, the venture capital firm he'd helped found back in the seventies. He and his partners were the money men that business people sought out when they needed major financing for start-up companies and spin-off ventures. She knew from reading The *Post and Courier* that Victory Capital had funded companies such as Windcare Pharmaceuticals, Obata Telecom, and Axion Software. The men at Victory, not unlike the gnomes of Zurich, were the financiers that helped new companies spread their wings and soar. They were the dream makers.

Theodosia also knew that a would-be entrepreneur would have to have his ducks in a row when approaching Victory Capital. You had to make a formal presentation in which you laid out your business plan. And that business plan had better be extremely well thought out. Victory Capital would require a carefully crafted corporate mission statement and executive summary. And they'd want to see nitty-gritty details, as well. Start-up expenses would have to be carefully detailed, as well as source of volume, competitive market data, projected revenues, and staffing plans.

Theodosia had done her own mini business plan when she'd first laid plans to open the Indigo Tea Shop. And even with her extensive marketing background, constructing a theoretical company and then running the numbers on it hadn't been a simple task.

So . . . could Duke's murderer have been someone whose financing had been turned down by Victory Capital? she wondered. *A would-be entrepreneur whose plans had been deemed shaky? One whose dreams had been derailed and was now seething with anger and resentment?*

Maybe. Anger and festering rage can be powerful motivators.

On the other hand, Theodosia knew that Duke Wilkes had also been fiercely involved in civic activities. He was a member of the Heritage Society, headed a huge group of Civil War reenactors, and served on the board of directors of several non-profit organizations. So possibilities lurked there, too. Duke had often been outspoken and opinionated to the point of being crusty. So he certainly could have ruffled more than a few feathers.

Theodosia set her soup bowl down on the coffee table and closed her eyes. Let her mind free associate over the information she'd managed to pick up so far.

Why, she wondered, *had the murder weapon, or at least part of it, been left in the basement? Because the killer came back upstairs to join the crowd? Hmm. Maybe.*

The telephone's ring interrupted Theodosia's musing.

Leaning over, she reached for the phone. "Hello?"

"Theo," came Drayton's excited voice. "I'm glad you're home."

"What's wrong?" she asked him.

"Are you serious?" asked Drayton. "My ears are still burning. I just this moment got off the phone with Timothy. To say the old fellow was agitated would be a complete understatement. And, I must say, I share his nervousness."

Uh oh, Timothy told Drayton about Delaine and I going into the Chait House this afternoon. And about finding the dirk.

"You went back to the Chait House," Drayton continued, managing to sound both excited and disapproving at the same time.

"The plan was to have a little peek," said Theodosia. "I was hoping the trail might still be hot."

"Sounds like it might have been a little *too* hot," said Drayton.

Somehow, Theodosia had known that would be Drayton's exact response.

"Hold on a minute, Drayton," she countered. "You were there today, you saw how upset Pookie was. Delaine and I were just trying to help. In fact, you thought my jumping in to lend assistance was a perfectly *good* idea at the time."

"Silly me, I thought you were just going to keep an ear to the ground," said Drayton. "But now . . . well, you've certainly managed to shuffle things around. Now it would appear that the focus of the investigation has turned completely back on the Heritage Society."

"No way did I engineer that on purpose," replied Theodosia. "But once I saw that old Heritage Society label on the dirk, I couldn't *not* follow up." She paused for a moment. "Besides, Timothy is pretty well convinced that the murder weapon was stolen from the Heritage Society's storage room."

"I know he is," was Drayton's hoarse response. "Still, this is all deeply disturbing."

Theodosia could feel Drayton's fear and worry. After all, the Heritage Society was his baby, his pride and joy. He'd served on the board of directors for many years and derived enormous pleasure from its many accomplishments.

Wait until Drayton finds out I'm probably going to have a photo spread on the front page of Shooting Star, *thought Theodosia. Then he'll really have a cat.*

"Listen, Drayton," said Theodosia, deciding to strike while the iron was hot. "Can you lay your hands on the Heritage Society's membership list?"

"You're going to *continue* pursuing this?" asked Drayton. "Is that really wise? You've shaken loose what would appear to be a major clue, now shouldn't you step back and let the professionals take over from here?"

"Well . . . uh . . . I thought I'd nose around a little bit more," replied Theodosia. "For Pookie's sake."

"Uh huh," said Drayton.

"Don't you think it's *worth* pursuing?" asked Theodosia.

Drayton seemed to be mulling over his thoughts. Finally he said, "I suppose I do. Pookie is the dearest soul that ever walked God's green earth. And to be honest, she was quite correct about wanting someone *on the inside,* as she so delicately phrased it."

"That's you and me, then," said Theodosia.

"Am I to understand you want *me* to be complicit in this as well?" asked Drayton. He sounded a little surprised.

"You're one of the smartest people I know," replied Theodosia. "And, unlike Delaine, you can keep a confidence."

Drayton gave a nervous chuckle. "Ah, flattery will get you everywhere."

"What I really want to know is, will you get me that list?" asked Theodosia.

"Of course I'll do what I can," replied Drayton.

Twenty minutes later Theodosia was outside with Earl Grey. Friday was the Ainsworth Kennel Club Show and they were supposed to be part of the halftime entertainment.

Earl Grey was going to retrieve a dropped book, pick up a pencil, and demonstrate how he could walk alongside a wheelchair. Although Theodosia didn't have use of a wheelchair tonight, there'd be one available on Friday. So Earl Grey could show the crowds how he could carefully maneuver alongside one without getting his paws clipped by the wheels.

They were busy practicing in the back alley when Haley's window suddenly slid up and her face appeared between the curtains.

"Is that you out there?" she called.

"Me and Earl Grey," Theodosia replied. "He says thanks for the nice walk."

"Tell him he's very welcome," said Haley. "He conducted himself like a perfect gentleman . . . gentledog . . . whatever. Say, what are you guys doing putzing around outside at ten o'clock on a school night?"

"Just brushing up on our service dog skills," said Theodosia. "Earl Grey's got his big demo on Friday."

"Earl Grey doesn't need to practice." Haley laughed. "He's perfect."

"Practice makes perfect," whispered Theodosia as she shortened up Earl Grey's leash and walked him smartly beside her.

9

❧

"*What I want* to know," said Haley, "is why the Chait House sat empty for so many years."

It was Tuesday morning and Theodosia had finally brought Haley up to speed on the events of yesterday. Now, as the three of them scurried about the tea shop, setting tables, lighting candles, and giving silverware a final wipe, they tossed out their random questions and comments.

"The Augustus Chait House has a checkered past," said Drayton in a somber tone. He placed two Crown Ducal saucers on one of the smaller tables, followed by matching teacups.

"I thought only women had checkered pasts," said Haley. She grinned sheepishly when Drayton raised a single, quivering eyebrow at her. "Not that I *know* anyone like that," she added. "Personally, I mean."

"Let me amend my statement then," said Drayton.

"I should have said that the Chait House has a strange and haunted history."

"Haunted!" exclaimed Haley. "Now you're talking."

"Tell us," urged Theodosia. "I thought I pretty much knew all the legends and lore on the houses in the historic district. But this is a new one for me."

"It's true the house was built by Augustus Chait, a pharmacist whose patent medicines were sold all over the country," said Drayton. "But the house has never had a particularly happy history. After the old pharmacist passed away, ownership remained in the Chait family, but the house became a hospital, then an orphanage, and finally a funeral home in the forties and fifties."

Which explains the old casket, thought Theodosia. *And if it had been an orphanage, maybe the dolls, too.*

"Don't quote me," said Drayton, "but I believe that, until now, it's been unoccupied for some thirty-five years. Not that's it's actually occupied at present."

"At least not owner occupied," said Theodosia, thinking about the lantern that had been left on the table in the hidden room, the dust that had been wiped clean, the broken dirk handle they'd found in the basement.

"And it's really got a secret passage and a secret room?" asked Haley.

Theodosia nodded. "I'll give you the fifty-cent tour if you want."

"Just say when!" exclaimed Haley as Drayton vehemently shook his head in protest.

"Absolutely not!" he told them.

"Why not?" asked Haley, ever the adrenaline junkie. "Creepy crawling that old house would be a gas."

"I'm sure the police have once again deemed that house

off limits," said Drayton. "And for good reason." He glanced at Theodosia, who had suddenly gotten very busy positioning a newly decorated grapevine wreath on the brick wall. "Now, please, let's try to remain focused. We have a *huge* day ahead of us."

Haley waved a hand. "We'll be fine. No problem."

"You're absolutely positive Miss Dimple will be in to help?" asked Drayton. "You did tell her we're hosting a major tea this afternoon?"

"Cool your jets," advised Haley. "She knows we have a big event planned. She'll probably pop in any minute."

"Because Theodosia and I are still planning a quick run to Le Nest this morning," explained Drayton.

"I'm hip to the program." Haley chuckled. "Honestly, Drayton. Calm down."

"Can we at least run through the menu?" he asked.

"Our luncheon menu or the afternoon tea?" asked Haley.

"Afternoon tea," said Drayton. "I know it's perverse of me, but I can only worry about one thing at a time."

"You've never been big on multitasking," said Haley. "And the tea for that bigwig congressman just happens to be your major worry du jour."

"Could we please just *do* this?" asked Drayton. Fiddling with his bow tie, he glanced across the room where Theodosia was trying mightily not to let the corners of her mouth twitch upward. "Theodosia?" Drayton called. "Can you join us?"

"First course," said Haley, all business now as they sat together at a table, "is Crab Carolina. It's a small puff pastry amply stuffed with crab meat and gruyere cheese."

"Sounds wonderful," murmured Theodosia.

"Check," muttered Drayton, uncapping his Montblanc pen and making a notation in his black notebook.

"Second course is apple-raisin soup," continued Haley. "Served in those little soup bowls with the matching plates." She glanced up at Drayton. "The ones you picked up in Savannah when that French place went belly up?"

"Yes, yes," said Drayton. "Now what about scones? Our guests always adore our scones."

"I'm getting to that," said Haley. "I'm doing almond scones today. And we'll probably serve them right alongside the fruit compote."

"With the usual complement of Devonshire cream, lemon curd, and jelly?" asked Drayton.

Haley nodded. "In our three-sectioned cut glass bowls."

"Excellent," said Drayton.

"Then, per your request," said Haley, breezing along, "*two* luncheon entrees. Our guests will have their choice of a chicken breast with wild rice stuffing or trout almondine. Both will be drizzled with white wine sauce, a classic velouté, and served with gingered green beans."

"And for dessert?" asked Drayton, tapping his pen.

"Four different desserts presented on tiered serving trays," said Haley. "A veritable *pasticcio* of miniature pastries and candy."

"So no tall parfait glasses?" asked Drayton.

"Not for this tea," said Haley.

"Harumph," remarked Drayton.

Haley looked up at Theodosia and grinned. "Drayton's certainly got himself in a mood today, doesn't he?"

"He sure does," she agreed.

"I'm not in a mood," protested Drayton. "I'm just extremely busy. We're all busy."

"For your information," continued Haley, "our desserts will include tuxedo brownies, Charleston cream cheese cookies, white fudge, and chocolate leaves."

"Wonderful," proclaimed Theodosia. "Sounds like a superb finale."

Haley fingered the page containing her notes. "I thought so, too."

"Now what about favors?" asked Drayton. "Has anyone thought about favors?"

"All taken care of," said Theodosia. She'd come in early this morning and dispatched with that little chore. "Handmade chocolate caramels, tiny glassine bags of Jasmine tea, small straws filled with raw sugar, and cinnamon sticks."

"Tea party in a bag," said Haley.

"And they're all put together?" asked Drayton.

"In my office," said Theodosia. "All tied up in little gold mesh bags, ready to go."

"Hey, Miss Dimple," called Haley as the front door burst open and Miss Dimple came chugging in. "Right on time."

"Glad you could make it," said Drayton, looking somewhat relieved as he peered over tortoiseshell half glasses. "Come join us. We're just making sure we're all on the same page."

Pulling a pale pink scarf from around her neck, Miss Dimple shrugged out of her nubby sweater. "Still so worried about your big tea this afternoon?" she asked.

"Yes," said Drayton.

"No," said Haley. "But Drayton seems to have pre-party jitters."

"Take a look at Haley's menu," said Theodosia, sliding the page across the table. "It's fantastic."

After trading her sweater for one of the long black Parisian waiter's aprons that hung on the coat rack, Miss Dimple came over to their table. "Wow," she said, gold bangles jangling on her chubby wrists as she scanned Haley's notes. "Five courses. No wonder you wanted me to work all day today."

"And you can, can't you?" asked Theodosia. Miss Dimple was a dear who rarely said no.

"You have me from now until whenever," said Miss Dimple. "Although I have to be home by five to feed my kitties. Sampson and Delilah get very huffy if their dinner is delayed. By the way, this fancy schmancy tea you're catering . . . who's it for anyway?"

"Congressman Clive Bonham and about forty prominent female guests," said Drayton. "And please understand, we're going all out in our effort to impress."

As Miss Dimple stared at the menu, her penciled brows suddenly knit together in a frown. With her plump cheeks and sparkling blue eyes her face had the appearance of a grandmotherly cabbage patch doll, albeit a worried one.

"What's wrong, Miss Dimple?" asked Haley. "You see a problem with the menu?"

Miss Dimple paused, patting at her flyaway white hair, obviously gathering her thoughts before she spoke. "Congressman Clive Bonham," she said slowly. "Wasn't he called to task a few months ago about some shaky campaign contributions?"

Drayton sighed, unhappy Miss Dimple had brought up

what he saw as a messy political issue that had no bearing on his tea. "Seems to me I might have heard something about that," he said abruptly. "But that's all in the past now."

But Miss Dimple was not about to let it go. "You know who the whistle-blower was, don't you?"

"Who?" asked Theodosia, her curiosity suddenly aroused.

Miss Dimple glanced about nervously. "Duke Wilkes."

"You're kidding," muttered Drayton.

"Say it ain't so," said Haley.

"Hmm," said Theodosia. Up to this point, her suspect list had been sketchy at best. But, she decided, this accusation or rumor or whatever it was, was definitely worth checking on.

10

❧

Theodosia *was locked* in the throes of indecision about
which table linens to buy. There was the diamond damask
pattern, inspired by rich fabrics originally used at medieval
banquets. And then there was the floral pattern, subtle, in-
tricate, and oh so elegant. Both designs were equally spectacular, both amazingly expensive. What a dilemma!

Wandering about Claudia Chait's linen shop, Le Nest,
Theodosia decided the place was everything Corky had told
her it was. Specializing in antique and high-end linens, this
small, elegant jewel of a shop was also stuffed with duvet
covers, woolen throws, aprons, and tea towels. And not only
was it merchandised perfectly, the shop itself was gorgeous.

Claudia had hired Perkin Parsons, a genius of a local dec-
orator. He had swooped in and immediately declared that
all four walls, as well as the ceiling, must be painted. Parsons had whitewashed on a creamy alabaster-colored paint,

then wiped it down until the woodwork showed through slightly but the alabaster still imparted an amazing glow. An enormous glittering crystal chandelier had been hung in the center of the store. And Claudia had scoured antique shops and tag sales throughout the South Carolina countryside until she'd amassed a marvelous assortment of antique furnishings.

Now down comforters billowed from old trunks, table linens were stacked on antique breakfronts, and tea towels spilled out of cypress cupboards and cabinets.

As Theodosia happily explored, Drayton and Claudia were seated at a small Sheraton table that Claudia used specifically for tabletop displays and hands-on demonstrations. They seemed to be engaged in some sort of game that could only be called "dueling napkin folding."

"My favorite is still the knotted fold," said Claudia. She was petite with tidy brown hair and warm brown eyes. And her small hands worked quickly, as she folded and knotted her napkin, then set the finished piece in front of Drayton.

"The tailored fold isn't bad either," said Drayton. Not to be outdone, he grabbed another napkin and began a complicated fold.

"You prefer the pleated and tied?" Claudia asked as she continued to fold table napkins at super sonic speed. "Or the party fan?"

"Love the fan," said Drayton as he, too, folded and tucked. "But I really adore the bishop's hat."

"Ah, so you know the tricky ones, too?" Claudia laughed. "Cuffed roll fold, cat's paw . . ."

"And the triangle pocket fold," said Drayton, squinting at her last arrangement. "I'm familiar with most of them," he told her. "But my technique isn't quite up to snuff." He wiggled his hands in the air and laughed. "I think my fingers are too big."

Wandering about the store, Theodosia, meanwhile, had discovered an herb section. Three metal tubs perched atop a wrought iron garden bench. In each tub were loose herbs and a large metal scoop.

"Oh, you've got lavender bundles and herbal bouquets, too," Theodosia called to Claudia.

Claudia smiled as her nimble fingers continued to work. "We import our lavender, chervil, and ylang-ylang from Provence. And you see those wheat sheaves? Also from Provence. They're created on a shuttle loom and are very cute when used as wall decor."

Theodosia studied the wreath of Mediterranean oak leaves, the array of olive oil soaps, the sateen pillows filled with lavender, and the French market baskets with leather handles. Clearly Claudia had found a niche.

Moving along, eyes taking it all in, Theodosia came to a cabinet that housed antique linens. She fingered a pair of antique linen pillowcases. They were gorgeous. Old, hand-stitched, hand embroidered, too. She glanced at the price tag. The pair was marked at ninety-nine dollars. "How old are these pillow cases?" Theodosia asked.

Claudia wrinkled her nose, thinking. "I suppose sixty . . . maybe seventy years?"

"Wonderful." Theodosia thought how romantic it would be if some pre–World War II bride had lovingly included them in her trousseau. "And it smells so heavenly in here, too," said Theodosia, picking up a sheaf of dried lavender and inhaling the fragrant aroma.

"When we designed the store, we tried to come up with ways to appeal to all the senses," Claudia told her.

Theodosia nodded. She was also a huge proponent of aromatherapy. In fact, the Indigo Tea Shop, with its vast array of tins, canisters, and jars filled to the brim with tea, also seemed to impart an aromatherapy-type affect on customers. Shoulders seemed to relax, facial expressions seemed to soften, voices suddenly lost that hard-edged, world-weary tone. She'd always chalked it up to the chamomile, hibiscus, and jasmine tea that seemed to permeate the air. Even as the simple act of sipping tea served to calm the nerves and inspire tranquillity, so did inhaling a tea's rich scent.

"What do you think of my tea towel assortment?" asked Claudia. She noted that Theodosia was lingering in front of a large mahogany sideboard, hungrily gazing at ample stacks of tea towels.

"I'm in awe," admitted Theodosia. "Truly, I've never seen such an extensive collection."

"Most are French," Claudia told her. "Alsace was and still is home to the best artisans and fabric printers. And, of course, they use only the finest cotton yarns. Take a look at those Bequvillé towels."

Theodosia gently fingered a stack of towels. The fabric was exquisite, the weave soft and pliable under her fingertips. And the designs . . . oh, my.

"These designs are incredible," Theodosia told Claudia. "I particularly like the butterflies. Well, the iris is very charming, too . . . oh, and here's a terrific one with a brush stroke sketch of Chartres Cathedral!"

"Now take a gander at the stack next to it," instructed Claudia. "Those are by Moutet, which as you probably know is a rather famous company located in the French Basque country."

Theodosia gazed at the Moutet line and grinned. These tea towels were far less formal and featured whimsical, French-inspired doodles. Some carried snippets of stanzas from Bach's music compositions and what looked like part of an opera program for *Cyrano*. One towel was stenciled with joyful, bouncing type that proclaimed. *"Jo m'éveille, le matin, avec une joie secrete."*

Checking some of the price tags, Theodosia caught her breath. Forty-five dollars a towel. An awful lot of money. Still . . . she was a collector and these imported tea towels were a rare indulgence.

"Good heavens," exclaimed Drayton, gazing toward the back of the store. "We didn't expect to see *you* here today!"

Theodosia turned to see Corky Chait bounding toward Drayton, his hand extended, a smile on his placid face.

"Drayton, good to see you again." They shook hands, and then Corky turned and favored Theodosia with a wave and friendly smile. "Theodosia, you, too."

Then, obviously aware that Theodosia and Drayton had been admiring the store, and very proud of his wife's accomplishments, Corky rocked back on his heels and asked: "What do you think of Claudia's little shop? Hasn't she done an amazing job?"

"I'm blown away," declared Drayton. "There are stores in *Europe* that aren't this good."

"Claudia cajoles vendors and haunts the *marchés* on all her buying trips," said Corky. "It's taken a while to build a solid base of suppliers, but I'd say she's almost there. Last time across the pond she charmed the sales director at Les

Olivades. Their traditional Provençal styles haven't changed since the sixteenth century."

"Which is why I'm having a difficult time making a choice," said Theodosia. She had at least a dozen different tea towels draped over her arm. All good candidates.

"But you found *something* you like and you're having fun," said Claudia. "That's what's important."

"I'm in heaven," replied Theodosia.

"Say . . . I never got a chance to thank you folks the other night," said Corky. "You were so kind and generous to come in and handle the catering. Of course . . ." His voice trailed off. Obviously Sunday evening was still painful and embarrassing for him.

"Not your fault," Drayton quickly assured him. "A tragic event, to be sure, but nothing that would reflect on you and your lovely wife."

"But it does feel as though our family's endowment to the Heritage Society is a little tainted now," said Corky.

"Like a dark cloud is suddenly hanging over everything," added Claudia. There was sadness in her voice.

"Not at all," said Theodosia. "I know for a fact that Timothy is thrilled to have the house."

"It's kind of you to say that," said Corky. "But, quite frankly, our family is just as happy to be rid of that place. It's a strange house, kind of a sad place, really. And now with Duke's death . . ." He shook his head.

"Thank goodness the police are working so hard," said Claudia, jumping in. She'd seen how choked up Corky had become. "And Detective Tidwell has been so helpful. We have complete faith in him."

"You've talked with Tidwell recently?" asked Theodosia.

"Oh, yes," said Corky. "Just this morning, in fact. The

police are apparently interviewing all the guests from Sunday night. They're quite sure that someone will recall seeing something."

There were a few moments of pregnant silence among them.

"Well," said Drayton, trying to interject an upbeat note. "It's still a lovely house and the Heritage Society is especially grateful. And once it gets fixed up . . ." he said hopefully.

"Maybe," said Corky. "But to be perfectly honest, I'm not even sure how much fixing needs to be done. The possibility exists, you know, that my grandfather may have stuck the Heritage Society with a real white elephant."

"Jock Rowley didn't think it was a white elephant," murmured Claudia.

"Pardon?" said Theodosia.

"That real estate developer," said Claudia. "He wanted to buy the place."

"Really?" said Theodosia. "I wonder why."

Claudia shrugged. "Don't know."

"My grandfather's will was pretty much ironclad," said Corky. "So, of course, selling was never an option."

"Would you have sold if you could?" asked Theodosia.

Corky scratched his chin thoughtfully. "No. It's an old home with, I think, significant historic value. So it belongs exactly where it is. Under the care and protection of the Heritage Society."

"Have you spent much time inside the old house?" asked Theodosia.

Corky shook his head. "Truth be told, I've only been inside that old place twice. The first was with my attorney when we made the initial arrangements with the Heritage Society. And then, of course, this past Sunday evening."

Corky's earnest look turned into a pained grimace "And now . . . well, I can't honestly say I'd relish stepping inside again." His discomfiture seemed genuine.

"You probably won't have to," said Theodosia. *So you'll never have the bizarre pleasure of getting trapped in that secret room, which you don't even know about. Or fumbling your way out via the basement.*

Claudia breathed a deep sigh, then picked up a linen napkin and twisted it in her hands. "I can't tell you how bad we feel . . ."

Corky put a hand on Claudia's shoulder. "On a more upbeat note, my dear, four new cases of merchandise have just arrived at the warehouse."

She clapped her hands together. "The shipment from Deauville. Thank heavens!" She turned toward Theodosia and Drayton, explaining. "I signed up for a small booth at the Women's Expo on Thursday and I've been worried sick I wouldn't have anything new to show!" She leaped from her chair, pivoted, and rummaged around in the desk behind her. "Here," she said, pulling out two oversized postcards and handing them to Theodosia and Drayton. "Stop by if you can."

"I'm sure I'll see you there," said Theodosia, still deliberating about tea towels.

"We have to choose," said Drayton. "Table linens." His eyes went toward the two different patterns they'd been tossing around earlier.

"You decide," Theodosia told Drayton. She was confident of Drayton's unerring eye.

But Drayton merely shook his head. "You're the one who wears the various titles of CEO, head dishwasher, and keeper of the checkbook."

"The exchequer," joked Corky.

Theodosia held up a napkin with the medieval design. "Do you have four dozen of these?" she asked.

Claudia gave a quick nod. "We do. Just."

Things were in a tizzy when Theodosia and Drayton got back to the tea shop. Miss Dimple had a brown betty teapot clutched in each hand and was scurrying about, pouring tea as fast as she could. Haley wore a slightly panicked look on her normally happy face and seemed to be turning customers away at the door.

"Someone requested a pot of oolong," Miss Dimple told Drayton, breathlessly. "I let the leaves steep four minutes, but I wasn't sure if that was correct."

"Thai or Formosan?" he asked.

She thought for a couple seconds. "Formosan. The extra fancy in the green tin."

"Not to worry," Drayton told her. "That particular oolong is an aromatic, fruity tea, so a little extra brewing will only enhance the flavor."

As Theodosia pulled on an apron and grabbed a teapot to help with refills, she suddenly noticed Detective Burt Tidwell seated at one of the tables. Hunched over like a giant, glowering bear, he was tucked in next to the small stone fireplace.

"How long has he been here?" Theodosia whispered to Haley.

Haley blew a strand of hair out of her face and shrugged. "Long enough. I think he's even managed to intimidate a few people."

"Did you feed him?" asked Theodosia. All their other

guests were contentedly enjoying tomato bisque soup, cucumber tea sandwiches, and croissants stuffed with chicken salad.

Haley rolled her eyes. "What do you think?"

Theodosia didn't get around to talking to Tidwell until all their lunch patrons had been tended to. When she did drop by his table with a pot of tea and a dessert plate that held a tuxedo brownie and a piece of toasted walnut fudge bread spread with cream cheese, his manner was formal to the point of being abrupt.

"Miss Browning," he began as his large fingers immediately reached out to tow the dessert plate closer to him. "I warned you to back away from that nasty incident at the Chait House."

She touched a hand to her heart. "I haven't done anything." She poured out a stream of Dragon's Breath Puerh tea into his empty teacup. "Try some of this. It's exceedingly smooth but carries a nice earthy flavor."

Tidwell took a quick sip. "Lovely. But please, Miss Browning, do not try to dodge the subject. Or smoke screen the fact that you bullied poor Timothy Neville into throwing open the doors of his storeroom last evening."

"I bullied Timothy?" Theodosia laughed. "That's rich." Usually it was crusty old Timothy who did the bullying, as Tidwell was well aware. "Timothy's a friend," continued Theodosia. "When he traveled to England last year to do genealogy research, I stayed at his house and fed his cat Dreadnought."

Tidwell's head bobbed imperceptibly. "Yes, yes. I remember."

"Timothy opened the store room last night because I *asked* him to," continued Theodosia. "Because I thought there might be a problem concerning that knife we found. And I felt Timothy should be the first to know."

"You didn't think *I* should have been informed first and foremost?" asked Tidwell, not bothering to mask the annoyance in his voice "And we *are* talking about the label on the knife."

"Technically it's a dirk," said Theodosia. "A Civil War–era . . ."

"I *know* that," said Tidwell, his patience straining.

"And Timothy did call the police last night," said Theodosia. "He brought you into the loop almost immediately."

"Almost," replied Tidwell. "Of course, Timothy's a man of honor and principles."

Theodosia resisted the impulse to strike back. Tidwell was needling her and no doubt enjoying himself. But, right now, she was too busy, too preoccupied, to allow him to irritate her.

Tidwell delicately broke off a piece of chocolate walnut bread and popped it into his mouth. "The fact is, you really should have told me about the label yesterday afternoon." He pursed his lips and continued to munch.

"I wasn't sure that's what it was." Theodosia tried to keep her expression neutral.

"You weren't sure that's what it was," parroted Tidwell. He waggled a pudgy finger in Theodosia's face. "Don't be duplicitous with me, Miss Browning. I will not tolerate such actions and it will curry no favor." Tidwell continued to munch away with considerable gusto.

"Have you matched the weapon to the knife wound yet?" Theodosia asked.

Tidwell stared at her. "We have," he said.

Theodosia waggled her fingers, gesturing for him to give her more.

Tidwell belched a deep sigh. "The incised wound had no bridging tissue and was horizontal in character, rather typical of a victim who was stabbed from behind. Death undoubtedly resulted from asphyxiation and air embolism."

"Whew," said Theodosia. It was more than she'd hoped to know. She thought for a moment. "Did you find the secret passageway?" she asked.

Tidwell nodded. "We actually found two."

"Good heavens," said Theodosia. "Do you think Duke knew about them?"

This time Tidwell shrugged. "Doubtful."

"Could Corky and Claudia have known?" Theodosia asked.

Tidwell almost chortled. "Are you serious? She can't stop leaking tears and he just keeps apologizing."

"Do you think there's a layout of the Chait House at the Heritage Society?" asked Theodosia.

"I'll have to find out." Tidwell gave her a condescending stare. "*I'll* find out," he repeated.

"Did you know that Jock Rowley, the real estate developer, tried to buy the Augustus Chait House?" Theodosia asked.

Tidwell put his cup down suddenly and gazed at her with hooded, questioning eyes. "How did you come across that information?" he asked in a sullen tone.

"Claudia Chait mentioned it," said Theodosia. *Ah, I certainly captured Tidwell's attention with that little tidbit.*

"So you've been pestering Corky and Claudia Chait," said Tidwell. "Trying to ferret out more information for your ill-advised and highly amateurish investigation."

This accusation, compounded by an insult, was just too much for Theodosia. "Please be serious," she said in a voice dripping with ice. "Drayton and I stopped by Le Nest to purchase table linens." She threw him her best look of haughty disapproval. "Honestly, why don't you just put me under house arrest if it'll make you feel better? Or implant a microchip in my neck so you can track my every move?"

"Don't push me," cautioned Tidwell.

Theodosia shrugged, decided to attempt a different tact. She'd try the innocent-Southern-lady ploy. After all, it usually worked exceedingly well for Delaine. "Going back into that house yesterday," Theodosia told Tidwell, "I was just poking around. Really . . . my intentions were quite innocent."

This time Tidwell favored her with a full-fledged glower. "With you, Miss Browning, nothing is ever completely innocent!"

11

❧

The romantic strains of Cole Porter's *"C'est Magnifique"* wafted through the perfumed air and mingled with the low buzz of women chatting, the jangle of charm bracelets, and the pleasant clink of teacups against saucers. Congressman Clive Bonham's tea was well underway and the Indigo Tea Shop was so packed with women wearing large, stylish hats that Haley whispered to Drayton that the place looked like a *Flying Nun* convention.

Pleased at what had to be the largest event they'd ever staged at the tea shop, Theodosia, Drayton, and Miss Dimple efficiently wove their way between tables, pouring cups of Darjeeling and Keemun, serving their first course of Crab Carolina, and accepting compliments about how lovely everything looked.

At the very last moment, Theodosia had opted to use their gold and cream brocade tablecloths. Which perfectly set off the Crown Ducal china, their cut glass cream and sugar sets, and the new damask napkins which they'd tucked demurely into simple gold napkin rings.

Floral arrangements, which had earlier been in question, remained small and tidy. But thanks to magic wrought by Hattie Boatwright, owner of Floradora, bouquets of pink tea roses, pink larkspur, and white freesia were now artfully tucked into towering long-stemmed glass goblet–type vases.

As afternoon light filtered through the leaded glass windows, the tea shop seemed to take on a glow that reflected in the faces of the guests. This was a phenomena Theodosia had observed several times before. She was pretty sure it meant their guests were in a joyful, relaxed state, but their sensory awareness was slightly heightened. Of course, the contributing factors of amiable companions, animated conversation, and the mingled aromas of succulent crab, fresh-baked scones, and steaming tea had something to do with this, too. She decided that, for all practical purposes, the planets seemed to be aligned favorably this afternoon. And wasn't that a blessing?

"A wonderful tea, Drayton," exclaimed Congressman Clive Bonham as Drayton carefully transferred an almond scone from the silver tray he was carrying to the congressman's plate. "Your staff seems to have outdone itself."

"Care for a cup of Assam, Congressman?" asked Theodosia, moving around the table to stand at his left shoulder.

Clive Bonham pointed to his teacup. "Is that what I was drinking before?"

"No, you started with Darjeeling," Theodosia told him.

"What's the difference?" The congressman's rich, throaty laugh echoed throughout the tea room.

"That particular Darjeeling, a Goomtee Garden Darjeeling, is fairly light-bodied and brisk," explained Theodosia. "This Assam is far less so. In fact, it's rather sweet and flavorful."

"Pour away then," said the congressman, flashing a winning smile at the women seated with him at the largest of the round tables. "Goodness," he went on, "I see now why you ladies are such raving fans of these formal teas. The portions look tiny, but they're amazingly filling!" He glanced at his watch, then turned toward Greg Killman who was sitting directly to his right. "You're sure we'll have time for a little schmoozing?" he asked in a low voice. "I've got a meeting at Charleston Memorial right after this." Then to Theodosia, who had just finished pouring his tea: "Killman probably told you, this is a critical audience for me. Power of the purse and all that. With the election less than two months away, we're into the final big push."

"Aren't you starting your final push a little early?" Theodosia asked, pointedly ignoring his "power of the purse" remark. Her former marketing firm had handled several political campaigns. And standard reasoning held that the final *two weeks* were reserved for what Congressman Bonham had deemed "the final push." In other words, media blitzes, all-out campaigning, and whistle-stop speech-making.

"Not at all," responded Killman, who had been observing Theodosia with hooded eyes. "The congressman is in the big leagues. We don't stop pushing until we win."

Interesting choice of words, thought Theodosia. *Push until you win, not just until the election's over. Well, at least Killman has a positive, can-do attitude. Rather essential in South Carolina politics, I'd say.*

"Oh, Drayton dear," called Delaine, who'd managed to wrangle an invitation and get herself seated at the same table as Congressman Bonham and Greg Killman. "Can you come over here?"

Drayton, who'd just signaled Haley to begin plating the entrées, hurried back over to the congressman's table.

"I was telling everyone about how you worked for Croft and Squire in England," said Delaine. "And were so fortunate to attend the wholesale tea auctions in Amsterdam."

"That must have been fascinating," piped up Celerie Stuart, who sat beside Delaine. "What would you say was the most important thing you learned from your experience?"

Drayton thought for a moment. "That tea is both celebration and ceremony."

"Wonderful." Celerie smiled shyly at Drayton. "Delaine tells me you have a favorite tea poem that you sometimes quote. Would you consider favoring us with a short recitation today?"

"Ah, the one by Robert Ford?" asked Drayton.

Delaine nodded.

"Perhaps I could manage a quick stanza before the entrées are served," said Drayton.

Congressman Clive Bonham, pleased by this impromptu entertainment, tapped a spoon against his water glass. Although it was a rather inelegant maneuver, it did cause conversation to quickly cease.

Then, looking very much the Heritage Society parliamentarian that he was, Drayton faced the room and began:

> *I like a dry wine whenever I dine,*
> *And it's mid-morning coffee for me.*
> *But the liquor I crave, to which I'm a slave,*
> *Is the God-given nectar tea.*

It pleases me so when I sip orange pekoe—
Such color with taste crisp and clean;
But for sheer relaxation and quiet contemplation
It's the clear amber tea known as "green."

Celerie Stuart clapped enthusiastically. "Is there more? Could we have another stanza, please?"

Drayton was only too happy to oblige:

A cup of Earl Grey adds some zest to my day—
The aroma of bergamot oil
Or I hear Ceylon Bop and my heart takes a hop;
I can't wait for the water to boil.

"How delightful," remarked Angie Congdon as Theodosia circled back to the far table and placed one of the chicken breast entrées in front of her. The presentation was phenomenal. Haley had added purple lettuce and tulip-sculpted tomatoes as accents.

"Drayton's totally in his element today," said Theodosia, smiling down at Angie. "And how nice to see *you* here."

"Bet you didn't know I was so important to Clive Bonham's reelection, did you?" Angie laughed.

Angie and her husband Mark had been Chicago commodity brokers who'd fled their stressful life and the icy winter gales off Lake Michigan to engineer a midlife career switch in a much warmer clime. Now they were the proprietors of the Featherbed House, a fashionable bed-and-breakfast near the Battery, that most famous promenade where the Cooper and Ashley Rivers converged and the Atlantic surged in to meet them.

"Doesn't matter," said Theodosia. "I'm just delighted to see you here. Usually I know most of my guests. But today . . ." She glanced around. "Well, Delaine's sitting over there with Celerie Stuart. But other than a few familiar faces, it's pretty much a whole new group."

"A fairly well-heeled group, I'd say," said Angie. She grasped at Theodosia's sleeve. "But seriously, honey, my name is only on the guest list because Mark was so active in the mayor's campaign. I don't know if you've heard yet, but Mark went back to being a commodities broker again." Angie shrugged. "He finally got tired of playing innkeeper."

"But you're going to keep running the Featherbed House, aren't you? asked a surprised Theodosia. "You're the coziest place around."

"It's full steam ahead," said Angie. "I just went out and hired an assistant. A fellow by the name of Teddy Vickers. He's an absolute whiz. Now our reservations, bookkeeping, and guest list are even computerized!"

"That's terrific," said Theodosia.

"I hadn't planned on attending today," said Angie, "but then I thought about seeing you and Drayton and meeting a few new people, so I thought *why not?*"

"I'm so glad you did," said Theodosia as she heard a click and a whir behind her.

"Okay, ladies, turn this way, please," ordered a familiar male voice.

Theodosia and Angie's heads snapped in the direction of the voice and suddenly found themselves staring into the wide angle lens of Bill Glass's Nikon.

"Smile, hold that pose, and say . . . tea." Bill Glass chortled as a strobe light exploded in their faces.

When Theodosia's retinas finally recovered from the barrage of light, she edged closer to the unwelcome photographer. "This is a private party," she told him in a quiet but firm voice. "You'll have to leave immediately." She was outraged that Glass had crashed the congressman's tea, but didn't want to stage a major knock-down-drag-out scene. Hopefully, obnoxious clod that he was, the man would take his cue and depart quietly.

"Honey," said Bill Glass as he fumbled with a second lens. "Don't get your tea bags in a twist. Because I'm an *invited* guest." He plugged in a cable and fiddled with a couple switches on his camera, then nodded when he heard the telltale high-pitched squeal that signaled his battery had powered up again. "They want me here."

"I hardly think so," said Drayton. Radiating disapproval, he moved in quickly on Glass's other side.

"Talk to the man over there," said Bill Glass, casually aiming his camera into the crowd and snapping two more shots.

"You mean Congressman Bonham?" asked Theodosia, unhappily noting that Glass was the very picture of a glib, slightly bored paparazzi.

Bill Glass gave a brusque shake of his head. "Nah. His handler, his head honcho, Killman. He's the one who asked me to drop by. Said the congressman was entertaining some hoity-toity, high-society women today." He looked out over the crowd and gave a crooked yet appreciative smile. "Women with good connections, old families, and powerful husbands. The kind of stuff *Shooting Star* readers really eat up."

Shaking his head, Drayton moved off. Once he did, Bill Glass focused his laser gaze on Theodosia. "Solved the murder mystery yet?" he asked her in a taunting voice.

Outraged, she busied herself with pouring tea.

Then, just as quickly, Bill Glass seemed to lose interest in her. His dark head swiveled as Haley brushed past him, carrying out a tray of desserts. "Say, sweetheart," he called after her. "Think you could spare a couple of those chocolate things?"

As the tea continued, Theodosia was hard-pressed not to toss Bill Glass out on his keester. He slipped from table to table, chatting, chortling, and snapping pictures. Most of the women were politely obliging and Congressman Clive Bonham seemed not to notice that Bill Glass was the single jarring note.

Oh, well, what can I do? thought Theodosia. *Nothing, that's what. If this is the congressman's idea of publicity, all I can do is keep smiling and get those dessert trays on the tables.*

Haley had taken their three-tiered trays and twined sprigs of real ivy around the brass handle that arced over the top tier. Then she'd added a silk bow at the top, let the ivy tendrils trail down the sides, and piled each level full of deserts. As an afterthought, she'd sprinkled edible flowers amongst the brownies and truffles. Which elicited appreciative *oohs* and *aahs* once the dessert trays were all ferried out and presented at each table.

"Your dessert trays are a hit," Theodosia told Haley.

But as Haley lurked in the doorway, it was obvious she had other things on her mind.

"You see that lady over there?" Haley asked, pushing a hunk of stick-straight hair behind her ears. "That's Sydney Chastain. She's the one who's heading up that new TV network, Viva Media. The one they call VTV." Haley snuck another surreptitious glance in Sydney Chastain's direction. "That's the kind of executive I'd like to be some day."

Theodosia gazed across the room where a tall woman wearing a red power suit seemed to be holding court. Her blond hair was pinned up in an old-fashioned French roll. Yet somehow it looked perfect on her. Maybe it was the woman's height or her impeccable grooming or her commanding presence. Whatever, the overall impression was one of supreme competence and a smatter of TV glitz. Theodosia patted her own auburn hair. Thick, bordering on raucous curls and waves, framed her face, giving her not a sophisticated look, but certainly quite a lovely one.

"Keep taking those business courses," Theodosia told Haley, "and you'll be honchoing your own company some day. I have the utmost faith in you."

"But wouldn't it be exciting to head up a new *TV network?*" Haley obviously had stars in her eyes.

Theodosia, who'd logged a dozen years as an account executive for one of Charleston's top marketing firms before she'd fled that industry to open a tea shop, wasn't so quick to agree. "Maybe," she told Haley. "But it's a tough, volatile industry where everything can change overnight."

Haley let loose a small sigh.

"We're finished serving," said Theodosia. "Things are beginning to wind down. Why don't you go over and talk to her?"

Haley stared back at her with saucer eyes. "You really think I should?"

"Absolutely," urged Theodosia. "Introduce yourself and tell her you're studying for your masters degree in business administration. Then ask a few pertinent questions. She'll probably be flattered. All business people adore talking about their business." *Do they ever. Don't I love talking about tea? Until the cows come home.*

"Hold my apron?" asked Haley as she pulled it from around her neck, then thrust the ball of fabric into Theodosia's hands.

"Of course," said Theodosia. There was approval on her face as she watched Haley speed happily across the room. Then Theodosia turned and headed back to see if Drayton needed any help.

He didn't. But even as Congressman Clive Bonham began making the rounds at each table, shaking hands, and asking for support, a few of his guests were already starting to wander about the tea shop. Chatting, renewing acquaintances, and doing a little shopping.

Shopping. Such a lovely diversion. For some reason the act of sipping tea and enjoying scones, tea sandwiches, and savories could put almost any woman in the mood for a nice little recreational shop. Thus, Theodosia had loaded their shelves with T-Bath products, her own line of tea-scented bath oils, lotions, and moisturizers that she had specially designed. Plus she and Haley had hauled out a stack of pretty floral hat boxes that had been in her back office forever, then propped them with tea cozies, miniature teapots, trivets, and two grape vine wreaths decorated with teacups.

Theodosia was just wrapping up two bottles of green tea lotion, bought on impulse, when Sydney Chastain sauntered up to the counter.

"That lovely young woman who works for you suggested I talk with you," said Sydney. She extended a hand and a wrist full of gold bangles that clanked loudly. "I'm Sydney Chastain."

"The new CEO of VTV," said Theodosia. "Nice to meet you."

"I understand you worked in media before you opened your tea shop," said Sydney.

"Worked in marketing, dabbled in media," said Theodosia. "Now I'm afraid my only contribution to the business is helping garner a little publicity for the Spoleto Festival."

"Still," said Sydney, "you're a female entrepreneur. Exactly the kind of woman our new network is gearing up to appeal to." Sydney gazed intently at Theodosia. "Do you know what percentage of small businesses are started by women?"

"Not precisely," replied Theodosia as she popped her package into an indigo blue bag and tied a puff of white ribbon at the top. "But I imagine it's a goodly amount. Fifty, maybe sixty percent?"

"Seventy percent in the last decade," said Sydney. "Amazing, don't you think?"

Theodosia smiled at her. "I think most women are natural born entrepreneurs. They don't always have the supreme ambition to build a Fortune five hundred company, but they're very skillful at creating small businesses."

"Absolutely," said Sydney.

"But," said Theodosia, holding up a finger. "Women want the work environment they create to be both nourishing and rewarding. The other thing about women entrepreneurs is that they prefer to grow their business in a hands-on way. Which I suppose is why they often choose smaller ventures such as bookstores, needle craft stores, or antique shops."

"Or tea shops," said Sydney, smiling. "*Touché.* I understand from talking to a few people that you're very talented. And I would truly love to sit down with you and get your input on a few things." She turned her megawatt smile on Theodosia. "Any chance of making that happen? I wanted to chat with you the other night at the Candlelight Concert, but . . ."

"You were there?" asked Theodosia.

Sydney nodded. "Afraid so. I didn't know Mr. Wilkes personally, but I certainly knew of him." She shook her head. "A terrible thing."

"Yes, Duke was well-known and well-loved," said Theodosia.

"So . . . do you think we could get together?" asked Sydney.

"Why not?" said Theodosia. Sydney seemed like a smart, on-the-move business woman. And Theodosia was of a mind that you can always learn a thing or two from talking with people. Maybe she'd pick up a few pointers from Sydney Chastain. And while she was at it, ask her a few questions about Sunday night. Who knows? Sydney might have seen something.

"Wonderful!" exclaimed Sydney. "My office, tomorrow night," she said, pressing her business card into Theodosia's hand.

"Whoa . . . that's pretty short notice," said Theodosia. "I've got an awful lot on my plate right now." She still hadn't planned her talk for the Women's Expo. And then there was the demo with Earl Grey on Friday.

"Please try to find time," said Sydney. "Believe me, there's a good chance I can make this extremely worth your while. One of the programs I'm tinkering with is a new show in a magazine format that profiles successful women and their small businesses." She looked around the tea shop, obviously liking what she saw. "Like yours, for example."

"Okaaay," said Theodosia. "Tomorrow night it is." She was still enough of a marketing pro to know that you never, ever turned down a shot at publicity. Especially publicity of that magnitude.

"Excellent," said Sydney. "I'll be sure to order in some food."

An hour later Theodosia sat by herself at the front counter. She'd just finished tallying the receipts for the day and the results were staggering. Besides the $24.95 per person they'd charged for Congressman Bonham's tea, they'd managed to sell a whopping $750 in extra merchandise. Dozens of tins of Drayton's custom-blended teas, tea cozies, baskets of T-Bath products, both grapevine wreaths, and, remarkably, all the hat boxes!

So when the phone shrilled and Theodosia grabbed it, she was feeling tired but fairly exuberant, too.

"What are you doing?" asked a male voice.

"I think I'm about to celebrate," was Theodosia's flippant answer, her eyes still on the column of numbers. Then she hesitated. "Parker?" she asked, sounding a little unsure. "Is that you?" It had *sounded* like him, but now she wasn't so certain.

"Yes'm it's me," came Parker Scully's enthusiastic reply. "Who else phones a dozen times a week to ask you pesky little restaurateur questions?"

Parker Scully was a fellow restaurant owner who owned Solstice, a French- and Mediterranean-influenced bistro over on Market Street. For some reason their paths kept crossing.

They ran into each other at gallery openings, Heritage Society events, and, most recently, a wine tasting. She'd even dropped by Solstice a couple times. And ever since her old boyfriend Jory Davis had moved out of town (and, she assumed, out of her life), Parker Scully was beginning to look more and more interesting.

"What's up?" Theodosia asked. Parker *was* forever calling with quirky little questions. *When you make a dessert glaze do you mix your powdered sugar with lemon juice or cream? What's the absolute best chocolate to use when you're making truffles? Can I steal your recipe for she-crab soup?* And *Are you okay? I heard you guys were the ones catering that Candlelight Concert.*

"How would you like to go to an oyster roast tonight?" Parker asked her. "Help take your mind off this past Sunday night's nastiness."

Sliding off the high stool, Theodosia shrugged. Not because she was indifferent to his invitation, but because she was trying to wriggle a knot of tension from her shoulders. She was tired. Beat, in fact. Had been ready to trudge upstairs and flake out for the evening. Take a hot bath, sip a cup of tea, curl up with her pup, and probably lose herself in a good book. That is if she could muster enough energy to turn the pages.

But the prospect of going to an oyster roast, generally a get-down, good-time, traditional low-country event, was suddenly intriguing.

"Wait a minute," came Parker's cautionary voice. "That's an extraordinarily long pause. Please don't tell me you don't partake of oysters. Shame! And you, a native daughter!"

"No, no," protested Theodosia as she slipped off her shoes and curled her sore toes under. "I adore oysters in any shape or form. Raw, Rockefeller'd, and, especially, roasted."

The large oysters native to South Carolina's salt marshes and streams were some of the tastiest, most succulent bivalve mollusks on the planet. Theodosia even found them preferable to briny Long Island bluepoints, small, sweet Fanny Bay oysters from British Columbia, or the more aristocratic French Belons which were now being farmed in Maine.

"Wonderful! You *do* imbibe in oysters," enthused Parker Scully. "Which means you'll come with me tonight?" He hesitated. "Listen, there's this guy Dell who's hosting this shindig. He's one of my seafood suppliers, okay? But he didn't mention the oyster roast until this morning, so you can see I'm kind of a B-list invitee."

"What does that make me?" asked Theodosia.

"I know it's last minute," said Parker. "So apology, apology, apology. But here's the thing . . . I was breaking in a new *sous*-chef today, so I just now thought seriously about going myself. And, of course, you were the only one I would consider inviting. Doesn't that count for something?"

"When you put it that way, so seriously," she told Parker, "how can I possibly refuse?"

"Terrific," enthused Parker.

I can soak in the bathtub, walk Earl Grey, and get primped in an hour, can't I? wondered Theodosia. *No, I think perhaps I need a little more time.*

"Uh . . . can you give me a couple hours to depressurize and get ready?" asked Theodosia. "It's been a crazy day here, too."

"No problem," said Parker. "How about I pick you up around seven? And be sure to dress casual. Your best oyster-eating duds."

12

❧

Jumbo oysters popped and sizzled over hot glowing coals as two chefs outfitted in heavy asbestos gloves, fisherman's aprons, and workman's boots shoveled black, briny oysters from a huge metal tub onto a heavy metal grate suspended over a six-foot-long fire pit. As flames from burning logs licked at the grate, the oysters steamed and bubbled inside their shiny, black shells.

Theodosia was in seventh heaven. As tired and frazzled as she'd been a few hours earlier, she'd immediately perked up once she and Parker Scully had left Charleston behind and arrived at Dell Harper's Palmetto Boulevard beach house on Edisto Island.

Now she and Parker were seated at a picnic table. The Atlantic Ocean surged just beyond and the North Edisto River was just a mile to their north. Colored lights dangled and swayed above them, strung between palmetto trees.

Dozens of other picnic tables, inhabited by denim-wearing, oyster-eating folks, were clustered about. Under the gnarled branches of a giant live oak, The Four Craw-Dads, an enthusiastic quartet of middle-aged rockers, cranked out tunes that also blended strains of blues, country, and Caribbean rock.

The evening was cool, the darkness soft and languid, settling around them like a luxurious cashmere sweater.

"You're a purist," observed Parker as Theodosia snapped open an oyster shell and dug into it with the rather homely-looking metal fork they'd been provided with. "No Tabasco sauce, cocktail sauce, or ketchup?" he asked her. "Not even a dab of horseradish?"

"Just straight up." Theodosia laughed. It was the way her father had always eaten them when they'd had oyster roasts at Cane Ridge. So she did, too. "Although," she told Parker, "there are various low-country schools of thought regarding oyster-eating accompaniments."

He waggled his fingers at her. "Enlighten me."

"Some folks favor saltines and sweet pickles, others prefer chips with *pico de gallo* sauce. And then a few holdouts say melted butter is the only accompaniment worthy of these briny delights."

"I think I'm in the camp that holds you should wash the little darlings down with a nice white wine," said Parker. He held up his glass of wine, poured from one of the bottles he'd brought along. "And this Sauvignon Blanc is particularly fine on the palette."

"Agreed," said Theodosia, clinking her glass against his in an impromptu toast. "Even a Pinot Gris would taste rather splendid." Although she considered herself a wine neophyte, Theodosia was becoming more and more intrigued with wines and wine tasting. Parker Scully's wine cellar at Solstice was an oenophile's dream and one Theodosia regarded with awe. In the few times she'd visited Solstice, she'd had the pleasure of sipping a Redigaffi Italian Merlot and a Napa Valley Syrah from JC Cellars. Fantastic!

Parker had told her she was a natural wine connoisseur. That wine tasting was very comparable to tea tasting because it required the same discerning palette to identify sugars and acids and tannins. Theodosia wasn't sure whether Parker was just being polite in paying her the compliment or if he was genuinely serious. Oh well, time would tell.

"You recovered from Sunday night?" Parker asked her.

"I suppose so," said Theodosia.

Parker peered at her. "You had a funny look on your face just now."

"Did I?" asked Theodosia.

"Are you . . . um . . . involved in some way?" he asked.

Theodosia wrinkled her nose. "A little."

"You're *investigating*," said Parker, "aren't you?"

"A little," Theodosia admitted.

"Hey, spy girl, better be careful," cautioned Parker. "Remember what happened last time you got all balled up in a murder investigation?"

"I'll take care," Theodosia replied. "Don't worry about me."

"Ah, but I do," said Parker in a softer tone.

"*How you folks* doin'?" This from Dell Harper, Parker's seafood supplier and host of tonight's roast, who'd just ambled over to their picnic table. Dell was a hail-hearty bear of a man. Tall, barrel-chested, with a shock of unruly red hair. Besides the fact that he was brimming with ebullience, Dell was also slightly intoxicated.

"We're doing great," said Theodosia. "I love that you just piled the oysters on top of big grates and let 'em cook."

"They cooked all right." Dell chuckled. "Some of 'em even exploded."

Theodosia nodded. When you didn't cover the oysters with wet burlap that was one of the rather dramatic side effects. Exploding oysters and shells all over the place. Dangerous, of course, but awfully darned colorful. Unless, of course, you were one of the poor devils who happened to be in the line of fire.

"No casualties?" asked Parker.

"None yet," said Dell. " 'Course, we just set another batch to sizzling, so the shelling's not quite over." He swiped at his hair and laughed. "We allotted a bushel for every five people." He laughed. "So you'd better eat up." Glancing at Theodosia's almost empty plate, he said, "C'mon, miss. Let's get you another helping while they're pipin' hot."

"Go on," urged Parker as Theodosia raised her eyebrows at him. "I'll run grab us another bottle of wine."

Standing at the grill, basking in the warm glow from the embers, Theodosia was suddenly aware of a vaguely familiar face. She peered at the man standing in line a few feet down from her.

Who is that? she asked herself. *I know him from somewhere.*

She stared at the man, noting his clipped mustache and

his suntanned look. And as she ruminated, his name suddenly popped into her brain.

That's Jock Rowley. The real estate developer Delaine pointed out to me at the Candlelight Concert. The one that Corky Chait said wanted to buy the Augustus Chait House.

She sidled over to him slowly. "Jock Rowley?" she asked, arranging her face in a friendly smile and mustering her best Southern drawl. "I'm Theodosia Browning, a friend of Delaine's?"

"Hello," he responded with what could only be called a blank stare.

"We met at the rather ill-fated Candlelight Concert the other night?" They hadn't really met but Theodosia figured it was a darned good opening.

Light finally dawned for Jock Rowley. "Of course," he said, a faint smile of acknowledgment flickering across his darkly handsome face. "You're Delaine's friend."

His face had taken on a slightly pinched look at the mention of Delaine's name and Theodosia figured Jock had either shelled out a rather princely sum for Delaine's restoration project or else she was still working him over.

Jock shook his head. "That was a tragedy the other night, a real tragedy. Old Duke was quite a legend in these parts."

"Yes, he was," said Theodosia.

"Let's hope the police are making headway in their investigation," said Rowley, glancing about.

"I understand they're busy interviewing all the people who were in attendance at the Chait House Sunday night," said Theodosia.

"That so?" said Rowley, eyes darting around, searching for something over Theodosia's shoulder.

"I understand *you* had some interest in that property," said Theodosia.

Jock Rowley snorted. "Don't believe everything you hear."

When Theodosia got back to the picnic table, Dell was clearing a stack of empty oyster shells into gunny sacks. "Spent shells." He chortled. "We'll return 'em all to the marshes."

"You're gonna dump empty shells back into the river?" asked Parker. "Why on earth would you do that?"

"Helps restore the oyster population," said Theodosia.

Dell nodded. "When oysters reproduce, they release free-swimming larvae that generally get carried along by tidal currents. But after two or three weeks; the larvae start looking for a surface to latch onto so they can begin building their shells. As crazy as it sounds, the young oysters prefer attaching to already existing oyster shells."

"Cool," said Parker.

"How do you know Jock Rowley?" Theodosia asked Dell.

Dell favored her with a wide grin that showed off crooked teeth. "That old pirate? He bought some land off me a couple years ago. Worthless tract of sand across the river from here. Over on Wadmalaw Island. Course, then Jock Rowley put up a couple hundred condos and made himself a cool thirty million. Around these parts we call him the condo king."

"The condo king," said Theodosia. "That's pretty much what a friend of mine said, too."

"Here," said Parker, popping the cork on a second bottle of wine and pouring glasses for Theodosia and Dell. "Enjoy."

* * *

Sated with oysters, relaxed from the wine she'd imbibed, Theodosia was snuggled comfortably in the passenger seat of Parker Scully's Lexus. Cruising down Highway 174, they were headed toward U.S. 17 and back toward Charleston.

Charleston was a large enough city that you could often see a glow from its lights when the clouds hung low. But right now, zooming through stands of pines and skimming the road where swampland stretched out to either side, all that was visible was the road ahead.

So when Parker Scully suddenly cranked his steering wheel to the right, Theodosia was caught completely off guard.

"Hang on!" exclaimed Parker as he fought to gain control of the car.

Automatically bracing herself, Theodosia was jostled roughly from side to side. Then she felt their speed ebb as Parker gained control and slowed the car. "What was *that* all about?" she asked as they sat in the dark car as it idled at the side of an even darker road.

"Holy smokes," said Parker Scully. "I think I might have hit something." He looked shaken and apprehensive, a little scared.

"What?" asked Theodosia. "Oh lord, it wasn't a person, was it?" She had her hand on the door, ready to jump out. "A hitchhiker?"

"No, no. Hold on," said Parker. "I'm pretty sure it was some kind of little animal." He eased open the car door, gave a nervous laugh. "I know *something* bounded across the road in front of us."

"You're going to go check?" asked Theodosia. "It's pitch-black out there. Even if you hit something, you'll probably never find it." She grimaced at her own words, hating the idea of some poor animal lying wounded in the road behind them.

Parker gestured at the glove box. "Pop that open. I'm pretty sure there's a flashlight inside."

There was. "Be careful," Theodosia told Parker as she handed him a silver and black high-tech-looking rubber flashlight.

Parker grabbed it and flicked the switch. Nothing. Parker smacked it against the palm of his hand and the light flickered on. "We're in business," he told her.

"Remember," said Theodosia, feeling a little jumpy. "An injured animal's first reaction is to bite."

"I'll be careful," Parker told her. And then he was gone, melting into the darkness.

Squirming about in the front seat, Theodosia pulled herself around until she was kneeling backwards, elbows resting on the headrest of her seat, staring intently out the rear window. Now she could see the beam of the flashlight bouncing along as Parker searched the side of the road. She could just hear his faint footsteps on pavement. And then he was on the shoulder of the road, probing the bushes, poking his flashlight beam into a scraggly stand of crepe myrtle.

"Be careful," she said out loud, but doubted he could still hear her.

Theodosia waited two minutes, maybe three minutes. Was just about to hop out of the car and go looking for him, when the rear door flew open.

"What?" she cried.

"Found him," said Parker. He had something furry cradled up against his chest.

"What is it?" asked Theodosia.

"A kitten," said Parker. "More scared than hurt. In fact,

I doubt if I even grazed him." He opened the top of his empty wicker wine hamper and tucked a towel in. There was a quick flash of fur as the kitten was quickly but gently deposited inside. Then Parker closed the lid on the hamper.

"You think the cat's going to be okay in there?" Theodosia asked.

"Well, it's wicker," said Parker. He closed the door then climbed into the driver's seat. "So the cat's going to be able to breathe okay. And I'm pretty sure it's not hurt."

They both stopped talking and listened. There was a faint rustling sound as the little cat seemed to be circling and scrunching up the towel to make a nest. Then nothing. Not a peep. Not a meow.

"My best guess is it'll just curl up and go to sleep," said Parker. He turned the key over and restarted the car. "Probably a stray. Or maybe what happened was somebody didn't want him anymore and just dumped the poor little beastie out here in the boonies." Parker maneuvered his car back onto the road, accelerating to pick up speed. "Man, I really hate that. People can be so darn cruel." Soon, they were zipping along at sixty miles an hour again.

"We could take it to Delaine's house," suggested Theodosia. "She's a real cat person, knows all about them. Delaine could probably help find it a good home. Or at least a place in an animal shelter."

"No, no," said Parker. "I *want* to take the cat home with me. It's really cute. Very cute with little spots. A kind of tabby, I'd guess. I've been meaning to drop by one of the local animal shelters to adopt a cat or dog. Some nice little critter to keep me company. I work such crazy hours and get home so late, it'd be nice to have a kitty meet me at the door. Besides, there are perks. Leftover shrimp and such."

"You think cats like shrimp remoulade?" asked Theodosia. "Or grilled catfish with red pepper puree?"

"Fresh always beats canned," said Parker.

"So you really do like animals," said Theodosia. It was a statement, not a question.

"I *love* animals," said Parker. "I never had one before, but I'm a pretty fast learner." He paused. "And I'm counting on you for pointers."

In the darkness of the humming auto, Theodosia just smiled to herself.

13

❧

"*Time for an* autumnal shift," announced Haley, dragging a straw basket out from the kitchen. "Our own tea shop equinox."

"What are you mumbling about?" asked Drayton. "And why are you all hunched over and what on earth do you have secreted in that enormous basket?"

Straightening up, Haley muscled her basket onto one of the wooden tables, then proceeded to dump out its bounty. Orange squash, egg-shaped gourds, and bottle gourds spun across the table. A small white pumpkin skittered over the edge and landed on the floor with a dull thud.

"Careful," warned Drayton.

"Looks like Haley's advocating a bountiful harvest theme," remarked Theodosia. She was sitting at one of the tables, enjoying a nice afterglow from the oyster roast last night before she switched into high gear for the day. Before she started worrying about the promise she'd made to Pookie Wilkes, but hadn't yet been able to keep. *I think I let my mouth write a check I can't cash,* she told herself.

"I hit the farmer's market bright and early this morning," Haley was explaining to a mildly interested Drayton. "Shopped my little heart out and picked up all this stuff. Plus I've got stalks of bittersweet, Indian corn, and bunches of grapes stashed out back. I thought we'd use those caramel-colored tablecloths you hate so much, top 'em with straw baskets and then fill the baskets with gourds, eggplant, white pumpkins, and fruit."

"I don't actually *hate* those tablecloths," said Drayton, fingering a speckled gourd. "As long as they work thematically."

To Theodosia, Haley's abundant enthusiasm was contagious and a welcome relief to fretting over crime-solving. So she jumped up to help. "We've got cinnamon-scented candles in the cupboard, too," Theodosia told Haley. "And I'm thinking we could pull out those pottery tea mugs."

"Love it," chirped Haley. "And what about using that old silverware with the bone-colored handles." She stopped abruptly when she saw Theodosia grimace. "Oh, no," she said quickly. "I didn't mean to remind you of . . ."

Theodosia waved a hand in the air to indicate it was nothing. "Not a problem, Haley. I woke up this morning with Duke's murder running through my mind anyway. Turning every detail over and over, thinking about how I promised Pookie to keep my eyes and ears open." She sat down in one of the chairs heavily. "Well, I've thought about everything all right. But I haven't been able to unravel a darn thing. Not a rock-solid clue I could take to Pookie or the police. In other words, nothing that points to a particular suspect."

Haley could see Theodosia's dilemma. And she was in total sympathy. "Maybe you should . . . oh, I don't know . . . talk to Timothy Neville again?" she suggested, a hopeful expression on her face.

"Maybe," said Theodosia, but she didn't sound convinced.

"Perhaps you should just bow out of this investigation entirely," proposed Drayton.

That's what Burt Tidwell would prefer, thought Theodosia.

"You would take a let's-not-rock-the-boat attitude, wouldn't you?" Haley accused Drayton.

"No," he replied, remaining calm in the face of Haley's words. "Theodosia's done her best and still not turned up much of anything. There's no shame in trying."

"You haven't dug up any suspects at all?" asked Haley. "That's so not like you, Theo. Once you start snooping around you usually have a gazillion ideas."

"Well, I suppose I have a *few* ideas," Theodosia admitted.

"Of course you do," said Haley, turning back to her tabletop scattered with produce.

Duke was a whistle-blower on Clive Bonham, thought Theodosia. *So I still want to check that out. And I need to look over the Heritage Society's membership list that Drayton gave me as well as the guest list from Sunday night that Delaine finally faxed over.*

Theodosia sat and thought for another minute. *That's it exactly. I've got to scan those lists and then let everything percolate for a while. Or better yet, gently steep.*

Seeing the look of supreme concentration on Theodosia's face, Drayton turned to address Haley. "So you're suggesting the tea shop institute a menu change as well?" he asked her.

"Sure," said Haley. "Like today I'm baking sweet potato muffins. And since I also picked up some nice apples from Long Creek at the market, I'm going to prepare a turkey, grape, and apple-walnut salad for lunch. And probably squash soup for tomorrow."

"Well, in the spirit of a somewhat heartier menu," said Drayton, "I'll be happy to suggest some new tea options to our guests. Maybe some Shou Mee white tea or Kandoli Garden Assam."

"Atta boy, Drayton," said Haley. "Probably time to recommend some Lung Ching, too. That's always so rich and smoky tasting."

"Don't forget the Chun Mee tea," added Theodosia, pulling herself out of her fretful mind-set. "Folks always love that plumlike flavor."

Click, click, click. Theodosia's fingers flew across the computer keyboard as she searched through The *Post and Courier* archives. She'd already found two short articles about Congressman Clive Bonham accepting money from special interest groups to fund his upcoming bid for reelection. Bonham had been quoted in each article and, each time, had lobbed back a rather neutral reply. Duke Wilkes had not been mentioned.

Hmm. Could Miss Dimple have been wrong? wondered Theodosia. *Maybe Duke Wilkes hadn't been that much of a whistle-blower after all. Well, there are a few more articles to check, so . . .*

The third article Theodosia scanned was more or less a rehash of the first two, so that was no help at all. But, in the fourth and last article that Theodosia found looking through the *Post and Courier* archives, she hit pay dirt.

An article written by C.S. Lewis, one of their regular staff writers, also included an interview with Duke Wilkes. Lewis had done a one-paragraph bio on Duke, characterizing him as "a colorful, crusty gadfly in a political arena that was shaky at best."

Hmm. Interesting phrasing. And not that far from the mark.

That article went on to cite corporate contributions that had been made to Congressman Clive Bonham's campaign. And then Duke's argument as to why they were highly inappropriate.

Bonham had defended himself fairly well, citing various precedents. But then, according to the article, Bonham had ended up returning the money to escape any semblance of impropriety. The article had concluded with a fiery quote from Greg Killman, Congressman Bonham's aide. Something to the effect that it was a free country and supporting your candidate of choice was the American way.

Theodosia thought about this campaign contribution brouhaha for a moment. Bonham must have been furious to have to hand back large sums of money. And Duke Wilkes, a man who had a soft spot for the underdog, but was tough as nails when it came to fighting on his own turf, must have been gleeful about forcing Bonham's hand.

So obviously there had been bad blood between the two men. *The question was,* Theodosia wondered, *had Duke's blood been spilled on account of this?*

Lifting her eyes from the computer screen, Theodosia stared at the wall across from her, letting her mind wander as she enjoyed a quick perusal of the photos, framed tea labels, and various memorabilia that hung on the wall. She picked up her mug of rapidly cooling tea and took a sip. Dayton had given her a cup of Hiki Garden Sencha. It was one of her favorite Japanese green teas. Refreshing aroma, delicate taste, toasty undertones. Maybe, she decided, it would help clarify her thoughts, too.

•

Greg Killman, Bonham's aide, also presented a slight wrinkle, she realized as she sipped. When she thought about her dealings with Killman he always seemed to come across as—how would one characterize it?—as the man behind the man. A hard-driving, tough-nosed political operative who probably got his jollies by manipulating the puppet strings. Maybe Killman was even one of those H. R. Haldeman true-believer types. A fruitcake who was willing to prove his loyalty and devotion to his boss by puting his hand in an open flame.

But how far would Greg Killman *really* go for his boss? That was another big fat question sitting out there.

Maneuvering her cursor, Theodosia closed out Netscape and switched off her computer. She took the fax Delaine had sent her and laid the pages on her desk. Then she spread out the membership list Drayton had given her.

For practical purposes, Theodosia decided that pretty much everyone on Delaine's guest list was a suspect. Since they'd attended the Candlelight Concert, they'd had ample opportunity to murder Duke Wilkes. And because the murder weapon itself seemed to have been appropriated from the Heritage Society, she figured the smartest thing to do was cross-reference the two lists. So anyone on the guest list who was also a Heritage Society member would get a red check beside their name.

The cross-checking was futsy but, because the Heritage Society membership list was alphabetized, Theodosia got through the whole thing in about half an hour.

When she finished, Theodosia leaned back in her chair, shrugged her shoulders to work out the kinks, and stared at her list. She'd put thirty-eight red check marks on Delaine's list of about one hundred people. Thirty-eight people who had a known connection with the Heritage Society.

Interestingly, Congressman Clive Bonham rated a red check mark, but not Greg Killman. Of course, Drayton's list was comprised of paid members only. It didn't include board members, people who'd used the Heritage Society's meeting hall or outdoor patio for special events, or folks who'd toured the place.

Would volunteers and docents also be members? she wondered. *Probably. Probably you start out as a member and then, as you get more and more interested, you trade up to becoming a volunteer.*

"Hmm," Theodosia said out loud. She wasn't sure what she'd just proved. Or disproved. She obviously couldn't go running around investigating thirty-eight people. And there was always the chance the murderer wasn't on the list at all.

This murderer had to be particularly clever, she decided. He'd known the peculiar layout of the house, had managed to separate Duke Wilkes from the rest of the crowd, and then, after committing his foul act, managed to slip away undetected.

Okay. So who would have known the layout of the house? What if I start from that premise?

Theodosia reached for a fat black marking pen as her eyes slid down her checked-off list. When she came upon one name, she thought for a moment, then circled it. Jock Rowley. He was a contractor who had ongoing access to the tangle of deeds, records, and blueprints that were filed at City Hall. He'd made overtures to Claudia and Corky Chait, expressing interest in buying the Chait House.

But if Jock Rowley had stabbed Duke Wilkes, what had his motive been? Anger, greed, revenge?

Theodosia knew those were all powerful motivators that could drive people to commit murder. But for now, she had no clue if she was even remotely in the ballpark concerning Jock Rowley.

By two o'clock, activity in the tea shop had slowed to a lazy pace. Drayton had spread out a clutch of tiny I-hsing teacups on one of the large round tables and was conducting an impromptu tea tasting of Chinese green teas.

Haley was making the rounds of the shop, topping off teacups for the rest of the guests. Once she'd finished, she slid quietly into a chair opposite Bill Glass.

Pushing her way through the green velvet curtains that modestly shielded the kitchen and back office from the tea room, Theodosia did a double take.

Wait a minute, is that Bill Glass again? What's that clod doing back here?

Theodosia was across the room in a heartbeat. "Fancy seeing you here again," she purred.

Glass swiveled his dark head and looked up at her. "You. Tea lady. How do." He favored her with a perfunctory smile.

Theodosia directed her inquisitive gaze toward Haley. "You two look like you're busy plotting something."

Haley's face lit up with an excited grin. "We're talking recipe books," she told Theodosia. "You know how I've been babbling on about doing a recipe book for the last couple years? Well, Mr. Glass is a *publisher.*" She paused, obviously reveling in her news. "And he says he's interested in my recipes!"

"Sounds pretty exciting," said Theodosia, slipping into a chair between them.

"He says my desserts would tempt the devil himself." Haley laughed.

"Those would be the desserts Mr. Glass appropriated yesterday?" asked Theodosia. Glass had gone crazy over Haley's tuxedo brownies and Charleston cream cheese cookies. So much so that one table of guests had been slightly short-shrifted.

Glass gave a low chuckle. "You don't miss a trick, do you tea lady?"

"I try not to," said Theodosia.

"Mr. Glass . . ." began Haley.

"Bill," said Bill Glass. "Call me Bill."

"Bill has published almost a dozen different books over the past couple years," expounded Haley. "All having to do with Charleston and Charleston-related subjects. He was telling me all about them. He did a book about Pinckney Island and a book about some of the old plantations out Ashley River Road."

"That plantation book was really a coffee table book," interjected Bill Glass. "More glamour shots than text."

"Plus a bunch more books," continued Haley, happily. "He even put one together for the Heritage Society."

"Really," said Theodosia, trying to sound noncommittal. "The Heritage Society. How nice."

"They have it for sale in their gift shop," offered Glass. "Thirty-nine ninety-five."

"I'll have to check it out," Theodosia told him.

"Oh, oh," cried Haley. She suddenly sprang up from her chair. "Gotta hustle. Drayton's making eyes at me. He probably needs that other pot of Dragon Well tea. S'cuse me." And she was gone.

"Haley's pretty excited about this," said Theodosia as she

watched Haley measure out tea leaves into a blue and white Chinese teapot, then pour in a steady stream of hot water.

Bill Glass nodded. "Hey, she's a kid. How many kids get offered a book deal, especially to publish recipes?"

"You think her recipes are that good?" asked Theodosia. She was trying to keep an open mind about this. Even though she didn't care for Bill Glass personally, she didn't want to stand in Haley's way.

"Listen," said Glass, leaning forward, looking serious. "I hear nothing but good things about this place. About the tea you folks serve and the unbelievable food. In particular, the scones, muffins, breads, and desserts. And as I understand it, Haley does all the baking."

"She's an incredibly gifted baker," murmured Theodosia.

"And she tells me she has tons of recipes," said Glass. "Apparently handed down from her grandmother. So if it's not a problem with you . . ."

"It's not," said Theodosia. "I'd tell her to go for it. If the terms of the contract are right, that is."

"Wonderful," said Glass, leaning back in his chair. "Mind you, I'm not making any *promises* here. This recipe thing is still an awfully loosey goosey concept. One that needs a lot more exploring."

"Of course," said Theodosia. "I'll make sure Haley understands that."

"T-riffic," said Glass.

Theodosia let a beat go by. "You know," she said. "I was wondering about something."

"Shoot," said Glass.

"Those photos you took Sunday night? I was wondering if I could take a look at them."

Bill Glass was instantly on the alert. "The ones from the Candlelight Concert?"

Theodosia nodded.

"And your interest is . . . what exactly?" asked Glass.

"Let's just call it curiosity."

"About Duke Wilkes?" he asked.

"Well . . . yes," said Theodosia.

Glass's dark eyes bore into her, obviously expecting more.

"I made a promise to Pookie, Duke's wife," explained Theodosia. "She's a good friend, visits the tea shop a lot. I told her I'd sort of look into things for her."

"Concerning the murder," said Glass.

"Right," said Theodosia. She didn't think she was tipping her hand too much by revealing this. Unless Bill Glass was the murderer, and she didn't think he was. Hoped he wasn't anyway.

"Sure," said Glass finally. "You can look at em."

"Great," said Theodosia, surprised he'd agreed so readily.

"But let me warn you, you won't find anything out of the ordinary," said Glass, peering at her carefully. "I've already looked through them with that very same thought in mind. And obviously the police were extremely interested, too."

"Really?" said Theodosia. She had hoped the police might have overlooked the photo angle.

Bill Glass nodded. "You bet they were. I even had to hand over the film canisters so their lab could process 'em. Give 'em the first look-see."

"Good for you," said Theodosia, sounding deflated. *If Tidwell's already seen the photos, then chances are I'm probably not going to discover anything new. Rats.*

14

❧

"When did you get so cozy with Bill Glass?" Drayton asked Haley. His table of tea tasters had departed and only one small group still occupied a table in the tea shop.

Haley straightened up from where she was emptying tea pots behind the counter. "Are you serious?" she asked. "Since he was all over the place yesterday taking millions of pictures I could barely turn around without bumping into him. Plus, he asked me what I did and I told him."

"You told him what?" asked Drayton, sounding miffed.

"That I was a studying business administration in school, but worked here as a baker and caterer."

"And how did that lead to the recipe book concept, pray tell?" asked Drayton.

"He snuck a few brownies from the kitchen." Haley laughed. "And wanted to know if my recipes were proprietary."

"He actually used that term?" asked Drayton. "Proprietary?"

"He was just being inquisitive," said Haley. She rolled her eyes and cast a glance over at Theodosia, who was sorting through the day's receipts. Clearly, Haley was beginning to regard Drayton as a bit of a killjoy.

"This from a man who appropriated some of our desserts," said Drayton. "Leaving us a tad short for our final course."

"I'm sorry about that," said Haley, letting out a huge sigh. "But honestly, Drayton, you act as though I'm about to give away trade secrets or something."

"You never know," said Drayton. "He publishes that awful rag, *Shooting Star.* So obviously he's not the most reputable person in town." He glanced over toward Theodosia. "Right, Theo?"

Theodosia offered a noncommittal nod. She'd suddenly remembered the photo Bill Glass's photographer had snapped of her when she was passing the dirk to Tidwell. And wondered if it was still going to grace the front page of Friday's *Shooting Star. Heaven forbid. Hopefully he's found something timelier or frothier to appeal to his gossip-loving audience.*

"You know, Drayton," said Haley. "An awful lot of people are delighted to get publicity."

"Not the *Shooting Star* kind," said Drayton derisively.

"Actually," said Theodosia, "Haley's pretty much right on. Since we live in such a media-frenzied world, publicity, even negative publicity, is often considered a major coup."

"See, Drayton." Haley smirked. "Theo knows. She *worked* in advertising and PR."

"Which she got tired of and left," said Drayton. And with those final words ringing in their ears, Drayton promptly grabbed a plastic tub of dirty dishes and ducked into the kitchen.

"Drayton's certainly got his nose out of joint," said Haley. "You think he's jealous?"

"Drayton doesn't have a jealous bone in his body," said Theodosia. "But he is a rather cautious sort. I'm sure he doesn't want to see you get all worked up over something that might not come to fruition."

Haley peered at Theodosia, weighing her words. "Maybe so." She hesitated. "You don't mind if I do a recipe book, do you?"

"Goodness no, Haley," said Theodosia. After all, they're your recipes."

"Technically, an awful lot of them belonged to my grandmother," said Haley.

"But she passed them on to you, then you adapted them," said Theodosia. "Over time you've given each recipe your own little twist. Like the she-crab soup with the mustard in it. Or adding molasses to your Caribbean sweet potato pie. Or your wonderful plum sauce with mulberry wine."

"I'm just going to keep my fingers crossed," said Haley, glancing over at their last remaining guests. "Bill Glass may be a strange duck, but he's also a publisher who's got his finger in a lot of pies." She picked up a pot of tea and headed toward their lingering customers. "And just maybe he can help make my dream come true," she murmured under her breath.

Theodosia watched as Haley refilled cups, then chatted with their last table of guests. And she thought about what Haley had just told her.

She knew Bill Glass was a strange fellow. But he must also be guided by a lucky star or possess the skills of a darn good prognosticator. Because Bill Glass had carefully stationed his young photographer Gep outside the Chait House the day after the murder.

Could that have been mere coincidence? Theodosia wondered. *Or if it wasn't coincidence, then what? Had Bill Glass been setting something up? Had he set something up?*

Theodosia stood up and carried her teacup over to the counter. She lifted the gingham tea cozy off a white porcelain teapot decorated with lavender pansies and poured out a fragrant stream of gunpowder green tea.

Is Bill Glass the kind of journalist who'd do anything to get a story? she wondered. *Is he just like those rabid Hollywood paparazzi who hunt down stars, prompt a nasty confrontation, and thus create a story? Is he of the same ilk as the paparazzi who chased poor Princess Diana?*

Theodosia let her mind wander, thinking about Bill Glass. The one Drayton had once called "old smooth as glass." She was aware that Glass's name appeared on Delaine's guest list, but not on the Heritage Society list. Although Glass had almost certainly attended gallery openings and galas there.

On the other hand, Bill Glass had obviously cooperated with Burt Tidwell. With the Charleston Police. He'd handed over his film to them, allowed them to develop and print his shots in their lab.

Theodosia was about to take a sip of tea, when a thought struck her. *Did Bill Glass also let the police take a look at the digital photos he'd snapped? Good question. And a darned good excuse to get in Burt Tidwell's face again.*

"*Are you up* for this?" asked Drayton, staring across the table at Theodosia. It was four o'clock and the Indigo Tea

Shop was formally closed. Haley had retreated to her apartment across the alley to curl up with her business textbooks.

"We've got to do it sometime," said Theodosia. "Last year we were almost a month late and probably missed out on a lot of sales."

Drayton nodded. "People are already asking about holiday tea blends. Seems like the holidays get started earlier and earlier every year."

"Halloween is getting to be the kick-off point now," agreed Theodosia.

"So," said Drayton, paging through the black ledger that served as his journal. "Holiday blends." He glanced up at Theodosia. "I've jotted down ideas for four different teas."

"Good," said Theodosia, trying to stifle a yawn. "Let's go ahead and do all four."

Drayton lifted a single eyebrow. "Don't you even want to hear my ideas? Shouldn't we *discuss* them?"

"If you wish," said Theodosia pleasantly. "But you know I have complete faith in you. After all, you're the master tea blender, not I."

"You're not without certain skills," said Drayton. "Your idea for our house blend of Earl Green was superb."

"Pure luck," said Theodosia. "Or perhaps a touch of your brilliance rubbed off."

"Rubbish," said Drayton, adjusting his glasses and looking pleased. Then he cleared his throat and gazed at Theodosia earnestly. "What I'd love to do this year is a sort of *homage* to the Charleston area."

"Okay," said Theodosia. "Lay it on me."

"First tea blend I call Angel Oak. A tribute to our beloved

fourteen-hundred-year-old live oak out on Johns Island. A blend of Chinese green tea and jasmine with a hint of vanilla."

"Sounds fantastic," said Theodosia. "And very fresh."

"Next blend, Santee Soothing Tea," said Drayton. "Chamomile tea combined with peppermint and cloves."

"I predict that will be a huge seller," said Theodosia.

"Idea number three," continued Drayton. "Broad Street Blend."

Theodosia gave an encouraging nod. "Everyone from Charleston proper will adore it." Broad Street was the cross street that pretty much defined the peninsula proper. Anything "below Broad" was considered "real" Charleston.

"Our Broad Street Blend would be a medley of Ceylon and Indian black teas with flavors of peach and cinnamon."

"Love it," said Theodosia.

"And finally, a wild card blend I call Her Majestea. *T-E-A* instead of *T-Y* for the ending," added Drayton.

"I thought as much," replied Theodosia. "And the blend is . . . ?"

"Black tea with bits of roses, orange peel, and wild cherry," said Drayton, consulting his notes.

"I amend my earlier prediction," said Theodosia. "Her Majestea will be our biggest seller."

"I'm betting on the . . ." Drayton hesitated as a loud pounding started up on the front door.

Theodosia raised her eyebrows. "Latecomers?"

Drayton rose and hurried to the door. "Insistent ones at that. I'll tell them we're closed."

"Let me in," came the muffled cry of a familiar-sounding voice.

Drayton peered through the leaded pane windows, then gazed back at Theodosia. "Delaine," he said.

"Better let her in," said Theodosia. "She's not the type who'll just give up and go away."

Delaine came steamrolling across the tea shop like a race horse out of the gate. "What are you two up to?" she asked as she plunked herself down at the table with Theodosia.

"Drayton's been working on the new holiday tea blends," Theodosia told her.

"We were trying to get a jump on things," said Drayton, emphasizing the word *trying.*

"In that case, I have a fantastic idea I've been saving just for you," volunteered Delaine. "Black tea blended with poinsettias! Nothing screams the holidays like poinsettias."

"Poinsettias are poison," replied Drayton in a dry tone. He was almost, but not quite, amused.

Delaine looked shocked and supremely disappointed. "Poison? Are you positive? Good heavens." She frowned. "Well, another brilliant idea bites the dust. I suppose you can't whip up a brew that would *poison* half of Charleston."

"Delaine," said Theodosia, trying to cut to the chase. "What's up?"

"Well," said Delaine, putting her hands flat on the table and drawing a deep breath. "I've just come from Pookie Wilkes's house. She needed something suitable to wear to the memorial service. You know that's tomorrow, don't you?"

"We know," snapped Drayton.

"As luck would have it," continued Delaine, "I had the most *adorable* black boucle jacket just hanging in my shop. Totally elegant and a bit understated. Certainly suitable for . . ."

"Delaine," said Theodosia, staring pointedly at her.

"Okay, okay," said Delaine, throwing up her hands in mock surrender. "I hear you. Long story short, Pookie is *dying* to know what you've come up with. Suspects, motives, conclusions, the whole ball of wax." With that, Delaine positioned her elbows on the table, dropped her chin in her hands, and stared fixedly at Theodosia. A stare that said, *Surely you've got this all figured out by now.*

"I've been noodling around a few ideas," admitted Theodosia, "but nothing I can really share yet."

"What?" wailed Delaine. Obviously she'd been expecting a more concise, buttoned down answer. "Certainly, you're harboring some deep, dark suspicions. After all, Pookie's counting on us!"

Us, thought Theodosia. *Delaine says Pookie's counting on us. But I'm the poor schnook who's stuck doing all the grunt work.*

"What about that broken piece of knife we discovered?" asked Delaine. "Have you followed up on that with Detective Tidwell? Has he shared anything new with you? Did you even *look* at the guest list I faxed over? Come on, Theo, *talk* to me!"

"Theodosia's been working very hard on this in her spare time," said Drayton, coming to her rescue. "But this is an extraordinarily tough case. There are simply no concrete leads to speak of."

That shut Delaine up. She sat there, a slight frown on her face, staring into space.

"Delaine," said Theodosia finally. "How much do you know about Jock Rowley?"

Delaine drifted back. "Him," she sniffed. "Jock Rowley hasn't contributed a single cent yet to my restoration campaign."

"Really?" said Theodosia. "Because I got the feeling you might have worked him over pretty well."

"Me?" said Delaine. "My dear, I beg to differ. I called Jock Rowley yesterday morning, trying to play catch-up on my fund-raising. And all he wanted to know was, *Is the deal still going through?*"

"What deal?" asked Drayton.

"The Chait House and the Heritage Society, of course," said Delaine. She picked at a bit of fuzz on her yellow cashmere sweater. "From the rather probing questions he asked, I got the distinct feeling Jock Rowley would have liked to buy that old place."

"Buy the Chait House?" Drayton snorted. "And do what with it?"

"Maybe build condos?" offered Theodosia. *Rowley is, after all, the condo king.*

"But that house was never for sale," said Drayton. "And even if it was, you certainly couldn't convert it into condos. It's listed on the historic register."

"Not yet, it isn't," said Delaine. "We're still working on that."

"Whatever," said Drayton. "It's a big old stately home. Hardly the sort of thing you could convert into condos."

Theodosia thought for a moment. "What if it was zoned commercial?"

"Well, it's not," snapped Drayton. "The Chait House is a private residence."

"You told me yourself that place was used as a hospital, an orphanage, and then a funeral parlor," said Theodosia. "That sounds awfully commercial to me."

"Good grief," said Drayton, suddenly realizing Theodosia's assessment was quite correct. "Jock Rowley. You don't suppose . . . "

15

Live oaks stretched their signature gnarled boughs overhead as Theodosia and Earl Grey jogged through the heart of Charleston's historic district. Gigantic homes, huge as medieval castles, loomed on either side of them. The faint crash of the sea echoed up ahead.

This is the plus of living here, Theodosia told herself. *I enjoy all the benefits of this grandeur and grace without paying the price of maintaining one of these gigantic money pits.*

Timothy Neville, who owned one of the largest mansions over on Archdale Street, was forever complaining about how much *financial resources* were required to maintain his huge Italianate home. She'd stayed there before and found it wonderfully sumptuous. But to hear it from Timothy, the wiring was terrible, heating nonexistent, the lawn and formal gardens demanded meticulous care, and tuck-pointing on the outside brick work was never-ending.

"Timothy . . . " Theodosia panted alongside Earl Grey, who was more than matching her stride for stride. In fact, the dog had slowed to a gentle lope in order not to outpace her. "Lets make a quick stop at the Heritage Society and talk to Timothy."

"Hello, doggy," said Timothy Neville as he stretched a wizened hand toward Earl Grey's twitching nose. "Long time no see. You should drop by some time and see if you can track down Dreadnaught. That old cat seems to disappear for days at a time."

"I bet I saw him maybe three times during the entire two weeks I stayed at your house," laughed Theodosia. "But he did manage to clean his dish every day."

Timothy looked down his nose. "Are you sure that wasn't you?" he inquired of Earl Grey.

Seemingly offended by the implication, Earl Grey gazed solemnly at Timothy as if to say, *Pardon me, sir, but a canine such as myself would never indulge in cat food.*

Theodosia backed him up. "Earl Grey is much too finicky an eater," she assured Timothy. "Most of the time I have to top his dog food with hamburger or rice just to get him to consider having a nosh."

They were sitting in Timothy's palatial office at the Heritage Society, Theodosia enjoying a cooldown after her run, Timothy finishing some paperwork.

"I wanted to ask you about a book that Bill Glass published for the Heritage Society," began Theodosia.

Timothy favored her with a sharp gaze. "I hope you're not thinking about using that charlatan's services," he began.

"Not me," said Theodosia. "But Haley received a somewhat tentative offer from Bill Glass. He's expressed interest in publishing some of her recipes. Bragged to us that he put together a nice book for the Heritage Society."

Timothy snorted. "Not nice at all. The book Glass did for us was a compendium on modern day Civil War reenactors. It was a lifelong dream for many of us but ended up being nothing short of disaster."

"What went wrong?" asked Theodosia. If Haley was headed for trouble she wanted to know.

"A better question might be what *didn't* go wrong," said Timothy. "The paper stock was flimsy, several photos were incorrectly identified, and two battlefield maps got transposed. If that wasn't enough, getting a look at the final proof was akin to pulling teeth."

"What I hear you saying is you definitely wouldn't recommend Bill Glass as a publisher?" asked Theodosia.

"I wouldn't wish that man on my worst enemy," said Timothy. He stood up from his chair and walked stiffly over to a wall that was floor-to-ceiling bookshelves. Timothy fumbled around amidst leather-bound volumes for a moment, adjusted his gold-rimmed glasses, then found what he was looking for. "This," he said, walking back to his desk and handing an oversized book to Theodosia, "turned out to be an absolute travesty."

Accepting the book, Theodosia gazed at its cover. The visual was an old etching of Civil War troops charging into battle. Above the etching was the title in boldface type: *Sabers & Swords: The Story of Modern Day Civil War Reenactors.*

She opened the book in the middle and thumbed through a few pages. Timothy was right. The paper stock was a little flimsy. The reproduction quality wasn't bad, but it just should have been printed on *heavier* stock. And the kerning, the spacing between each line of type, seemed a little too generous to her as well. Then again, Theodosia was a stickler on production quality. She'd produced hundreds of brochures and catalogs for her former clients.

"What else went wrong?" asked Theodosia. The book, though it might not possess the heft Timothy wanted, didn't seem all *that* bad.

Timothy's thin mouth twisted into a grimace. "One of our overzealous board members signed a contract he didn't fully comprehend," said Timothy. "With each sale, most of the profits go to Glass Publishing. The Heritage Society retains something like five percent royalties."

"Ah," said Theodosia. "I had a feeling Glass might be a bit of a sharpie." *Now I know he is. Better watch out, Haley. Your dream could easily turn into a complete nightmare.*

Theodosia handed the book back to Timothy. "Too bad," she said. "This really could have been terrific."

"We learn from our mistakes," replied Timothy. "The problem is, of course, the older I get, the less value I seem to glean from these ridiculous trip-ups."

Theodosia nodded. She could agree with that. "Have the police been bothering you much?" she asked.

Timothy waved a hand. "They seem to have finished their business. But the crime scene people were a dreadful nuisance for a couple days. Skulking about, fingerprinting employees and volunteers, sniffing around inside the basement storeroom, looking for lord knows what."

"Sorry," she replied. "Like I said before, I didn't mean to drive the investigation right to your front door."

Timothy sighed heavily. "Couldn't be helped. Since, apparently, the dirk came from right here, from our own store-

room. But even though the police followed their set proto-
cols for collecting evidence, I don't see that they actually
came away with anything useful."

Same problem I'm having, thought Theodosia.

"Did you hear that Jock Rowley wanted to buy the Chait
House?" Theodosia asked.

Timothy shrugged. "I heard a rumor that Jock might
have made a run at Corky Chait, but Corky has always been
committed to making sure that the house passed on to the
Heritage Society. He's a good man, Corky. Possesses a genuine social conscience. Unfortunately, there's not enough of
that in the world today."

"Have you thought any more about Duke?" asked Theodosia. "And what he'd been up to? Can you think of any enemies Duke might have had? Why someone might have
wanted to kill him?"

Timothy's face fell. "No, not really," he replied.

Theodosia could see that, once again, her visit was bringing Timothy down. Ten minutes ago he'd appeared to be in
a fairly decent mood, now he looked tired and dispirited.

Okay, she told herself. *Just one last question. Then I'll quit
pestering this poor man.*

"Do you know what Duke had been working on recently?" she asked. "I mean, did Duke have any pet projects
that you knew about?"

Timothy thought for a moment. "Duke was constantly
involved in projects," he finally answered. "Volunteerism
and community action were part of his basic philosophy.
Get involved, stay involved, try to make things better."

"Right," said Theodosia. She glanced at her watch. *Time
to get moving. I've got to go home, take a shower, feed Earl Grey,*

and then hustle off to my meeting with Sydney Chastain tonight.
She stood up, tugged at Earl Grey's leash. "Well, if you think
of anything," said Theodosia, starting for the door.

"There might be one thing . . . " said Timothy slowly.

Theodosia stopped and turned. "What?"

"There was a small tract of land that Duke . . . oh, what
would you call it? That Duke managed to *rescue.* A little
piece of woods outside of Mount Pleasant that was going to
be sold to a developer and turned into an industrial park. A
place nicknamed Chatham Field. Duke did his usual due
diligence and found out it had historical significance. Seems
it had once been a part of Francis Marion's old stomping
grounds."

"The Swamp Fox?" asked Theodosia. The Swamp Fox
had been a major hero during the Revolutionary War, appearing out of nowhere to cut down redcoats.

"Mm hmm," said Timothy.

"And did Duke Wilkes manage to save this Chatham
Field?" asked Theodosia.

"Oh, yes," said Timothy. "Duke not only persuaded the
property owner not to sell to the developer, he ended up
purchasing the land himself. If I recall, Duke was planning
to turn the little tract of land over to the South Carolina Department of Natural Resources." Timothy sighed. "Perhaps
he already has."

"Do you know who the developer was?" she asked. "The
one Duke thwarted?"

"No idea," said Timothy.

In the midst of blow-drying her hair, Theodosia decided to
call Pookie Wilkes. The last bit of information Timothy had

given her about Chatham Field was weighing on her mind and she wanted to find out more. Probably, she could wait until tomorrow, when she'd see Pookie at the funeral. But, somehow, questioning the bereaved widow at her own husband's service seemed more than a little crass. And might be potentially upsetting to Pookie, even though she had asked for help.

Pookie was nothing but gracious when Theodosia called.

"I'm so sorry to disturb you," began Theodosia.

"But you're not really, my dear," said Pookie. "In fact, it's rather refreshing to hear your voice. All of Duke's relatives are sitting around downstairs looking angry and morose. And, frankly, it's a bit more than I can stand."

"It must be very hard for you, what with the funeral tomorrow."

"I'm managing," Pookie assured her. "The fact that Duke and I had many wonderful years together helps sustain me." She paused. "Now, what can I do for you?"

"What can you tell me about Chatham Field?" asked Theodosia.

Pookie hesitated. "Now isn't that funny? The police asked me the exact same question."

"They did, really?" A jittery feeling had suddenly insinuated itself inside Theodosia. Maybe she was on the right track! Maybe she was keeping pace with the police!

Theodosia forced herself to remain calm. "So what do you know about it?"

"Exactly what I told the police," replied Pookie. "Duke had done research on the little tract of woods and then when a developer made motions to purchase it, he stepped in."

"Did Duke have some sort of notes or file regarding the Chatham Field transaction?"

"Of course," said Pookie. "But most of that's been handed over to the police."

Oops, thought Theodosia, *I'm treading old ground now. The police are already investigating that angle. Well . . . heck.*

"I'm really sorry to bother you," said Theodosia, "but I've got just one more question. Do you know who owned this Chatham Field?"

"A company by the name of Tiburon Enterprises," said Pookie.

"Never heard of them," said Theodosia.

"Neither have I," said Pookie.

"Okay, thanks so much," said Theodosia. "Sorry to disturb you."

"You didn't disturb me," said Pookie. "If anything, you've helped uplift my spirits. And strengthen my faith in my fellow man. Especially now that I know you're really trying to investigate this. Thank you, Theodosia, you have no idea what this means to me."

Theodosia was starting to feel slightly beleaguered. If she didn't pick up the pace, she'd really be running late. And then what kind of smart businesswoman would she look like in front of Sydney Chastain? She wouldn't. She'd look like a *goof.*

But . . . she had just one more phone call to make.

Pulling out Tidwell's business card, Theodosia punched in his office number. And was surprised when he answered the phone himself.

"I didn't think you'd still be there," she stammered.

"Then why did you call?" he asked in a petulant tone.

Theodosia fought to recover her composure. *Why does this man frustrate me to no end?* she asked herself.

"I have a quick question for you," she told Tidwell.

"Then ask," came his gruff rumble.

"Who owns Tiburon Enterprises?" asked Theodosia.

"I was wondering when you'd get around that," replied Tidwell. Now a hint of amusement had crept into Tidwell's voice. Or was it a hint of superiority?

"Why do you say that?" Theodosia asked him.

"Because it's a holding company owned by Jock Rowley," said Tidwell.

Theodosia was dumbstruck. "Are you serious?"

"And, I'm sorry to have to tell you this, but you're ten or twelve steps behind us in making that particular connection," goaded Tidwell. "Which is exactly where you *should* be," he added.

"Jock Rowley owns Tiburon Enterprises," Theodosia repeated. She was shocked beyond belief.

"Is there an echo in here?" asked Tidwell. "Because I thought we already covered that material. Could we possibly move on?"

"You're enjoying this, aren't you?" said Theodosia. *Of course he was.*

"Really relishing it," replied Tidwell, rolling his *r*'s.

"I see that, Detective," said Theodosia. *You want to zing me? I'll zing you back.* "By the way, have you thought to look at *all* the photos Bill Glass took the night of the Candlelight Concert?"

"Please," said Tidwell, in a condescending tone. "Our police lab *developed* that film. Standard black-and-white publicity shots, nothing out of the ordinary. Certainly nothing that would lead to the apprehension of a suspect." Now he sounded almost bored, as though he were about to indulge in a good yawn. Of course, once the cat-and-mouse part of a conversation had been concluded, Tidwell almost always lost interest.

"What about the digital photos?" asked Theodosia.

There was a moment of shocked silence.

"Digital photos," repeated Tidwell.

"You know, there *is* an echo in here," said Theodosia.

"What are you talking about?" huffed Tidwell. "*Digital* shots. What exactly are you implying?"

"Glass was shooting with *three* cameras that night," Theodosia told him. "Two Nikons and a small digital camera."

"Hmph," said Tidwell. "News to me." He sounded far from happy.

"Are you going to contact Bill Glass?" Theodosia asked.

"Obviously," replied Tidwell.

"In my book, Glass withheld evidence," said Theodosia. "Right?"

"Digital," snarled Tidwell one more time.

"Will you tell me what happens? What he says?" asked Theodosia. "Will you let me look at the photos?"

But Tidwell had already hung up.

"Creep," she yelled, slamming down her phone. And Earl Grey, who'd been snoozing next to her bed, suddenly twitched and jumped to his feet, wondering what on earth the uproar was all about.

16

❧

"*So you've just* launched a brand new network," Theodosia said to Sydney Chastain, "right here in Charleston."

Draped in her leather executive chair, wearing a stunning eggplant-colored suit with three-strand pearl necklace, Sydney favored Theodosia with a dazzling smile. "My goal is to do for Charleston what Ted did for Atlanta. Put us squarely on the map broadcast-wise."

"I think Charleston's already on a few maps." Theodosia laughed. "What with our history, hurricanes, and hospitality. What I call the three *H*'s."

"You mean, four point four million visitors can't be wrong?" asked Sydney. That was the number of tourists who flocked to Charleston every year to tour the historic district, ply the markets, and enjoy the superb restaurants, shops, and hotels.

"Something like that, yes," replied Theodosia as a soft knock sounded on Sydney's office door.

"Come in," called Sydney. Sitting at her desk, surrounded by stacks of papers and files, she looked every inch the high-tech CEO. Theodosia was positioned across from her in a comfortable leather chair, feeling slightly drab in her black pencil skirt and matching Chanel look-alike jacket.

An attractive dark-haired woman in a dove gray suit entered the room, carrying a large tray. "I thought I'd bring this back to you," she said with a smile. "The delivery boy dropped it at the reception desk, but most of the secretarial staff has gone home for the evening."

Sydney pushed aside papers to accommodate the tray.

"Theodosia, meet Sarah Jane Sigrid, my number one producer."

"Nice to meet you," said Theodosia as Sarah Jane smiled at her.

"Great to meet you," responded Sarah Jane. "And now, if you'll excuse me, I've have a preproduction meeting that's probably going to drag on forever."

"Go make the magic," Sydney told Sarah Jane.

Theodosia smiled to herself at their little exchange. There was definitely chemistry at work here. And she knew that good chemistry was the first step in making a business vigorous and viable.

In fact, when she'd first arrived for her appointment with Sydney Chastain, she'd been impressed and a little surprised by the number of women who were striding about in spiffy-looking business suits, working late, and obviously holding key positions in management.

Well, she told herself, *it is a new network exclusively for women.*

They helped themselves to sandwiches and bottled water, then Sydney settled into her high-backed chair.

"Imagine when VTV really takes off," enthused Sydney. "Think about the impact on our community. We live in a high-tech, high-speed world. And there's no reason why Charleston shouldn't bite off a nice fat chunk of it." Sydney leaned forward and flashed a broad smile.

The smile, Theodosia noted, of a *true believer*. One who believes she can move mountains just by her sheer will. *Well, good luck.*

"We already have streaming video on the Internet," continued Sydney. "Imagine the possibilities when a complete convergence of technologies is achieved. And wouldn't it be wonderful," she purred, "if VTV was the pioneer network that delivered that first fine-tuned merger of TV and Internet? VTV would be instantly global. There'd be no stopping us!"

"Is that what you're working on?" asked Theodosia.

Sydney reached up and patted her blond hair. "It's one of the things."

"Then bravo," said Theodosia. "I wish you all the luck in the world." She was all for technology, too, but was still aware that one fourth of the globe's inhabitants had not yet made a phone call.

"VTV is up and running now with twenty-eight affiliates," said Sydney. "Eight are major market."

"Very impressive," Theodosia told her. "But it sounds like you have your work cut out for you. Captaining a brand new network has to be an incredibly demanding role."

Theodosia knew for a fact that business today was tough and getting tougher. As an account executive for a marketing firm, she'd been obliged to produce revenues of ten to twenty times her salary. What then, did the head of a TV network have to produce? Hundreds of thousands? Millions? And what were the brutal pressures that hung over you like the dangling sword of Damocles? Obviously you had to develop meaningful programming, sign up affiliates, generate revenue, generate *more* revenue . . .

Theodosia shuddered. No thank you. Running a network might seem like a hip, hot career choice. But running a tea shop was challenging enough these days.

Theodosia smiled at Sydney Chastain across the broad expanse of her executive desk. Sydney seemed like a genuinely sincere woman, she really did. It was just that she had this super *macho* (or was it *machess?*) thing going. Sydney was so sure, so positive, that she possessed all the answers. The problem was, Sydney probably hadn't yet asked all the questions. But she for sure had the stats, numbers, big talk, and big ideas.

As if reading her mind, Sydney shoved the sandwich platter across the table at Theodosia. "Another?" she asked. "And be sure to try those little wrap things, too."

"Thank you," said Theodosia, helping herself.

"Sorry we don't have any tea," said Sydney.

"Bottled water is fine," replied Theodosia. "More than fine." After her jog earlier in the evening, she was feeling the need to replenish her fluids.

"So," said Sydney, "you've given up your evening to come here and let me pick your brain. I appreciate that, I really do." She reached for the notebook that sat next to her plate. "Can we get started?"

"Fire away," said Theodosia.

Over the next half-hour, Sydney asked Theodosia some very probing and thought-provoking questions. Why Theodosia had left marketing to get started in the tea shop business? How had her customer demographics broken out? What kind of niche marketing did she do? What trends did she see happening? What were the important issues that seemed to be on women's minds these days?

They found they were both "demographic junkies." And began tossing interesting facts back and forth.

"Did you know that, right now, fifty-six percent of college students are women?" asked Sydney.

Theodosia nodded. "I think it's another testament to the emerging power of women. And not just as educated consumers, but as investors, employees, managers, and corporate leaders."

"I read an IRS study that said women enjoy a higher net worth than men," said Sydney.

"And they own something like fifty-five percent of all stocks and bonds," said Theodosia.

"Did you realize that when women comprise half the management team on companies that go public, the stock price rises twenty-three percent higher than companies with no women?" Sydney asked.

"Wow," said Theodosia. "That is impressive." She thought for a moment. "*You* just went public."

Sydney made a face. "We did. Although I'm sad to say it took some hard finagling. We shopped VTV around to several regional venture capital firms and found only one that was willing to work with us."

"Are you serious?" asked Theodosia. She was impressed with Sydney and beginning to revise her earlier assessment of the woman. She had pegged Sydney Chastain's management style as cowboyish. Eager and anxious to cut a wide swathe. Instead, Theodosia found Sydney to be thoughtful, aggressive, yet carefully tempered.

Sydney spun her chair around and grabbed a stack of booklets off her gleaming teak credenza. She spun back and slapped them down hard on her desk. "Look at this," she said, sounding more than a little angry. "We put together what I thought was an absolutely *brilliant* pitch. And four venture capital firms wouldn't deign to touch us with a ten-foot pole!"

Theodosia gazed across the table at Sydney's rejected proposals. Reading upside down, a skill she'd honed in dealing with her marketing clients, she saw that the top booklet read *A Venture Capital Request from VTV to Goldfinger Ventures*.

"Goldfinger," she said. "I've heard of them."

"Two-bit operation," Sydney said bitterly. "Oh, well. We eventually got our expansion capital and that's all that matters."

"From . . . who?" asked Theodosia.

"Nobilus Financial. Down in Savannah," said Sydney. "We couldn't be happier with them. And now the rest of those visionless jerks are simply a lingering bad taste in my mouth." She downed the last of her bottled water, then sprang to her feet. "I better let you get going. I've kept you here long enough."

But as Sydney strode around her desk, her sleeve caught the stack of proposals, causing them to spin across her desk then flutter to the floor. "Oops," she send, starting to bend down.

But Theodosia had already bent forward to retrieve the folders that were scattered everywhere.

"Here you go," said Theodosia, grabbing the folders and scooping up her handbag at the same time. But as she placed the folders back on Sydney's desk, her smile froze on her face. Because one of the pitches, the one that had been on the bottom of the stack and now was on top, caught her eye.

The title page read: *A Venture Capital Request from VTV to Victory Capital.*

Victory Capital. Isn't that Duke Wilkes's company? Sure it is. So Duke's company turned Sydney Chastain down. Wow. That seems like a very unique coincidence.

Sydney was already across the room and gesturing at two architect's models that were mounted on pedestals beside the door. "Take a look at these models before you go," Sydney was saying. "We contracted with two different architectural firms to come up with ideas for our new headquarters."

Theodosia walked over to the models, still thinking about the strange coincidence. Did she mistrust coincidences? Yeah, sometimes.

Sydney was pointing at a super contemporary-looking model complete with glass walls and a soaring roofline. "This is the one from Greystone Architects," she told Theodosia. "An amazing showpiece, but very expensive. Greystone was *extremely* disappointed when they didn't get the job." Sydney gestured toward the more boxy, conservative model that sat next to it. "This is the one we decided to go with. More practical, which translates into affordability." She sighed. "One of those tough business decisions you don't like to make."

"Who's the architectural firm on this one?" Theodosia asked.

"Morison Architects," said Sydney. She pulled open her office door, gestured for Theodosia to go ahead of her. "This has certainly been a fun, productive evening," she commented as they walked down the hallway toward the receptionist desk.

"I really enjoyed it," replied Theodosia. "I suppose I miss being part of the corporate team. Of course it drove me completely nuts when I was tangled up in all the ensuing problems of a big marketing firm."

"You ever think of jumping back in?" Sydney asked her. One carefully waxed eyebrow was raised in a mischievous arch.

"No, not really," said Theodosia, hoping Sydney wasn't about to extend a job offer. *Pour my guts out for somebody else's start-up company? Be on call practically 24/7? No, not anymore. Not on your life.*

"You'll have to sign out with the security guard," Sydney told Theodosia when they reached the reception desk. "Company policy." She smiled at the paunchy uniformed guard behind the desk who was skimming an old copy of *People* magazine. "How you doing tonight, Raleigh?"

"Just fine, Ms. Chastain," he replied, giving her a guilty smile and setting down the magazine.

"I had to get tough and lop off some heads recently," Sydney explained. "Which is why we now have a full-time security guard." She laughed. "When it comes to protecting this company I'm like a mama bear protecting its cubs."

Raleigh nodded as he slid the log book toward Theodosia.

"You never know what a disgruntled employee will do," Raleigh added helpfully.

While Theodosia signed her name in the log-out column, Sydney picked up a handful of pink message slips and flipped through them.

"Wonderful," she exclaimed.

"Good news?" asked Theodosia.

Sydney shrugged. "Ah . . . just more publicity," said Sydney. "This fellow I met the other night . . . well, you were there, too," said Sydney.

Theodosia bit her lip, wondering where she'd been the other night. The oyster roast? Suddenly it dawned on her. "You were at Delaine's Candlelight Concert?" she asked Sydney.

"Just for a very short time," said Sydney. "I left before the assault on poor Duke Wilkes. But I did have the rather dubious pleasure of meeting Bill Glass of *Shooting Star* fame. And, local publicity being in somewhat short supply these days, I agreed to let him do a feature story on us."

"Really," said Theodosia. Now the coincidences were coming fast and furious. She wasn't sure what they meant, but they must mean something!

"Bill Glass wants to drop by tomorrow," said Sydney. "I just hope I can steer him in the right direction."

"Which is?" asked Theodosia.

"Talking about the exciting lineup of shows we've got planned. One in particular, an investigative journalism series we're calling *Third Degree,* is my absolute pet project. The various segments will tackle issues like bio-identical hormones, illegal Botox parties, and mortgage scams."

"Mortgage scams," said Theodosia. "Now that sounds interesting."

17

A contingent of Confederate soldiers, dressed in gray and shouldering antique muskets, paraded silently down the aisle of Grace Episcopal Church. This was followed by a smaller cluster of Union soldiers, dressed in blue and wielding gleaming sabers.

Theodosia watched as the soldiers filed somberly past the flower-laden casket of Duke Wilkes and she was filled with a sense of reverence. Here were men who had been die-hard members of Duke Wilkes's Civil War reenactors group. Men who had shared his love of history, his respect for tradition, and who had come to pay their final respects to Duke in a personal, meaningful way.

Sitting next to her, Drayton gave her shoulder a gentle nudge. Pookie Wilkes and what had to be the rest of the Wilkes family were filing past now, walking slowly down the aisle toward the front of the church, many of them sobbing and clutching hankies to their faces. They filtered past, filling the first ten rows of pews on both sides of the great church.

Gazing about, Theodosia decided that Grace Episcopal Church was the perfect place to hold this funeral. Built in the Gothic style of architecture, Grace Episcopal imparted a staid and serious atmosphere. Soaring architecture, vaulted ceilings, and stained glass windows lent an old-world quality and recalled the great cathedrals of Europe.

As a choir sang "The Lord's Prayer," Timothy Neville took his place at the front podium to begin the eulogy. Gripping the front of the rostrum with his knuckles, dressed in a black suit, Timothy looked almost like a minister himself. One who would thunder out a sermon, decrying the death of this humble servant.

But Timothy didn't thunder. His was a eulogy of gentle remembrance. Recalling the life of Duke Wilkes. Recounting his many charitable deeds and contributions. Sharing a humorous anecdote here and there.

By the time Timothy had finished, there wasn't a dry eye in the house. Even Drayton had surreptitiously pulled out his hanky and was daubing and sniffling.

"What an orator," Drayton whispered to Theodosia. "I certainly hope Timothy's still around for *my* funeral."

"Shush," she whispered back. "Please don't talk like that!"

Two more people took their places at the podium to eulogize Duke: his sister, Hannah Dickerson, a tiny woman from Spartanburg, who spoke in a shaky voice; and Addison Luray, one of Duke's former partners at Victory Capital.

And then the minister imparted his final blessing over Duke's casket and the service was concluded.

As everyone filed down the aisle behind the family, Theodosia slipped out to the side aisle. Seeing Pookie looking so utterly bereft, remembering the promise she'd made to her, Theodosia needed a few moments to pull herself together. To figure out what she really could do to help.

Tiptoeing to the Epistle side of the narthex, she stood contemplating a small stained glass window. It was an angel, dressed in traditional flowing robes, but with the face of a young girl who had drowned on Sullivan's Island. There was something otherworldly about this image, yet the face of the girl made it highly compelling, too. As though, somehow, the two worlds had been bridged.

"Contemplating the inevitable?" asked a familiar voice.

Theodosia whirled about to find Burt Tidwell staring at her. "You!" she said, upset at having her moment of meditation ruined. "What is it with you, anyway? Do you enjoy sneaking up on people? Do you purposely wear crepe-soled shoes?"

"I take any edge I can get," Tidwell replied, obviously not one bit apologetic that he'd startled her.

Gathering her wits about her, Theodosia decided to confront Tidwell directly. "How is the investigation going?" she demanded. "Any new leads? Any new ideas?"

Tidwell puckered his lips and blew out. "I have carefully and thoroughly studied the Heritage Society's visitor log as well as the log book in their storage room and have arrived at only one possible conclusion."

"Which is?" asked Theodosia.

"Everybody and his brother has wandered in and out of that place. Hundreds of people. Nay, perhaps thousands."

Theodosia stared at him. "Well, we knew that already." *Good heavens, this man is maddening. Beyond maddening.*

"Did it ever occur to you," asked Tidwell, "that a die-hard Civil War reenactor might have a dirk in his possession?"

"Of course it did," replied Theodosia. *Actually, I didn't think of that angle at all.*

"Think about it," said Tidwell, as though he'd read her mind.

"More to the point," she said, "have you followed up on the information *I* provided? Were you able to get your hands on Bill Glass's digital camera?"

"Of course . . ." said Tidwell, beginning to edge away from her.

"Was Glass cooperative?" Theodosia asked, sticking close to Tidwell as he wandered down the side aisle toward the back of the church where a clump of people still milled about.

"What do you think?" Tidwell snorted. "Glass acted surprised, claimed to have forgotten all about it."

"So . . . ?" prodded Theodosia.

"And then he turned his camera over to us."

"Have you looked at the photos?"

"Lab's downloading them," said Tidwell. His eyes scanned the crowd of people lingering in the back of the church, then his head gave a slight bobble forward. "There he is now."

Theodosia followed Tidwell's gaze, then caught sight of Bill Glass moving through the crowd, pausing now and then to snap a photo. "I'm not surprised," she said. "This is his kind of venue."

"Glass does seem like a bit of a jackal," said Tidwell. "Sweeping in to see what carnage is left."

"I'm going to go over and talk to him," said Theodosia.

"Please don't," said Tidwell, suddenly looking concerned.

"Honestly," said Theodosia as she brushed past him. "I just want to ask him a few questions."

"Of course you do," muttered Tidwell.

But Bill Glass wasn't exactly thrilled to see Theodosia. Because when she finally caught up with him, outside on the steps, he was almost hostile to her.

"Thanks a *lot* for sicing the police on me," said Glass. "Especially that bulldog Tidwell."

"Why weren't you up-front with the police to begin with?" asked Theodosia. "Why didn't you turn over your digital camera as well?"

Glass flashed her a belated smile, his attempt at turning on the charm. "Because I wanted to *download* everything right away. All my best shots were on that camera. I was afraid those jerks at the police lab would screw things up."

"That's the only reason?" asked Theodosia.

"Sure," said Glass. He peered at her, his smile now devoid of any warmth. "What? You think I'd somehow hold the clue to Duke Wilkes's murder?"

"You said it, not me," replied Theodosia.

"Sweetheart, if I had any hard evidence I'd have either published the photos or sold 'em by now," said Glass. "Trust me." He glanced over to where Tidwell had positioned himself on the curb, watching the crowd that had just poured out of the church. "Boy, is that guy furious with me."

"You mean Tidwell?" asked Theodosia.

"Yeah," replied Glass, fiddling with his camera lens.

Theodosia stared at Bill Glass for a moment. "Listen," she finally said. "I still want to see your photos, okay?"

"Sure, okay," said Glass staring past her, his sharp eyes moving over the crowd.

"Then how about tonight?" Theodosia asked him. She was taking Earl Grey to the O'Doud Senior Home this evening, but she'd *make* time for this.

Glass's forehead pulled into a frown. "I've . . . uh, got something going tonight. Tonight's not good."

"Then when?" asked Theodosia as Glass began to drift off.

"Call me," said Glass, his back to her as he melted into the crowd.

Frustrated, Theodosia turned and glanced around. *Where did Drayton go?* she wondered. And then noticed that Drayton, along with Delaine, was standing on the sidewalk talking with Pookie Wilkes.

Theodosia hurried over to join them.

"Some of Duke's reenactor comrades wanted his ashes scattered over three different Civil War battlefields," Pookie was telling them. "But I decided the best thing was to have him interred at Magnolia Cemetery. Near the Civil War section."

"How fitting," murmured Drayton.

"Interesting," said Delaine, squirming slightly.

Theodosia put an arm around Pookie and gave her a hug. "How are you holding up?" she asked.

Pookie nodded bravely. "Doing okay," she answered.

"It's a good thing you have such an enormous family," said Drayton. "It must be very comforting for you."

Pookie gave a tiny shrug. "They're keeping me busy anyway." She swiveled her head toward Theodosia and stared at her with red-rimmed eyes. "You keeping busy, too?"

Theodosia knew what Pookie was implying. *Are you still working on this? Are you still willing to help?*

"Absolutely," said Theodosia.

Pookie grasped her hand. "Thank you," she said, her voice thick with emotion.

"Pookie," said Theodosia in a low voice. "One quick question."

Pookie nodded imperceptibly.

"Had Duke been active in Victory Capital?"

Pookie's brows knit together. "Yes. Well, for *some* things anyway. What are . . . ?"

They both turned at the sound of clattering hooves in the street. Two magnificent-looking black horses came into view, drawing a narrow wagon behind them.

"We're going to take Duke's body to Magnolia Cemetery on a horse-drawn catafalque," explained Pookie. "I hope folks don't think we're being too theatrical."

"Are you kidding?" said Theodosia. "I think it's extremely appropriate and fitting. And I know Duke would have loved it!"

"That's what I think, too," said a tearful Pookie as she pulled away.

"Hi, Corky, hello, Claudia," exclaimed Delaine, giving a little wave as Corky and Claudia Chait emerged from the crowd.

"Greetings," said a somber Drayton.

Corky seemed to echo Drayton's mood. "We feel so awful about this," he said, flapping a hand helplessly.

"None of this was your fault," Drayton assured him.

"Still . . ." said Corky. "If we hadn't been at the house . . ."

But Delaine would have nothing to do with the somber mood that seemed to engulf everyone. And she was well aware that any rehashing of Duke's murder would reflect badly on her Candlelight Concert.

"Did you see Pookie's jacket?" she asked suddenly. "Didn't it look spectacular? I knew that boucle would look extremely sharp."

"She looked very brave," replied Theodosia. Truly, she had not noticed the jacket Pookie was wearing.

Slightly miffed that Theodosia hadn't responded with more enthusiasm, Delaine turned to Claudia. "And I especially love your suit," she said, appraising the cocoa-colored tweed that Claudia was wearing. "Especially the collar."

Claudia fingered the dark fur scarf that was snugged about her neck. "It's really only faux fur," she replied.

"Well, it certainly has a nice sheen to it," said Delaine. "Not unlike some of the fur collars and scarves we carry at Cotton Duck."

"I truly do love your store," said Claudia, responding to Delaine's little prompt.

"Thank you, dear," said Delaine, finally looking pleased. "Your little shop is awful darn cute, too."

18

Theodosia and Drayton would have preferred to go on to Magnolia Cemetery with the rest of the mourners. Instead, they rushed back to the Indigo Tea Shop to help serve lunch.

"How was the funeral?" asked Haley as she skittered about her little kitchen, balancing stacks of plates, washing salad greens, and keeping a watchful eye on a pot of chicken in cream sauce that bubbled enticingly atop the stove.

"A packed house," said Theodosia. "And a very sad ceremony."

"I was beginning to think you guys would never get back," replied Haley. She squirted a dollop of oil onto her grill, then grabbed a large wooden spoon and gave her bowl of batter a final stir. "Today's the one day I probably shouldn't have planned such a complicated lunch. Making crepes isn't as easy as knocking out tea sandwiches."

"But making crepes always looks so effortless when you

do it," remarked Theodosia, as she watched Haley's skillful maneuverings.

Her grill greased and hot, Haley ladled a dollop of crepe batter onto the grill using a circular motion. As if by magic, the batter spread out in a thin, perfectly round pancake. Haley watched the bubbles on her crepe slowly pop and disappear, then after about forty seconds, she flipped the disk over to allow the other side to turn a golden brown. Then, when her crepe was perfectly cooked, she slipped it onto a plate, added a scoop of her chicken filling, then gently rolled it closed. Theodosia decided Haley had to be using slight of hand. Nobody could be that skilled, could they?

"What time do you have to be at the Women's Expo today?" asked Haley, as she ladled out batter for two more crepes.

"I've got the two to three o'clock stint," said Theodosia. "So there's really only time for a quick demo and tea tasting."

"Thank goodness you're only appearing at the hospitality booth," said Haley. "Remember two years ago when the Indigo Tea Shop took a display booth for the entire two days?"

"The promoters were all freaked out about wiring, so we only had a single hot plate to heat tea kettles on," recalled Theodosia. "What a hassle. And I thought Drayton was going to have an aneurysm."

As if on cue, Drayton stuck his head in the kitchen.

"What else do we have on tap for lunch besides your luscious chicken crepes?" he asked.

"Speak of the devil," murmured Theodosia.

"Harvest salad," replied Haley. "Field greens mixed with sautéed zucchini, sweet red peppers, eggplant, walnuts, crumbled blue cheese, and a sweet poppy seed dressing.

"Excellent," said Drayton, disappearing just as fast as he'd appeared.

Once all the luncheon plates were delivered and her customers were happily munching away, Theodosia caught up with Drayton as he hunched behind the counter, brewing a couple additional pots of tea.

"Smell that lilac aroma?" he asked, indicating a blue and white teapot. "That's Flower Dragon Pouchong. A spring-picked tea that's lightly oxidized."

"Heavenly," said Theodosia. "And this other pot is . . . ?"

"That lovely Russian Caravan blend I ordered from Benson and Blige." He inhaled deeply. "So nice and smoky." He turned over a tiny hourglass to time the brewing process. "Have you decided which tea you're going to use for your demo today?"

"Probably the White Peony tea," said Theodosia, reaching for a large silver tin. "Most everyone seems to enjoy it."

"Ah," intoned Drayton. "Pai Mu Tan. Made from a combination of two white tea plants. Lovely Chinese tea with a floral aroma."

"And I'll be serving Chinese moon cakes, too," said Theodosia. These were round sugar cookies filled with a sweet puree of lotus seeds.

Drayton nodded. "You're picking up on the Autumn Moon Festival theme. I like that." During this traditional Chinese festival people exchanged sweet moon cakes in hopes of a favorable, prosperous autumn.

"You know," said Theodosia, "I never got to tell you about my meeting with Sydney Chastain last night."

"I'm assuming she pried as much good information from your brain as was humanly possible," said Drayton.

"I gleaned a little information myself," replied Theodosia. "I found out that Duke Wilkes's firm, Victory Capital, turned Sydney Chastain down on financing."

Drayton frowned. "Turned her down on financing? What do you mean?"

"They basically torpedoed the underwriting application from VTV."

"Interesting," said Drayton, although he looked more perturbed than interested. "Do we know why?"

Theodosia gave a shrug. "Don't know. Maybe Victory Capital thought the airwaves were crowded enough. A lot of would-be TV entrepreneurs dream of building empires, but few accomplish it. Most so-called networks end up as also-ran cable channels that broadcast syndicated TV shows and generate most of their revenue by selling airtime for infomercials."

"Do you think that's what could happen with Sydney Chastain's outfit?" asked Drayton.

"I have no idea," said Theodosia. "All I know is I'd love to talk to her again."

Fidgeting with his bow tie, clearing his throat nervously, Drayton asked: "Do you think Sydney could be involved in Duke's murder?"

"Don't know," murmured Theodosia. "She doesn't *seem* like the murdering type."

But at the same time, Theodosia remembered the flash of anger she'd seen in Sydney's eyes when she talked about getting turned down on financing. *Had that anger flared into rage? Was Sydney capable of murder? She'd called herself a mama bear when it came to protecting her cubs. What exactly does a mama bear do to protect its cubs? It kills when it has to.*

"I'd definitely like to chat with her again," said Theodosia. "But I need a good lie."

Drayton lifted his chin and glanced down his nose at Theodosia. One eyebrow lifted, then quivered with disapproval.

"I mean a little white lie," explained Theodosia. "Some kind of *excuse.*"

At that moment, Haley popped out from between the green velvet curtains, carrying two plates and bound for the guests at the corner table who had demolished their salads then gone on to order crepes, too.

"I think I just found my excuse," said Theodosia, reaching for the phone.

"Please be careful," fretted Drayton, grabbing his teapots and hurrying off.

In a matter of moments, Theodosia called VTV headquarters and got Sydney Chastain on the line.

"Theodosia, what a pleasant surprise," said Sydney.

"Listen," said Theodosia, "I have a favor to ask."

"Shoot," said Sydney.

"I'm helping Haley . . . you remember Haley? Here at the tea shop? Anyway, I'm giving her advice on a term paper she's writing for one of her business administration classes. And I find that my knowledge about obtaining venture capital is woefully lacking." Theodosia paused, wondering if Sydney was buying all this. "And since you just went through the process, I figured you were the expert." She paused. "Realize, too, this information isn't just for Haley, it would be for my enlightenment, too. In case I ever get the crazy notion to expand or franchise or whatever."

Sydney was silent for a moment, thinking. Then she said, "Sure. Why don't you drop by again and we'll talk."

"Okay. When?" Theodosia was determined to hold Sydney's feet to the fire.

"Well, I'm supposed to go out of town on business tomorrow . . ." said Sydney.

"Could I possibly drop by your office later this afternoon?" asked Theodosia. "Around five-thirty maybe?" *I'll be finished with my demo by three, back here by four, so there should be plenty of time.*

"You're in quite a rush, huh?" said Sydney. "Then it might be better if you dropped by my house. Say seven, seven-thirty?"

"That's not so good," replied Theodosia. "I was planning to drop by the O'Doud Senior Home tonight. My dog, Earl Grey, is a therapy dog and I'm in the process of warming him up for a service dog demo he's taking part in this Friday." She paused. "I guess this is a big week for demos."

"Bring him along," purred Sydney. "I adore dogs. And hang on the line, Theo, so my secretary can give you my address."

From the moment Theodosia arrived at the Women's Expo, held in the Gaillard Municipal Auditorium, she was frantically busy. After locating the hospitality booth, she set her tea water to boiling—luckily, there was a real stove to use this time—then unpacked her small Chinese teacups. When they were arranged just so, she heaped her moon cakes onto a large silver platter. Glancing up, Theodosia was surprised to see that more than half the folding chairs in front of her booth were occupied by women eagerly waiting for her demo to begin. Heartened by their interest, she grabbed a large red marker pen and scrawled INDIGO TEA SHOP— THEODOSIA BROWNING on the white board behind her. Then, on a whim, she added the phrase: *So I must rise at early dawn, as busy as can be, to get my daily labor done, and pluck the leafy tea.* Underneath this little poem she added, *Ballad of the tea pickers, Early Ch'ing Dynasty, 1644.* A fun way to help springboard her into a talk on Chinese tea, she decided.

As it turned out, Theodosia had a very attentive audience. So her demo on brewing a perfect pot of tea and her talk about various and sundry Chinese teas was extremely well-received. But the big hit of the hour still came when she served small cups of White Peony tea and moon cakes. She figured if she'd brought three dozen of her shiny little blue bags filled with tea she could have sold every one of them. Ditto the moon cakes.

And, as her audience sipped and nibbled, they also asked a multitude of questions. What exactly is high tea? Are jasmine and hibiscus teas really teas? Which teas are best with milk, sugar, or lemon and which teas are best left plain? What does the term "bakey" mean? And which teas can be used as remedies?

Theodosia answered all their questions with grace and humor. Trying all the while to impress upon her audience that taking tea was supposed to be an enjoyable, relaxing ritual. There were recommendations, yes. But no strict, by-the-book rules one had to abide by. She tried to stress the fact that tea could be a solo pleasure to jump-start your day or expanded to a social celebration.

As Theodosia concluded her answers and passed out brochures, she saw Delaine and Claudia Chait edging through the crowd.

"I'm sorry I missed your demo," said Delaine, grabbing one of Theodosia's brochures and fanning herself. "But I've been busy setting up for the big fashion show. And Claudia's been going crazy, too!"

"You're racking up sales?" Theodosia asked Claudia.

"Surprisingly, yes," responded Claudia.

"Is all the merchandise in the fashion show from Cotton Duck?" Theodosia asked Delaine. She knew Delaine was a big believer in participating in fashion shows. It was a good way to get her current inventory in front of the buying public.

"No, no," said Delaine. "Sponsoring the whole thing would be way too much for me to handle. I've got six outfits in the show." She paused, thinking. "Still, that's an awful lot. All those models to dress, style, and accessorize, it's drivin' me crazy!"

"I'm sure you'll do great," Claudia assured her. "Charleston women always count on you for style advice."

But still Delaine fretted. "Would you two come take a look at my outfits? I've got a couple of those teensy little mohair sweaters. Very wide weave, but soft as angel hair. You wear them over tiny camisoles. Tell me what you think, okay?"

"They sound divine," said Theodosia, as she struggled to pack up. But Delaine's nervousness made it difficult. "Sorry I'm in such a rush," Theodosia told them. "But with this tea demo today and the service dog demo tomorrow I'm really not minding the store."

"Oh, you'll be fine, honey," said Delaine. "If you could just come take a peek . . ."

"I also wanted to stick around and say hi to Parker Scully," explained Theodosia. "He's coming into this booth right after me. Going to be doing a little wine tasting from three to four."

"Oh, great," said Delaine, rolling her eyes. "People are going to get soused on wine and then come to my fashion show. Wonderful."

"I don't think a few sips of wine are going to get anyone soused," laughed Claudia. "Delaine, honey, you *worry* too much," she said as she scurried back toward her booth.

"Maybe I should take a Xanax or a Lexapro or something," said Delaine, still radiating nervous energy.

"You don't need meds," said Theodosia in a reassuring tone. "Just a nice cup of tea to calm you down. Oh . . . hey!" she said as Parker Scully hustled up to the booth, carrying a large cardboard box filled with clinking wine bottles.

Parker leaned forward and gave Theodosia a quick peck on the cheek. "Hey, yourself," he said to her.

"Aren't you two cozy?" observed Delaine, peering at them with narrowed eyes.

"I wish," said Parker, smiling at Theodosia as he eased his burden onto the counter.

"Now don't go gettin' anyone too tipsy," warned Delaine. "My new inventory is riding on this fashion show today."

"I promise I'll be good," Parker told her. With his blond hair and earnest blue eyes, he looked like a frat boy promising to do the right thing. Theodosia wondered how much of that was real and how much of it was just pure charm.

"How's the cat?" asked Theodosia, deciding a change of subject might reduce the Delaine-induced tension.

Parker beamed at her. "Fantastic. A little sweetheart."

"Oh!" exclaimed Delaine, suddenly interested. "You have a new cat?"

"We found one that had been abandoned," explained Parker. "Coming back from Edisto Island."

Delaine, who was a cat lover of the first magnitude, shook her head sadly. "People can be so cruel! I don't know why they take their hostilities out on poor, defenseless little animals, but they do. It just breaks my heart."

"Well, this cat is living the life of Riley now," said Parker. "And eating like crazy."

"Poor little stray was probably half-starved," said Theodosia.

"Tiger Lilly's making up for it now," said Parker.

"Tiger Lilly?" asked Delaine. "That's her name?"

"Yup." Parker looked pleased that Delaine was so interested in his cat.

"Oh for cute," cooed Delaine.

19

❦

Theodosia and Earl Grey climbed the stone steps leading to Sydney Chastain's front piazza. They hesitated at the front door. Light shone from within, music played. She was home all right.

Theodosia bent down and addressed Earl Grey. "You," she told him, "have to be on your best behavior. This is a lady who could very easily put me on television. Or for that matter, could take a shine to you and produce a special program about service dogs and therapy dogs. And wouldn't that be lovely?"

Earl Grey, smart fellow that he was, placed a large paw on Theodosia's knee.

"Oh, you agree, do you? You are a smart cookie."

Earl Grey's ears pitched forward, his eyes lit up.

"Oops, I just said the magic word, didn't I." *Darn,* she

thought. *This dog must page through* Webster's *dictionary when I'm not looking. Honestly, the words he knows.*

Theodosia dug deep in her jacket pocket for a dog treat, found a liver snap, and held it out to him. "Here you go. Since I was dumb enough to utter the *c* word, you get the prize in the Cracker Jack box."

Earl Grey grabbed it and quickly gobbled it down.

"Okay now," cautioned Theodosia. "Best behavior." She stepped up to the door, pushed the bell. Deep within the old house, she heard it ring.

She waited patiently for Sydney to come to the door. But no footsteps sounded. No welcoming voice called out to her.

Hmm.

Theodosia punched the doorbell a second time. And waited.

Still no answer.

Earl Grey tugged at his leash, staring up at her.

"Hey, don't look at me," said Theodosia. "Sydney was *supposed* to be home."

Theodosia shifted from one foot to the other, feeling stupid. Feeling like she'd been blown off. *Maybe she's still stuck at the office,* Theodosia reasoned. *Still, you'd think she might have called.*

Frustrated now, just this side of ticked off, Theodosia rapped on the heavy wooden door. And watched it swing open a good six inches.

So her door isn't even locked or latched. Did Sydney come flying in and forget to close it? Did she leave it open for me because she's busy rummaging in the attic or the cellar for her suitcase?

"Well, we know she's home," Theodosia told Earl Grey.

Pushing the door open the rest of the way, the two of them stepped over the doorsill and into Sydney's entryway.

"Sydney?" Theodosia called out loud. "It's me. Theodosia. Are you home?"

Nothing. Just the sound of music. Louder now. From a radio or maybe a CD player.

"That's weird," said Theodosia. She tugged on Earl Grey's leash and walked another five steps in. Looking around the entry hall, she took in the antique sideboard with Sydney's briefcase and keys piled on top, a pair of oil paintings that hung on the wall, the parquet floor underfoot.

"Nice," she said. "Very elegant."

Earl Grey ambled ahead of her, pulling at his leash. Glancing down at him, Theodosia noticed that her normally placid dog seemed suddenly agitated. His ears were pitched forward, his nose twitched, his muscles tensed.

"What's up, boy?" she asked. She reeled out another few feet of Flexi Leash and Earl Grey immediately sprang forward pulling her down a hallway. Wondering why the dog was suddenly so bent out of shape, Theodosia gave him his lead. Earl Grey promptly spun to his left and Theodosia followed. Into what appeared to be Sydney's living room.

Theodosia blinked at the sight that met her eyes. Sydney was home all right. She was sitting on a low white couch, staring at them with blank eyes. Her hands were clutched in her lap and a slick of blood covered one side of her face.

"Good lord!" gasped Theodosia. Earl Grey chimed in with a commiserating yelp.

Tiptoeing up to Sydney, her heart thumping within her chest, Theodosia reached a hand out, touched it gently to Sydney's wrist.

Not only did Sydney not have a pulse, she felt cool to the touch.

Theodosia pulled her hand back quickly. She'd felt that

same coolness in a person before. When her Dad died. When she'd looked in on him to wake him from his nap. And found him curled up in bed, unnaturally cool under a heavy comforter.

How fast the body loses its human warmth, she thought to herself. *Once the life force is gone.*

Hands shaking, feeling vulnerable, Theodosia reached into her handbag and pulled out her cell phone. Calling 911, she gave a hasty, slightly excited account of what she'd found as well as Sydney's address.

Then Theodosia stood there, gazing at poor Sydney Chastain. And the only thought that ran through her overwrought brain like a string of theater chase lights was, *Sydney was murdered. Sydney was murdered. Sydney was murdered.*

Turning away, Theodosia focused on a white marble fireplace. *Get a grip,* she admonished herself. *Calm down.* She knew that in a few minutes a cadre of police and homicide detectives would come trooping in and she would be unceremoniously hustled out.

So . . . if I want to look around, I'd better be quick about it.

After giving Earl Grey a sit-stay command, Theodosia drew a deep breath then stepped up to Sydney's body again. This time she was going to try to remain cool and objective. To note and notice everything she possibly could.

Leaning forward, peering at Sydney's wrecked head, Theodosia decided there had been no antique weapon involved this time. From the looks of the small hole in Sydney's damaged scull, she'd been shot with a single bullet, close range, from a small-caliber weapon.

Had the shooter been someone Sydney had known? Theodosia wondered. *Someone who'd come tippy-tapping at her door this evening? Someone who could get close to her and not raise suspicion?*

Theodosia pondered this, even as she was aware of blatting sirens as police cruisers drew near. And then there was the squeal of brakes and the sound of miniature thunder on the verandah as a stream of officers came pouring in.

Detective Burt Tidwell arrived a few minutes later, just as the crime scene boys were taking pictures. He shoved past Theodosia and Earl Grey, pointedly ignoring them, as he stretched a pair of latex gloves over his chubby knuckles.

Tidwell looked, poked gingerly at Sydney's head, let out a loud, "Harumph," then surveyed the room.

Finally, in his own sweet time, Tidwell turned to regard Theodosia. "What are you doing here?" he asked. His dark eyes burned into her, his jowls sloshed as he spoke.

"I had a meeting with Sydney," she told him.

"Here? At her house?" he asked.

"Yes, here at her house," said Theodosia. "What do you think? That I have a police scanner in my Jeep and I just cruise around just waiting for crimes to happen?"

Tidwell's eyes wandered to Earl Grey. "A simple yes will suffice. Editorializing is superfluous," he commented.

"What do you think happened?" asked Theodosia.

"Gunshot," responded Tidwell brusquely.

"I know *that,*" Theodosia replied. "I mean, what do you think went on here? Had there been reports of a prowler in the area? Do you think a struggle took place? What does looking at this *scene* tell you?"

Tidwell shot her a quick glance. "Miss Browning, you watch entirely too much television for your own good."

"No, I don't," said Theodosia. "I read books."

"Mysteries, no doubt. Thrillers," said Tidwell.

Theodosia plunged ahead and posed the sixty-four-thousand-dollar question. "Do you think this murder is somehow connected to Duke Wilkes's?" she asked.

Tidwell slightly bulging eyes stared at her. "Do you?"

"I have no idea," she told him.

"And you think I do?" asked Tidwell, pulling his lips into a rather inelegant pout.

"You're the one who said I was ten steps behind you," said Theodosia. "I figure if the police have that much of a lead, you must know *something.*"

Now Tidwell waggled a fat finger in front of her face. "Flattery, even obtuse flattery, will get you nowhere, Miss Browning."

"Can you tell me anything?" she asked.

Tidwell took a step toward her, moving his bulk so quickly, so gracefully, Theodosia was taken aback.

"Whatever went on here constitutes a grievous and most serious situation," barked Tidwell. "You're in the middle of something, Miss Browning, but have no idea what it is."

Theodosia stared at him confrontationaly. "Do *you* know what's going on?"

Tidwell inhaled deeply, then let his breath out slowly. "Just back off, Miss Browning, please. For your own safety."

20
❦

"*I can't believe* you just found her like that." Haley looked more than a little stunned. "Shot through the head. Wow."

"I could just kick myself for allowing you go over there," said Drayton. "You could have walked right into a trap!"

"You couldn't have known that," murmured Theodosia.

"Right," said Haley, "it's not like you're psychic or anything."

"I had a bad feeling," insisted Drayton.

"You were just upset that I went over there on a ruse," said Theodosia. "Your sense of honor was offended."

Haley fixed Drayton with a steady gaze. "So get over it, will you?"

"This is no time to joke," responded Drayton. "Miss Chastain is *dead*."

"I know, I know," muttered Haley. "Believe me, I'm as upset as you are. She seemed like a terrific lady. But what can we do about it? Sit around and wring our hands? Go out and make a citizen's arrest?"

"I wish," said Theodosia.

"We could get cracking for one thing," said Drayton, glancing at his watch. "We're supposed to open our doors in eight minutes and we haven't accomplished a single thing yet."

"I've got banana chocolate chip scones baking in the oven," said Haley. "And the tables are set. What you really mean is you haven't brewed any tea yet."

"Just this pot of Irish Breakfast," said Drayton. He lifted his cup and took a sip. "Nice and strong. Fortifying, in fact."

"Come on," said Theodosia to Drayton. "Let's you and I pick out a couple house brews for today."

"As you wish," said Drayton, grabbing his cup and following her across the still-empty tea shop to the little counter where colorful tins and gleaming jars of tea were stacked to the ceiling.

"What do you think?" asked Theodosia, her fingertips skittering across the tops of several tins. "Maybe a Formosan Oolong?"

"The Tung Ting Oolong is particularly good," replied Drayton. "Smooth, almost peachy in flavor."

"Okay," said Theodosia, pulling out that tin. "And what else tickles your fancy this morning?"

Drayton's eyes roved over their vast selection. "Perhaps the Fujian Province Golden Needle? As you well know, it's a nice full-bodied black tea."

"Golden Needle it is," said Theodosia. She turned to face Drayton. "And believe me, I do hear your concerns. I'm well aware that if I'd arrived a little earlier I might have been caught in the cross fire. Or *whatever* it was went on there."

"What do you suppose happened?" asked Drayton. He slipped his half glasses off, gave them a polishing with the edge of his long white apron.

Theodosia lowered her voice. "I have no idea. For all I know it could have been an old boyfriend. Or an ex-husband. I didn't know Sydney well at all. Certainly nothing concerning her background."

"Is that what you really think?" Drayton put his glasses on, adjusted them, and blinked furiously. "An enraged boyfriend or ex-husband just suddenly appeared?"

Light furrows insinuated themselves in Theodosia's normally placid brow. "What I can't seem to get out of my mind is that Duke Wilkes's murder and Sydney Chastain's murder might somehow be connected."

"How so?" asked Drayton.

"Well, Sydney was at the Candlelight Concert that night," said Theodosia. "At least the early part of it. And her company was turned down for financing by Duke's firm."

"I hear what you're saying," said Drayton. "But those are awfully tenuous connections."

"I know they are," replied Theodosia. She glanced across the room as the tiny bell above the door tinkled and a spate of customers came tumbling in. "But it *feels* like there might be something there," she continued as the telephone now started to ring. "Noodle it around, will you? See if you can make sense of it."

"Okay," promised Drayton.

"Hello?" said Theodosia, putting the receiver to her ear.

"Theodosia?" It was Parker Scully. And he sounded mildly

upset. "I caught you on this morning's news! What the heck happened last night?"

Theodosia sighed, turned her back to the customers, and began a quick run-down of events for Parker's benefit.

At twelve noon, just as Drayton gave away the last table, just as Theodosia was serving bowls of low-country black bean soup accompanied by angel biscuits, Delaine came fluttering in.

"I am *so* late," complained Delaine. "Just as I was trying to duck out of the store, Velba Pennington showed up." Delaine wriggled her shoulders in a mock shudder. "Velba wanted me to *personally* style a couple outfits for her."

"That's good, isn't it?" asked Theodosia.

"Only to a point, dear," replied Delaine. She leaned forward in a conspiratorial gesture. "Velba's taste and judgment are somewhat questionable."

"In other words," said Theodosia, "she doesn't listen to you."

"Not really," said Delaine as she spotted her friends across the tea shop. "Hey, Brooke," she waved at Brooke Carter Crockett, a jeweler from down the street. "Be right there." Then she turned back toward Theodosia. "Did you see the issue of *Shooting Star* that came out this morning?"

Theodosia shook her head. She'd almost managed to forget about that.

"Remember that lovely picture of us in the backyard of the Chait House?" asked Delaine.

"I remember being surprised by that rude, young photographer," said Theodosia. "What was his name? Oh, yeah. Gep."

"Well, bad news, sugar, 'cause we got bumped," said Delaine, sounding profoundly disappointed. "The big hot story is about that TV lady who got murdered. Sydney something."

"Have you actually read the story yet?" asked Theodosia. She was pretty sure her name would be mentioned. After all, Glass wasn't a complete idiot. He'd probably sniffed it out.

"Not yet," said Delaine as she scurried off to join her friends.

Twenty minutes later, when things were really cooking, Bill Glass strolled in. He gazed about the tea shop, saw that Theodosia was ringing up someone's tab, and sauntered over to greet her. If that's what you'd call it.

"Here you go cupcake," he said, holding a large manila envelope out for her.

Theodosia accepted it tentatively. "What's this?" she asked.

"Contract for Haley," said Glass. "You said you wanted to have a lawyer look it over. So have at it."

"I understand you didn't waste any time in splashing the news about Sydney Chastain all over the front page of your paper," said Theodosia. She bent down, tucked the contract under the counter for safekeeping.

"Are you serious?" said Glass. "Murder is always hot news. In fact, a murder beats a garden variety scandal any day." He peered carefully at Theodosia. "Hey sweetheart, you look a little shaken. Guess finding a dead body does that to a person. You're two for two now, aren't you?"

Theodosia stared at Glass, feeling white hot anger bubble up within her, hating his smooth, glib tone. "And how would you know about that?" she asked, her voice dripping with ice.

"Cops," responded Glass. "Best place to get inside information is from cops."

Not for me, Theodosia thought. *Not lately anyway.*

"Pretty weird, huh?" said Bill Glass. "Sydney's murder I mean. Not a lot of suspects so far."

"What's really weird," said Theodosia, deciding to play hardball, "is that Sydney Chastain told me she had a meeting with *you* yesterday."

Bill Glass stared at Theodosia for a long ten seconds. "Yeah. We had a meeting scheduled. But she canceled at the last minute." He shrugged. "Maybe it was a lucky thing. Who knows what would have happened if I'd kept that appointment. I might have had *my* brains blown out, too." He let out a nervous cackle.

"Who said her brains were blown out?" asked Theodosia, hating the nasty sound of the phrase.

"Hey, calm down, cupcake," said Glass. "If you'd shown up five minutes earlier, *you* might've have had your brains blown out, too!"

Still miffed at her conversation with Bill Glass, Theodosia ducked into the kitchen just as Haley was ladling out the last of her black bean soup.

"Your soup is a huge hit, Haley," said Theodosia. "So are your angel biscuits with honey butter."

Haley glanced up and flashed a bright smile. "One of my favorite recipes," she said.

"Speaking of recipes," said Theodosia. "Bill Glass brought your book contract by."

"He did?" squealed Haley. "Great. Wonderful." She gave Theodosia a questioning glance. "That *is* good news, isn't it?"

"As long as we have a reputable attorney look over the contract and give his blessing," said Theodosia. "From what Timothy Neville told me, Bill Glass is a bit of a slicko."

"That could just be sour grapes," said Haley. "You know what a curmudgeon Timothy can be."

"Yes, and Bill Glass is a bit of an opportunist," countered Theodosia. "Apparently the front page story in *Shooting Star* is all about Sydney's murder."

"Really?" asked Haley as she reached for an oven mitt, pulled open the oven door, and took a peek at her cuppa cuppa cake. "Are you, by any chance, mentioned in the article, too?"

"I sincerely hope not," said Theodosia.

"I've been thinking . . ." Haley paused to slide bowls of soup for their second seating of customers onto a large tray.

"About?"

Haley scrunched her young face into a thoughtful frown. "Did you ever think that maybe Sydney might have been working on something?"

"Working on what?" asked Drayton as he pushed his way into the kitchen.

Haley shrugged. "I don't know exactly. Something to do with a show maybe? With VTV's programming?"

"And someone didn't want it to come to fruition," said Theodosia. "That's a very interesting theory. And Sydney *did* mention that she was working on a pet project."

"What was it?" asked Drayton. "Do you remember?"

Theodosia thought for a moment. "Some kind of investigative journalism show."

"You don't say," said Haley. "Maybe you should see if you can find out more . . ."

"And I know just who to call," replied Theodosia.

But Sarah Jane Sigrid was in no mood to talk.

"I'm so upset, I don't know *what's* going on around here." Sarah Jane's voice, even through phone lines, sounded shaky and panicked. "Rumors are flying like mad that the entire network might be put on hold!" Sarah Jane snuffled loudly. "So I don't think I can tell you anything!" she wailed. "Especially what she was working on."

"Look," said Theodosia. "I'm on your side. I was there at her house last night. I found her!"

"Oh, my goodness," exclaimed Sarah Jane. "You're *that* Theodosia Browning? Of course, of course . . . you're the one she introduced me to. Sorry I'm so discombobulated."

"Yes, we did meet Wednesday evening," Theodosia reminded Sarah Jane, trying all the while to interject a calming note into her voice. "And I'm doing my best to help figure out who might have been responsible for Sydney's murder."

"You're working with the police?" asked Sarah Jane.

"In the manner of speaking," said Theodosia. *That little white lie doesn't really count, does it?*

Well . . . in that case," said Sarah Jane. "Maybe . . ."

"Look," said Theodosia. "I understand if you can't turn over the files to me."

"No, I couldn't do that," said Sarah Jane hastily.

"But is it possible to get a list of Sydney's program ideas?" asked Theodosia. "Especially the ones she was championing right now?"

"I *guess* there's no harm in that," snuffled Sarah Jane.

"Good," cut in Theodosia. "Can I stop by today? Early this afternoon? Can you make up that list and maybe leave it at the front desk for me?"

"Yes . . . yes," mumbled Sarah Jane. "I'll leave it at the front desk."

Upstairs in her apartment, Theodosia pulled off her long white apron then shucked out of her black T-shirt and slacks. Venturing into her walk-in closet that was loaded with skirts, slacks, long dresses, and lots of fun clothes from Cotton Duck, she changed into a pair of khaki slacks and a white T-shirt with the Big Paw logo emblazoned on the front of it. She brushed her teeth, dabbed on a little more makeup, and tidied her hair. Then it was Earl Grey's turn. Theodosia gave him a quick brushing, finished with a rub-down using a damp towel to pick up any loose hairs, then snapped on his good leather collar.

Glancing about, Theodosia wondered if she was missing anything. She still had a good hour before she had to be in Hampton Park for the Ainsworth Kennel Club Dog Show.

Then her eyes fell on her laptop computer. Sitting on her dining room table, it was plugged in, ready to go. She'd brought it upstairs last night because she wanted to send a nasty, chiding E-mail to Tidwell. Then found she was too tired to compose even a single sentence.

Maybe I should . . .

She crept over to the table, slipped into a chair. And decided to do what she always did when she needed more information.

She googled Bill Glass. Typed his name into the search

engine, hit return, and waited to see what turned up. Just like she'd done on Clive Bonham.

Within seconds, a jumble of hits materialized before Theodosia's eyes. Hits that led to Glass's website, his on-line version of *Shooting Star,* and a dozen or so articles from the archives of The *Post and Courier.*

Hmm. Good place to start.

She started clicking and reading. Most of The *Post and Courier* articles were from the business section. Short blurbs that chronicled Glass's start-up of *Shooting Star,* others that gave two-sentence bios on key personnel, some on his publishing ventures. But another hit revealed an article about a harassment lawsuit that had been filed against Bill Glass, then settled out of court. It seems Glass had camped out in front of a TV anchorman's house, then followed him to determine if the TV news anchor was really having an affair with a fellow on-air personality. But it was the last sentence of this article that riveted Theodosia's attention. It said: "William Glass, publisher of *Shooting Star* and president of Glass Publishing, Inc., hosted the long-running Radio KDXL morning show in Asheville, North Carolina and was a former Special Forces intelligence operative."

Special Forces. Aren't those the guys who are trained to kill a dozen different ways? The ones who get dropped into hot zones armed with all the latest weapons and electronic gizmos?

Theodosia thought about that for a couple moments.

If Bill Glass was a Special Forces agent, he definitely had military training on how to, as they say, terminate with extreme prejudice. Which is something Detective Burt Tidwell might find very interesting.

*   *   *

As Theodosia clattered down the back stairs, Earl Grey tugging at his leash, her cell phone rang. She dug in her shoulder bag, fumbled her way past the dog treats, her makeup bag, and wallet until she finally found her phone. She punched the receive button, all the while trying to keep her balance. "Hello?"

"I take it you're sufficiently recovered from last night's unpleasantness?"

It was Tidwell. Perfect timing.

"Hey," said Theodosia excitedly. "Did you know that Bill Glass served in the Special Forces?" She hit the downstairs landing, then pushed open the back door.

"Forget Bill Glass," growled Tidwell. "We just unraveled a tangle of DBA's, LLC's, and holding companies. Which led to a rather interesting and enlightening discovery."

"What are you talking about?" asked Theodosia, struggling to reel in Earl Grey who was intent on scrabbling after a gray squirrel.

"Sydney Chastain was in charge of selecting an architect for the new VTV headquarters," began Tidwell.

"That's right," said Theodosia, recalling the architectural models she'd seen in Sydney's office.

"The company that she turned down?" said Tidwell, a note of nervous excitement in his voice "Greystone Architects." There was a slight pause.

"Greystone is one of several subsidiaries owned by Jock Rowley. We're on our way now to pick him up for questioning."

21

⊰❧⊱

Hampton Park was a veritable canine circus. Tiny bichon's strutted their stuff beside jumbo Great Danes. Somber-looking wolfhounds and alert German shepherds peered over their wire enclosures, surveying a contingent of wrinkley, cuddly shar-peis as they ambled by. Poodles stood at aloof attention on grooming tables, getting fluffed, trimmed, poufed, and pampered.

More dogs, dog handlers, Ainsworth Kennel Club members, judges, and interested guests milled about on a great green carpet of grass where three showrings had been set up using low white modular fences.

As sunshine poured down, Theodosia couldn't help but grin at the sight of all this. Seeing all these wonderful, bouncy dogs, being out with Earl Grey, her spirits were colossally lifted. On the drive over, her brain still racing from Tidwell's phone call, all she'd thought about was Jock Rowley.

He'd been a *sort of* suspect in her estimation, but she certainly hadn't thought about him in regards to the shooting of Sydney Chastain. Still . . . she'd stopped by VTV to pick up Sarah Jane's list. Because, in the back of her brain, she had remembered Sydney mentioning something about a program focusing on mortgage scams.

But now, as Theodosia led Earl Grey through this marvelous melee, she was overjoyed that she might not have to do any more investigating. Perhaps . . . probably . . . Jock Rowley *was* the killer. Of both Duke Wilkes and Sydney Chastain. And since Tidwell was hauling Rowley in for questioning, the slow, steady wheels of justice would begin to turn. And maybe, just maybe, Burt Tidwell would be able to wrest a confession out of Jock Rowley. At least she hoped Tidwell would. An answer, an explanation, would be a great relief and help bring closure to what had been a nasty, unsettling week for everyone involved.

As she searched for the Big Paw tent, a woman in a red blazer and red, white, and blue straw boater approached her and pressed a large, shiny button into her hand.

"Congressman Clive Bonham would sure welcome your vote this coming election," said the woman, a bright smile on her face.

Theodosia stared at the button that had been thrust in her hand. And when she looked up, the rather animated woman, along with Clive Bonham, were both beaming at her.

"Theodosia Browning," Bonham said with hearty enthusiasm. "Great to see you again!" He gazed down at Earl Grey. "You showing your dog today?"

"Earl Grey's going to be part of a service dog demonstration," explained Theodosia. "That's why he's wearing his service dog vest."

"Good. Excellent," said Clive Bonham. He gave Earl Grey a perfunctory pat on the head, then moved on with his front man for today, the smiling button lady in the red blazer.

"Yikes," muttered Theodosia as she approached the middle showring. "I guess petting dogs and schmoozing their owners is a lot like kissing babies. When it's an election year politicians do what they have to do."

She gazed into the showring where at least two dozen King Charles Spaniels were posing for the judge. With their beautiful tricolor coats and soft eyes, they were a wonderful sight to behold.

"See the third dog from the left?" asked a voice behind her. "That one's mine."

Theodosia cocked her head to find Bill Glass smiling at her. *Good lord,* she thought, *didn't I just see this creep a couple hours ago?*

"Cute dog," said Theodosia. She didn't want to be rude, but she didn't want to engage Glass in conversation either. There was something odd about him . . .

"His name's Winthrop of Highcrest," said Glass, "but I call him Winnie. I'm just starting to campaign him, but he's already earned eight points toward his championship." Glass held out his digital camera, pointed it at the ring, and rapidly snapped several shots. "For his scrapbook," explained Glass. "Hey, did you see today's issue of *Shooting Star* yet? Sorry again that you got bumped from the cover, honey."

"Not a problem," said Theodosia. "And please don't call me honey. Or cupcake."

Glass grinned and jabbed a finger toward her. "Spirit. Know what I mean? You've got spirit. Love that in a woman."

"Oh, please." Theodosia sighed as Glass dashed off to capture more shots from a different angle.

Glancing about, Theodosia spotted a white tent with a large blue and white Big Paw banner flapping in front of it.

Ah, there it is. Across the park.

She ambled over, greeted the other Big Paw volunteers who'd brought their dogs along for the demo, and found out she still had a good thirty minutes to kill.

"Take Earl Grey around back if you want," said Cleo, one of the volunteers. She was thirty-something and pleasingly plump with carrot-colored hair; a tireless volunteer who'd already trained three therapy dogs and two service dogs. "There's plenty of bottled water and coolers filled with ice."

Cleo was right and Earl Grey was most appreciative. He lapped up a bowl of water, then was delighted when Theodosia popped a large ice cube in his mouth to chew on. Earl Grey slurped, chomped, then lay down and spit the ice cube out between his front paws, proceeding to lick it like a popsicle. Seeing what fun he was having, Theodosia looped his leash over a tent peg and walked around to the front. *Let him have his fun.*

"Hey, Theo," called Brooke Carter Crockett as she walked across the grass. "I thought I might find you over here."

"Don't tell me you brought a dog," said Theodosia, surprised to see Brooke. "Wait a minute you don't *have* a dog."

Brooke grinned. "No," she said, "I'm more of a hermit crab person. No muss, no fuss. And if you get tired of your little crabby, you can always pop him in a pot and make chowder."

"That's awful." Theodosia laughed. "You wouldn't really do that, would you?"

"Not a chance," said Brooke. "I couldn't be that hard-hearted. I'd probably just use him as a model for one of my silver charms." As one of Charleston's premier jewelers, Brooke was well known for her Charleston-themed charms. Tiny oysters, wrought iron gates, palmetto leaves, sweet-grass baskets, bags of rice, and even carriages. String a few of them on a charm bracelet along with a few jangling coins and you had a lovely, custom piece of jewelry.

"So you're just hanging around the dog show?" asked Theodosia.

"Actually, I helped add a little pazazz to the Ainsworth Kennel Club trophies," said Brooke. They wanted to do something different this year, something really special. So they bought silver loving cups and asked me to decorate them with Swarovski crystals."

"Sounds spectacular," said Theodosia.

"They turned out really neat," said Brooke. "I basically glued on crystals in interesting patterns and then outlined them with thin strips of silver. The finished look was a little medieval, but the club went wild over them."

"I can't wait to see these loving cups," enthused Theodosia. "You are so *creative.*"

"And you're not?" said Brooke. "Seems to me I remember some grapevine wreaths with teacups tied into them that were fantastic. Are you still making those?" Brooke asked as the two of them strolled around toward the back of the tent.

Theodosia nodded. "We keep chipping cups, so I have an endless supply of material. And the grapevines keep threatening to overrun Aunt Libby's place . . ."

Theodosia stopped abruptly, blinked, stared at the patch of empty grass.

Where's Earl Grey?

She glanced left, then right, saw plenty of dogs, but no

Earl Grey. No Dalbrador with a mottled coat wearing a blue service dog vest.

"Earl Grey's not here!" said Theodosia abruptly.

"He's got to be around here somewhere," said Brooke, picking up on Theodosia's panic.

"We've got to find him," insisted Theodosia.

"Of course," said Brooke. "Oh, honey, I'm sure he just wandered off somewhere. He's such a friendly guy. Probably just snuffling around, saying hi to other dogs."

"You're probably right," agreed Theodosia, fighting to still the fear in her heart. *He's still got his collar on,* she thought. *And my phone number's on his ID tag. And a chip, he's got an implanted ID chip, too.* She knew her mind was starting to race, but she couldn't seem to slow it down.

"I'm going to grab some of the Big Paw volunteers," said Brooke. "We'll launch a quick search party."

"Earl Grey!" shouted Theodosia as she ran over toward a small group of canopies that had been set up by the Doberman contingent.

Cleo caught up with her in a matter of moments. "Earl Grey's still got his collar on? And his vest?" she asked.

"Yes, he does," said Theodosia. She was stunned. Nothing like this had ever happened before. Earl Grey usually stuck to her like a burr.

"Then we'll find him," Cleo assured Theodosia. "I've got our volunteers spreading out all over the park. And Brooke is going to have them make an announcement over the loud speaker." She patted Theodosia's shoulder. "I'm sure he's not the first dog to wander off today."

But ten minutes later they still hadn't found hide nor hair of Earl Grey.

"We've canvassed the whole park," Cleo told her, frowning. "And still nothing."

"Can you do it again?" asked Theodosia. "Please?"

Cleo gazed into Theodosia's eyes, saw she was close to tears. "Sure," she said. "No problem."

Maybe Earl Grey wandered out of the park, thought Theodosia. *Maybe he's a block away, chasing somebody's cat. Or sitting in a nice sunny spot wondering where the heck I am.*

Theodosia jogged over to Mary Murray Drive and sprinted across it, calling Earl Grey's name. Then she whistled. And clapped her hands. And called again.

Still no sight of him. But she did hear a faint barking.

Is that him? Did he wander off even farther than I thought? That's not like him, she told herself, but decided she had to keep moving, keep searching.

Ruff, ruff, ruff, came the barking.

I'm coming, Earl Grey.

But the closer she got, the more she realized it didn't sound like Earl Grey at all. And when she ran up to the blue Chevy van, she saw there were two sheepdogs inside. No doubt waiting for their turn in the showring.

Gotta keep trying, Theodosia told herself. *Gotta keep searching.*

One block away, Theodosia found Earl Grey's blue vest lying neatly on the ground.

Oh, good lord. It's his vest. He got this far and now he's completely disappeared. But where? Where did he go? Better yet what should I do now?

Theodosia spun on her heels and jogged back toward the park. Halfway there, she remembered the stables at the far end of park.

That's where the mounted police keep their horses, she thought. *Maybe I can get the police to help!*

Veering left, Theodosia sprinted her way toward the stables, hoping she'd find someone from the mounted patrol grooming his horse or, better yet, getting ready to go out on patrol.

She was in luck. Two officers were tightening the cinches on their saddles as she ran up.

"Can you help me?" she asked, trying to catch her breath. She gestured toward the park where the dog show was in full swing now. "My dog, a *service dog* is missing. Wandered off, I think." She held up the blue vest. "I found his vest over on Sutherland Street."

The officers stared at her.

"Please," she cried. "I really need your help!"

One of the officers stared at her like she was crazy. "Lady, there's hundreds of dogs running around this place."

"Just take a quick look, okay?" asked Theodosia.

The second officer answered her more kindly. "Ma'am, with all these dogs around, it would be like looking for a needle in a haystack."

22

"These are excellent," said Drayton as he surveyed a stack of neon yellow posters. "How many did you have printed?"

"Three hundred," said Haley. "But if you think we need more, I can make a quick call."

Theodosia, Drayton, Haley, and three volunteers from the Big Paw organization were sitting in the tea shop. They'd rendezvoused there to formulate a plan that would help get the word out on the missing Earl Grey. Aside from the volunteers who were out searching right now, the posters were their number one idea.

"Okay," said Drayton as he passed out posters to the volunteers. "I'm giving everyone fifty posters. Put them up wherever you can. In store windows, on telephone poles, hand them out to joggers if possible." He murmured his thanks to the three volunteers, watched as they bid somber good-byes to Theodosia, then trooped out the door.

Not thirty seconds later Parker Scully came scurrying in, cradling his new kitty in one arm. "I came as soon as I could get away," he said breathlessly. Stroking the cat's back, he gazed into some very serious faces. "Someone left a message Earl Grey was missing? Was that for real?"

Seated at a table, looking utterly bereft, Theodosia nodded. Then she said, "He wandered off at the dog show this afternoon."

Parker walked swiftly over to her, leaned forward, and planted a gentle kiss on the top of Theodosia's head. Then, switching his kitty to the crook of his other arm, he sat down next to her. "You've got people out looking?" he asked.

Theodosia nodded. "Most of the Big Paw volunteers are out scouring the neighborhoods. And we enlisted three others to put up posters."

Drayton quickly pulled a poster from the top of the remaining stack and passed it to Parker. "Here," he said. "Day-Glo yellow. Not my taste, but easily seen and read."

"Have you called any of the TV stations?" Parker asked.

"Delaine's doing that now," said Theodosia, gesturing towards her friend who stood at the counter with her back to them, talking intently on the telephone.

"Good," said Parker. "A missing service dog is certainly newsworthy. A couple mentions on TV could boost public awareness and do the trick."

"That would be the general idea," murmured Drayton, as he wandered over toward Delaine to put on another kettle for tea.

At that moment, Delaine hung up the phone and came over to tell them the news. "Well," she said, posturing importantly. "Channel Eight is delighted to run a quick blurb on tonight's news." She gazed directly at Theodosia. "They like you because of those tea segments you taped. And Channel Three and Channel Ten said they couldn't *promise* anything, but they'd try to work in a mention if time allows."

"That's a positive start," said Parker.

Delaine's eyes flicked over to him, noticing Parker for the first time. "What's that?" she asked. Her gaze had shifted toward the cat and the tiny line between her eyes suddenly deepened.

"My new cat," said Parker. "I told you about her, didn't I?"

"That's not a cat," said Delaine in a disapproving tone.

"Well, technically, I guess she's still a kitten," said Parker. He held up a tiny paw and made it wave at Delaine. "Say *hi* to the nice lady, Tiger Lilly." Parker grinned sheepishly.

"I beg to differ with you," said Delaine, still staring intently at the furry little creature snuggled in Parker's arms. "That's a *cub!*"

"She sure is," said Parker, cuddling the kitten. "She's my little cubby."

Delaine stared at Parker as though he were insane. "I mean to say it looks more like a *jaguar* cub," she said forcefully.

That shushed the entire tea room.

"What?" said Parker. He stared down at the small cat in his arms.

"When I lived up north for a brief time, I worked as a docent at the Bronx Zoo," Delaine told him. "And if my recollection is correct, and I'm quite sure it is, I'm telling you that is definitely a jaguar cub."

Theodosia turned to stare at Parker's kitten. Feeling upset and more than a little distraught, she'd barely paid any attention to the little animal cradled in Parker's arms. Now she stared at it, too.

"I looked it up on a cat website." Parker laughed. "And

from the information I found, I'm fairly sure this is an Oci-cat." He held the little cat out. "You see," he explained, "it's a newer breed that's a blend of Seal Point Siamese, Ruddy Abyssinian, and American Shorthair. Ocicat's are even recognized by the Cat Fanciers Association." He paused. "Anyway, I can see where you'd be a little confused."

"And I still say it looks like a jaguar cub," said Delaine more forcefully. "Where on earth did you purchase it? And, pray tell, what exactly did it say on the bill of sale?"

"He didn't buy it," cut in Theodosia. "He found it."

"Good heavens where?" asked Delaine.

"Over on Highway 174," said Parker.

Delaine shook her head, as if clearing her thoughts. "That's totally weird," she said. "But if you don't want to take *my* word for it, Mr. Scully, why not get an expert's opinion. Talk to someone over at the Riverbanks Zoo, near Columbia."

"Maybe I will," said Parker, cradling his cat defensively. "But I still think you're dead wrong."

Shadows lengthened and Parker and Delaine had long since slipped away when evening finally arrived. Theodosia, Drayton, and Haley were alone and divvying up the remaining posters, deciding on which areas of town each of them should cover.

Fidgeting in his chair, Drayton glanced up at Theodosia and Haley, then licked his lips nervously. "All right, ladies, I'm just going to come right out and say this."

"Say what?" asked Haley, pushing a hunk of blond hair behind her ears and straightening up to listen.

Drayton's words came out in a rush: "I think Earl Grey's been abducted."

Theodosia's eyes widened as she stared at him. Then she dropped her head into her hands. "Please don't say that," she moaned.

"How can you even *imagine* a thing like that?" Haley gasped. "How *awful.*"

"Hear me out," said Drayton, holding up a cautionary finger. "Two reasons. The first one being that Earl Grey is a very well-trained yet playful canine. It's not in his character to just wander off from a dog show."

"You mean because so many other dogs were around?" asked Haley.

"Exactly," said Drayton. "He's going to be curious, he's going to want to interact with them."

"You're right about that," said Haley slowly. "Earl Grey loves his doggy play days. And for him that dog show probably looked like one gigantic play day."

"You said two things," said Theodosia, looking pained. "What's the second?"

Drayton gazed at her with sadness in his eyes. "His blue vest. You said it was lying there rather neatly?"

"Yes," said Theodosia, grabbing a tissue and daubing at her eyes.

"Almost folded?"

"Yes," she winced.

Drayton leaned forward and grasped one of her hands. "My dear Theo, Earl Grey is a very bright dog. But I've never known him to take off his own vest and fold it."

After brewing a pot of jasmine tea, his favorite remedy for relaxation and calming nerves, Drayton sat back down at the table and poured out cups of the steaming elixir for all of them.

"So," said Theodosia, looking apprehensive. "Where exactly is your kidnapping hypothesis leading?"

"Same place you're probably headed," replied Drayton. "Someone's intent on stopping you."

Haley screwed her face into a quizzical frown. "Stopping her from doing what?" she asked.

"My investigation," said Theodosia. "That has to be it."

"But you just told us that everything was pretty much over," said Haley. "Jock Rowley was taken in for questioning. And is probably going to be charged with murder."

Taking a sip of tea, Theodosia gazed off across the tea room, staring at the little stone fireplace and the teapot painting that hung above it. "You know something," she murmured. "Congressman Bonham showed up there this afternoon. So did Bill Glass."

"At the dog show?" asked Haley, clearly surprised.

"Interesting," said Drayton, his voice terse. "Convenient, too."

"Maybe you should give Tidwell a call," urged Haley. "Find out what's really going on. What went on. With Jock Rowley, I mean."

Pushing her chair back from the table, Theodosia stood up. "I'm going to go into my office, stuff a sock in my mouth, and scream my head off," she told them. "Then I'm going to phone Tidwell."

Theodosia came back ten minutes later looking subdued and shaken. "Rowley's off the hook," she told them as she slumped into her chair.

"Are you serious?" asked a stunned Haley. "I was hoping he was cooling his heels in jail by now."

"According to Tidwell, Jock Rowley had an iron clad alibi for last evening," said Theodosia. "Apparently Rowley gave a rip roaring speech to two hundred bankers at the Bayshore Club. After which he wolfed down a prime rib dinner then retired to the bar where he imbibed more than a few Manhattans."

"Rats," said Drayton, looking glum. "Did you tell Tidwell about Earl Grey?"

"I did," said Theodosia. "He said he'd try to get word out to the various squads. Send a radio broadcast, I guess."

"That's good of him," replied Drayton.

"So," said Theodosia, "unless Jock Rowley managed to generate a holographic image of himself that fooled two hundred bankers plus an overworked bartender, we're back to square one."

"Not necessarily," said Drayton. "I still believe that if, in fact, Earl Grey was kidnapped it was done as a ploy to stop you." He set his teacup down and stared at her. You *know* something."

"She knows something," repeated Haley. "But she doesn't know what she knows?"

"Something like that," said Drayton.

"Tidwell said pretty much the same thing last night," mused Theodosia.

"This is all very confusing." Haley sighed.

Theodosia straightened up, wiped at her cheeks. "Drayton might be right. I stumbled across *something*. The problem is, I'm not clear what it is. There's a big fat piece missing."

So you're saying Earl Grey's disappearance is linked to Duke's *and* Sydney's murder?" asked Haley.

"It certainly could be," said Drayton. He stared at Theodosia with bright eyes. "What do *you* think?"

"It's possible this is all linked," she admitted. *This isn't the first time I've had that niggling feeling.*

"But how does Duke's murder relate to anything that's going on?" asked Haley. "And where does Sydney's murder come in?"

"What do we know about Sydney?" asked Theodosia.

"What do we really know about Duke?" echoed Drayton.

They all sat and pondered those questions for a minute.

"Well," said Theodosia, "we know that Duke still sat on the board of Victory Capital. And that Pookie once referred to him as a professional gadfly."

Drayton nodded. "Which he was. Duke threw himself into everything he did. Gave a hundred and twenty percent."

"And Sydney had a pet project she was working on," said Theodosia. "The investigative journalism show." She turned to Haley. "You were the one who mentioned that as a theory."

"Did you ever follow up and find out about that?" asked Haley.

"The list of Sydney's possible topics is sitting on my desk," said Theodosia, "though I haven't had a chance to look at it yet." She thought for a moment. "Maybe Duke and Sydney somehow *intersect* in some way we don't know about."

"Let's pay a visit to Pookie," said Drayton. See if we can figure out what Duke was working on just before he was murdered. Do we have any idea what that might have been?"

"No," said Theodosia. "But it's high time we find out."

23

❧

Pookie Wilkes opened the door of her large Georgian-style home with a question on her face.

"So sorry to bother you," Drayton began. "But as I explained on the phone . . ."

Pookie waved a hand as if to shush him and ushered Theodosia, Drayton, and Haley into a large entryway covered in mauve-colored silk. Two framed watercolor paintings hung on the wall and they could see into a large front parlor that was decorated in tasteful, muted shades of mauve and dark green.

"Did you find your dog yet?" was Pookie's first question to Theodosia.

Theodosia shook her head. "Afraid not. Which is why, as Drayton probably explained to you on the phone, we're intruding like this and asking if we can snoop through Duke's files. We think there may be some rather strange coincidences at work."

Pookie stared at her, a hand poised delicately at her throat. "The disappearance of your dog might be related to Duke's death?" she asked.

"And that of Sydney Chastain," added Drayton.

"The poor lady who was heading up that TV network?" asked Pookie. "The one who was murdered?" She stared at them. "Are you *serious?*"

"I know this all sounds rather strange," began Theodosia.

Pookie let out a nervous, quavering sigh. "*Beyond* strange. I can't imagine . . ." She stopped, shook her head, tried to pull herself together. "But I do trust your judgment, Theodosia." Her eyes flicked over to Drayton and Haley. "And your cohorts here as well. So if you want to hunt through Duke's files, you are certainly more than welcome."

"Thank you," said Theodosia.

Pookie crooked an index finger. "This way," she said. "Down the hallway. Might as well get started right away."

Duke Wilkes's office was a large wood-paneled room at the back of the house, overlooking an expansive rose garden. Though two floodlights were on, Theodosia couldn't see much of the garden, but she figured that in summer, with full sunlight streaming in and a lush carpet of roses in bloom, it must be a spectacular view. Distracting, almost, for anyone who was trying to work in here.

"These are the files," said Pookie, indicating a two-drawer wooden file cabinet. "The police removed some of Duke's papers last Monday, but they brought everything back after a couple days. Said they made photocopies of any items they felt might possibly be relevant."

"You've talked to Detective Tidwell recently?" asked Theodosia.

Pookie nodded. "Yes, but . . . there's not been a whole lot of progress as you probably know."

Theodosia bent down on one knee and slid out the top drawer.

"Those are mostly household files," explained Pookie. "Insurance papers, taxes, utility bills, and whatnot. Not terribly interesting reading." She fidgeted, twisting her hands, obviously wanting to help, but not knowing what to tell them. "Would you like some tea?" she finally asked.

"That would be splendid," replied Drayton. "Haley, could you help Mrs. Wilkes?"

"Of course," said Haley.

Theodosia slid the top drawer closed and pulled open the bottom drawer. She walked her fingers down the row of file tabs. All were carefully labeled in what must be Duke's tight, block-letter printing.

"Anything?" asked Drayton.

"There must be fifty files in here," said Theodosia, suddenly feeling overwhelmed.

"Such as . . . ?" prompted Drayton.

She glanced up at him, a pained expression on her face. "I should be out looking for Earl Grey. I . . . I don't know what we're doing here."

"Searching for connections," replied Drayton. "Anything that seems to intersect, as you so eloquently phrased it."

"You really think that's the key to finding my dog?" asked Theodosia.

"Dear lord, I hope so," said Drayton. He put a hand on Theodosia's shoulder, squeezed gently. "Let's at least *look* at the files, okay? Then I'll help you search for Earl Grey. We'll drive around all night if we have to."

Theodosia swallowed hard. "Okay," she said, trying hard to concentrate. "There's lots of stuff in here, though." She suddenly remembered the *needle in a haystack* remark the police officer had made a few hours earlier and fervently hoped that wasn't going to be the case here.

"Pull out anything that looks interesting," urged Drayton.

"Duke has files on the Charleston Symphony, Gibbes Museum, and Heritage Society," said Theodosia. She was down on both knees now, hunched forward over the file drawer.

"Duke was a very generous contributor," replied Drayton.

Theodosia thought for a moment. "Remember when we were at the Candlelight Concert? Pookie was telling us about some of the causes that Duke did volunteer work for. Remember?"

Now Drayton was down on this knees beside her, glasses halfway down his nose, peering at the file tabs. "I think she mentioned something about housing?" he said, frowning.

"Citizen's Housing League," said Theodosia plucking the file from the drawer.

"And something about the people's . . ." he said slowly.

"People's Law Office or People's Food Shelf?" asked Theodosia.

"Grab 'em both," said Drayton.

"What else?" asked Theodosia, handing him the files.

"Take the Heritage Society file for sure," said Drayton.

"And here are at least ten different files that relate to Duke's Civil War reenactment group," said Theodosia.

"Grab all those, too," said Drayton, clambering to his knees. "Whoa, I'm getting too old for this," he moaned as one knee let out a loud pop. He grasped all the files Theodosia handed him, carried them to a large library table, and spread them out.

"It feels so futile," said Theodosia, joining him.

"We have to try," said Drayton. "Look for something, anything that might have to do with Sydney."

But forty minutes of searching through Duke's files and they were still nowhere. Even with Haley's help.

Pookie saw the frustration on their faces. "I'm sorry these aren't shedding any light," she told them.

"Not your fault," said Theodosia.

"Or ours," chimed in Drayton. "We tried."

"Do you know . . . ?" Theodosia asked Pookie. "Was Duke working on anything that had to do with Sydney Chastain?"

Pookie's face crumpled. "I have no idea."

"Okay," said Theodosia. *So Pookie doesn't even know that Duke's firm turned VTV down on financing. Well, maybe that doesn't even fit into this equation. Maybe nothing fits.* "We should head home now," she told Drayton and Haley. "I need to check in with Cleo and the other volunteers, then I want to drive around for a while."

"Take the rest of the folders with you," urged Pookie. "Maybe something will jump out at you."

"Maybe," said Theodosia as she gathered them up. But she didn't think so. Wasn't all that hopeful.

"I hope you find your dog," said Pookie as she bid good night to them at the door.

"I do, too," said Theodosia.

Drayton was true to his word. He rode shotgun with Theodosia while they drove around the darkened city searching for Earl Grey. They drove back to Hampton Park, up and down back alleys, all the while staying in cell phone contact with Haley who was camped out on Theodosia's couch, manning the phone line there.

But at eleven o'clock Theodosia dropped Drayton off at his house. He was yawning, rubbing his eyes, and visibly exhausted.

"You're a trooper," she told him. "Thank you."

"You go home, too," he said, yawning.

"I will," she promised.

But once she arrived home and sent Haley back across the alley to her garden apartment, Theodosia felt too anxious and keyed up to sleep. She wandered aimlessly about her apartment, opened the refrigerator, closed it when nothing appealed to her, was both grateful and hopeful when the phone suddenly rang.

"Hello?" Theodosia snatched it up on the first ring.

"Theo dear," came a hushed voice. It was her Aunt Libby who lived out at Cane Ridge Plantation. "I just found out about Earl Grey."

"You did?" said Theodosia, surprised. *How could she . . . ?*

"Haley sent me an E-mail," said Libby, filling in the blanks for her.

"You've got E-mail?" asked Theodosia. Somehow, she'd never thought of her Aunt Libby as being Internet savvy.

"Just got on-line last week," said Libby. "Kind of exciting. But how are *you* doing? Needless to say, I was absolutely shocked when Haley let me know what happened. I assume there's a search party out looking for your dear boy?"

"The Big Paw volunteers have been wonderful," Theodosia told her. "They promised to go out again tomorrow morning."

"I'm sure he'll turn up," said Libby. "I *know* he'll turn up. In fact I'm going to say a little prayer to Saint Francis."

"Thank you," gasped Theodosia, her throat constricting with emotion while tears filled her eyes.

"This hasn't been much of a week for you, has it?" asked Libby. "The Candlelight Concert last Sunday, then your finding that poor TV lady murdered . . ."

"It's been dreadfully strange," said Theodosia. Aunt Libby had been concerned for Theodosia when she'd learned about her close proximity to both murder victims and had phoned the tea shop twice this week to caution Theodosia about getting too involved. Obviously, she knew her niece rather well.

"Please take care," said Libby. "And come out to Cane Ridge when you can. Sometimes physically removing yourself from your problems can be highly therapeutic."

After bidding good-bye to Aunt Libby, Theodosia tucked herself into a large wing chair and gazed morosely into the dark of the fireplace. The fireplace Earl Grey always loved to lie next to. She thought about how much she detested the idea that Earl Grey was out there somewhere. Wandering around in the dark. He was her pup, her jogging companion, her best buddy. Now he was lost, scared, perhaps even injured. Wondering how to get home. Wondering where she was. Wondering why she didn't come for him.

Got to get to the dog shelters first thing in the morning, Theodosia told herself as her lids began to droop. *Got to find my dog.* And as the clock ground relentlessly toward dawn, Theodosia fell into a troubled sleep.

24

When Haley came clattering up the stairs early Saturday morning, Theodosia was already seated in her kitchen, sipping tea, the phone book sprawled open on the table.

"What are you doing?" asked Haley.

"Copying down the addresses for Bill Glass and Clive Bonham."

"You're going to go drive by their houses?" asked Haley.

"I'm going to take a good, hard look," said Theodosia. "Then I'm going to hit the animal shelters."

"Want me to come along?"

"No, thanks, but if you could stay here and hold down the fort I'd be eternally grateful."

"Not a problem," said Haley.

Clive Bonham lived in a brand-new high-rise condo with a security system. Theodosia hung around the front door until one of the residents, a young woman in her twenties, came back from her run, dressed in sweat clothes and looking red-faced and breathing heavily. Pretending to fish around in her purse looking for keys, Theodosia promptly followed the young lady into the building when she opened the door. Once in the lobby, Theodosia spotted an exit sign, pushed through that door, then followed the stairway down. She found a storage room with a warren of lockers separated by chicken wire and an underground parking garage. Theodosia poked around this lower level for a good ten minutes, calling Earl Grey's name. Nothing.

Bill Glass lived in a small bungalow in North Charleston. Theodosia cruised his alley slowly, then parked her Jeep at the end of his street. Hiking back up the alley, she peered through a dusty window into Glass's garage, poked her head over his fence, then boldly marched up to his back door and knocked. Nobody home.

Or at least nobody's answering the door, she decided.

Glancing around quickly, Theodosia bent down and rapped sharply on one of the low cellar windows, once again calling Earl Grey's name. Again nothing.

Okay. Neither of these guys stashed him at home. Which doesn't eliminate them completely, but I have to move on for now.

Theodosia drove to the municipal animal shelter. Stacey, the office manager, was sympathetic to her plight and helpful. Even offering to phone the other two area animal shelters for her.

"We stay in pretty close contact," Stacey told Theodosia. "In fact, new intakes are often up on their websites by now. Stacey sat down at her computer, clicked a few buttons, and scanned her screen. "No, nothing yet. But let me make those calls. You never know."

Theodosia wandered into the gift shop. Stared at the colorful balls, chew bones, plush toys, and leashes. *Bad idea,* she thought to herself, then turned on her heel.

Theodosia arrived back at the main office just as Stacey was hanging up the phone.

"Your dog's not at the other shelters, either," said Stacey. Then, seeing the look of disappointment on Theodosia's face, she said, "Sorry. I'll call you immediately if anything changes."

With a heavy heart, Theodosia drove home.

Haley and Drayton were waiting for her in her apartment.

"Nothing?" asked Haley.

Theodosia shook her head, too disheartened to speak.

"Cleo called about ten minutes ago," Haley told her. "The volunteers are out searching again."

"You look utterly exhausted," said Drayton. "Why don't you go lie down for a while, maybe take a short nap. I'll catch the phone if it rings."

"Good idea," said Haley. "Meanwhile, I'm going to drive around a little. Maybe cruise down to White Point Gardens, then pick my way back through the historic district. You know, kind of check out some of Earl Grey's favorite haunts."

"Okay," agreed Theodosia, too tired to argue.

But once she wandered into her bedroom, she found she was too jittery to lie down.

"You're back," said Drayton, as Theodosia walked into the living room.

"I can't nap," said Theodosia. "I'm going to go out and look for him again. Hit Hampton Park, see if I can figure out which direction he might have headed." She grabbed her purse and car keys. "But you'll stay here?" she asked. "In case the phone rings?"

"Count on it," Drayton told her.

For the next four hours Theodosia drove the streets and back alleys of Charleston. She called his name, stopped to ask joggers and bikers if they'd seen a stray dog, any dog.

Finally, frustrated and dejected, she went home.

True to his word, Drayton was still there.

"Anything?" he asked.

Theodosia shook her head. "Nope."

"I'm so sorry," Drayton told her. "Haley came up empty, too." He fidgeted for a moment, obviously aware of Theodosia's distress. "How about a cup of tea?" he asked her, pointing at the steaming teapot that sat on a silver tray on the dining room table.

"What have you got?" she asked.

"A Tippy Yunnan," said Drayton. "Nice and strong. Here," he said, "let me pour you a cup."

Theodosia sat at the dining room table, took a sip. "Mmm, good," she said.

"Are you hungry?" asked Drayton. "I bet you haven't had a thing to eat."

"Not really," admitted Theodosia.

Drayton hurried into the kitchen to grab a scone and some jelly. "Haley brought some scones and muffins in," he called to her. "Tell me what you want and I'll have it warmed up in a jiffy."

"A scone would be great," said Theodosia as she gazed at the stack of file folders they'd brought home from Pookie's last night. The ones they hadn't looked at yet.

The ones Pookie had urged them to take, just in case.

"Strawberry jam or apple butter?" asked Drayton.

"Surprise me," said Theodosia. She let out a sigh, rotated her head to try to ease the kinks out of her neck. "Maybe we've been going about this all wrong," she said suddenly.

Drayton hurried into the dining room, set the scone down in front of her. "What are you talking about?" he asked.

"Last night, when you told me you thought Earl Grey had been kidnapped, you thought it was because someone was trying to derail my investigation," said Theodosia.

"Yes," said Drayton.

"Using that as a jump-off point, we then made the assumption that the murders of Duke and Sydney were related."

"Right," said Drayton slowly.

"And when we went through Duke's files last night, we were specifically looking for clues that might pertain to Sydney," said Theodosia.

"Because you had a notion that the two of them somehow . . . what was the word you used? Somehow *intersected*," said Drayton.

Theodosia paused for a moment. "What if they did and didn't?" she asked.

Drayton shook his head. "I'm not following you."

"Maybe there was no one big sinister machination at work," said Theodosia.

"You're saying we simply went off on a tangent?" asked Drayton.

"In a way," said Theodosia. She pushed her scone to the side, extended her arms and scooped the files toward her. "Let's look again. But this time, let's not look for direct correlations. Let's look for . . . oh, call it touch points."

"Touch points," repeated Drayton. Clearly, he was still not following Theodosia.

"We need that list of investigative journalism projects Sydney was championing," said Theodosia, searching through the stack of papers on the table. "I think her TV show was going to be called something like *Third Degree.*"

Drayton pawed around. "Here it is," he said.

"Good," said Theodosia. "So we've got . . . what?" she asked.

Reaching into his jacket pocket for his glasses, Drayton placed them on his aquiline nose. "You want me to read them to you?" he asked, looking very much like a wise old owl.

"Please," said Theodosia.

"Huh-um," said Drayton, clearing his throat. "First thing on the list is bio-identical hormones. You see anything in Duke's files that comes close to that?"

Theodosia scanned the file tabs, trying to make out Duke's writing. "There's a file here on a children's clinic," said Theodosia.

"What's in it?" asked Drayton.

Theodosia opened the file. "A canceled check for five hundred dollars And a thank-you letter."

"A donation," said Drayton. "That's surely not related."

"I don't think so, either," said Theodosia, looking disappointed. "What's next on the list?"

"The glass ceiling," said Drayton. He peered over his glasses. "Anything?"

"Not really," said Theodosia. "Okay, read the next couple on the list to me."

"Illegal Botox parties and women in politics," said Drayton.

"This isn't looking good," said Theodosia, scanning the files.

"No touch points," said Drayton.

"None at all," said Theodosia. "At least nothing that jumps out at me."

"How about women's pay discrepancies, diploma mills, or mortgage scams?" asked Drayton.

"Not really," said Theodosia. She sighed. "I would've thought the mortgage scam thing might have tied in with Jock Rowley, but he's got an airtight alibi for the night Sydney was murdered. Darn, this isn't working at all."

"Bear with me," said Drayton. "There's just a couple more here. Child labor in third world countries, date rape?"

"Nothing that even comes close," said Theodosia. She reached for her scone, daubed a little strawberry jam on it, took a bite. It would have tasted marvelous if she wasn't so down.

"This is the tail end of the list," said Drayton. "False cosmetic claims and importing endangered species."

Theodosia flipped through the folders. "Not a darn thing." Pause. "Wait a minute. There *is* a file here labeled Wildlife Conservation Society."

"What's in the folder?" asked Drayton.

Theodosia flipped the manila folder open. "Not much. Another canceled check, a few newspaper clippings. I think this is a dead end, too," she said as she sifted through the papers. "Hold it, there's one more page." She rubbed at her eyes which were burning from lack of sleep, from scanning the streets for her beloved dog. "It's some sort of press release issued by the South Carolina Department of Natural Resources."

"Concerning what?" asked Drayton, reaching for the teapot.

"Looks like some kind of report on illegal importation of animals," she said.

"Huh?" said Drayton, staring across the table at her.

"This is actually pretty awful," said Theodosia, scanning the report. "It says here that unsavory importers are smuggling in endangered birds from South America."

"How dreadful," said Drayton.

"That's not the worst of it," replied Theodosia. "They're also reaping huge profits by bringing in exotic deer and large cats, then selling them to private hunting preserves."

"You mean so people can track them down and *shoot* them?" cried Drayton.

"That's the . . ." began Theodosia. She stopped abruptly, her mind suddenly flashing on a single, tenuous connection. Turning a startled gaze to Drayton she said, "Remember the little cat? The one Parker found? You don't suppose . . . ?"

"Call him," said Drayton. "This instant."

Theodosia checked her watch. "It's getting late, Parker's for sure at the restaurant and Saturday is their busy day."

"Call him anyway," prompted Drayton.

"Parker?" said Theodosia, once she had him on the phone and delivered a quick update on Earl Grey, which was really nothing at all. "Did you ever get your cat checked out?"

"Nah," he said. "Tiger Lilly's just a garden-variety kitty. That exotic cat stuff is just wishful thinking on your friend's part."

"Are you sure about that?" asked Theodosia.

There was a pause and then she heard Parker talking to

someone. Saying something about white wine and clarified butter. "I'm sure," said Parker coming back on the line. "Listen, can I call you back in a little bit? We're in the middle of prepping dinner."

"Okay, sure," Theodosia replied.

"Chin up, Theo," said Parker. "I'm positive Earl Grey's gonna be found."

"What did he say?" asked Drayton.

"He still says it's a garden-variety cat," said Theodosia.

"What do *you* think?" asked Drayton.

"No idea," replied Theodosia. "I've never owned a cat. I've always had dogs."

"But Delaine thought it might be something else," mused Drayton. "Although Delaine isn't exactly the most reliable source in the world."

"No, she's not," admitted Theodosia. Delaine was a dear, but she was a flighty dear, given to moments of exaggeration.

They sat and stared at each other for a while longer. Then Theodosia reached a hand out for her laptop and pulled it over in front of her.

"What are you doing?" asked Drayton, who was a complete technophobe.

"I want to check something," said Theodosia. She powered up, hit a few buttons, went to the MapQuest site. "Although I'm probably searching for that proverbial needle in a haystack again."

Drayton stood up, carried the teapot out to the kitchen. When he came back, he was carrying a plate with a plump banana muffin. "MapQuest," he said, sidling in behind Theodosia. "What does that do? Generate a map, I suppose?"

"Bingo," said Theodosia. "Here's the thing . . . we picked up Parker's cat, the one he dubbed Tiger Lilly, out on Highway 174." Her fingers flew across the keyboard. "Pretty close to where it intersects with Saint Elmo Crossing."

"Okay," said Drayton. For someone who disdained technology, he seemed fascinated by her every keystroke.

"So," said Theodosia, watching the graphics bloom on her screen, "this is the approximate area where we found Tiger Lilly." She studied the map and frowned. For some reason she'd had a tingling feeling that something might jump out at her. But nothing did.

Bummer, she thought.

Glancing over her shoulder at Drayton, Theodosia asked, "Does this ring any bells for you?"

About to take a bite of his muffin, Drayton bent forward and peered at the map. "Well, I'll be . . ." he said finally.

Theodosia was suddenly on alert. "What?" she asked him. *"What?"*

Drayton set his uneaten muffin down on the table next to the computer. He reached out a hand to point, his fingernail grazing the computer screen. "That's awfully close to where Claudia and Corky Chait live," he replied.

"Are you *serious?*" asked Theodosia. "They *live* out there?"

Drayton straightened up and squared his shoulders. "There's no *way* the Chaits could be involved," he muttered. "They're two of the nicest, most upstanding people who ever lived!"

But Theodosia was already on her feet, grabbing for her jacket and keys. "I'll get back to you on that," she told him as she flew out the door.

25

~❧~

Pink and gold lit the western sky, backlighting stands of cypress and tupelo as Theodosia turned off U.S. 17 onto State Highway 174. It had been an easy drive, a fast drive, her Jeep humming along as she kept the pedal to the metal and her speedometer a notch above sixty-five.

Breezing through the small town of Adams Run, Theodosia headed right into the heart of Edisto Island. It was here, in the eighteen hundreds, that local planters had given up on growing rice and indigo because of salty water intrusion. As luck would have it, though, these same canny planters stumbled upon the notion of growing sea-island cotton. Once planted, their cotton fields flourished and yielded bumper crops. This Edisto Island cotton, noted for its extra long, silky fibers, was reputed to be the finest sea-island cotton ever grown. And as their cotton crops commanded higher and higher prices from the lace mills of France, elegant manor homes also sprung up.

Since local growers religiously guarded their secret for growing sea-island cotton, the Edisto Island area remained a quiet, closed community. Much of it is still secluded and private to this day, and the entire area has managed to stay relatively untouched by outside development or heavy tourism.

Okay, thought Theodosia as the narrow blacktop road snaked through a tangled forest of live oaks, *Saint Elmo Crossing has to be coming up fairly soon.*

Emerging from the dark forest, Theodosia drove past a couple small wooden shacks where fresh shrimp and vegetables were being sold, then the road dipped down to reveal a large salt marsh stretching out on either side of her. Herons and terns sailed low over the sluggish waters as the last rays of sun glinted hypnotically on the golden marsh. This was the lair of snapping turtles, cottonmouth snakes, and the occasional alligator.

She was at Saint Elmo Crossing before she realized it. Sailing past the narrow gravel road and the tilting metal sign, Theodosia finally made the connection in her head, then slowly applied her brakes.

Pulling over to the side of the two-lane road, Theodosia sat in her idling Jeep, trying to figure out her next move. Finally, she dug into her handbag, pulled out the printed map from MapQuest and decided the Chait place was probably still up ahead.

She eased the car back on the road, but kept her speed low. Dozens of gravel roads spun off from the one she was on, but none were marked.

Hope this isn't a wild-goose chase, she thought to herself, but pressed on anyway.

Finally Theodosia spotted a single weathered, wooden sign at the mouth of a narrow drive. It had but one word on it. CHAIT.

This is it.

Parking on the side of the highway, Theodosia slipped out of her Jeep. She was about to lock the door, when she decided she just might have to beat a hasty retreat. So she left her vehicle unlocked and slung her shoulder bag crosswise across her body. Just in case.

Shoulders squared, firmly intent on pursuing this single, somewhat flimsy angle, Theodosia set off down the driveway.

Gravel crunched underfoot as she walked down a narrow drive that was almost overgrown with palmettos and oleander. Twenty yards, thirty yards, now fifty yards in, Theodosia finally saw a partial view of the house.

It was big. And white. A few more steps and she spotted a wooden pergola covered in grapevines.

Perfect cover, Theodosia decided, as she parted the leafy wall with her hands, then eased inside it. Vines caught at her hair and clothing, the late afternoon sunshine virtually disappeared, so dense was the vegetation on the trellises. The air inside the pergola was redolent with a sweet, spicy aroma and bunches of fat, purple grapes hung heavy and lush, brushing Theodosia's shoulders.

Tiptoeing the length of the pergola, Theodosia was able to come within fifty feet or so of Corky and Claudia's home.

No lights on, she murmured to herself. *Even though it's almost seven. Must not be home yet. Well, here's a piece of luck which, unfortunately, has been in fairly short supply lately.*

It was a lovely white elephant of a home. Stately, slightly ethereal in its dark, misty setting of pine and oak, badly in need of paint.

Large Ionic columns dominated the front of the structure, three brick chimneys rose from the roof.

Beautiful. And a little spooky, too, Theodosia decided. *I better take a quick look around and get out of here before Corky and Claudia come rolling in.*

Creeping forward, Theodosia parted the vines to scan the area. To determine if there were any out-buildings or barns.

Just as she was about to step out of the leafy pergola, a horrible, high-pitched shriek pierced the air!

Startled, Theodosia stopped dead in her tracks, her heart suddenly thudding inside her chest.

What on earth? Was that a woman's scream? If so, it sure sounded like she was being tortured!

Swiftly, Theodosia was out in the open and running toward the back of the house.

The scream came from back here, right?

Up a slight rise, she spotted a nearby cluster of three buildings. Two were small sheds, one was a more substantial-looking barn. The barn's lower foundation, constructed of sand-colored fieldstone, was partially nestled into the hillside. The top half of the barn looked to be board and batten.

Creeping from shrub to shrub to remain as inconspicuous as possible, Theodosia moved stealthily toward a wooden door that would grant her access to the lower half of the barn. She gave a quick look over her shoulder, then put an ear to the door and listened. Nothing.

Her hand on the metal handle, Theodosia gave a mighty tug. The door let out a low creak, but didn't budge. But she thought she could hear *something* moving inside.

Trying to stay low to the ground, Theodosia sprinted up the slight rise, hoping she'd find access to the top half of the old barn. But when she reached the opposite side, that door was locked, too. And the single window was so covered with dust and grime there was no way she could see in.

But if I can get this window open, I could shinny inside.

Grasping the window frame, Theodosia fought to slide it upwards. Nothing doing. Heart pounding, she searched around at her feet, looking for a rock.

There. A nice jagged hunk of rock. Should I? Do I dare?

She tapped at the window and was surprised to hear a strange, low sound.

Is someone hurt in there? Do they need help?

"Hello?" she called. And heard another low sound.

Balancing the rock in her hand, Theodosia slung it at the window and was rewarded with a sharp *crack*. A weblike pattern spread across the upper window.

Grabbing a good-sized tree branch, Theodosia swung at the window. There was a loud crash as she knocked a huge shard of glass inside. Then it was a matter of moments before she battered out the rest of the glass and was able to reach a hand up and twist the latch. Unlocked now, the window slid up easily.

Okay, let's see what that terrible scream was all about, Theodosia decided as she swung a leg over the windowsill.

The barn was dark inside. Darker than she'd feared. And a strange musty smell immediately assaulted her senses.

What the . . . ?

Pawing through her purse, Theodosia searched for the matches Delaine had given her when they were trapped in the Augustus Chait House, what seemed like eons ago. She caught her fingernail on the tip of a metal comb, flinched, finally found the small box of matches. Her hand shaking, Theodosia struck a single match and held it up.

And found herself staring into gigantic yellow eyes.

Dear lord! It's a freaking tiger!

Dropping the match, she flailed backwards in a panic until her back hit the rough wall.

Tiger . . . tiger . . . was all her mind could process. Cowering, she waited for its hot breath on her neck, for iron jaws to rip her apart.

Ten seconds later, Theodosia became cognizant that she was still alive. And realized there was a flickering light in the barn.

Fire! When I dropped the match it must have ignited a piece of hay.

Theodosia's eyes flew open. And saw that the tiger was actually inside a cage. A cylindrical wire cage, maybe twelve feet in diameter. As the tiger paced and turned on giant, padded feet, it let out a terrible cry. A high-pitched shriek, the same kind that had shattered the stillness just five minutes earlier. A cry that was most certainly a plea for help.

Realizing the poor beast was deathly afraid of the small fire that smoldered at her feet, Theodosia ripped her purse from her, then shrugged out of her khaki jacket and beat at the rising flames. Ten seconds later, there was only a curl of smoke. She'd been lucky. There could have been hay littered all across the floor, instead just the few patches outside the tiger's cage.

"Hey," she said to the tiger, who she could now see was a fairly young animal. "Take it easy, pal. No more fire, okay?"

The tiger stared at her with angry, blazing eyes. A low growl rose in its throat.

Okay," she said, realizing a bad case of the shakes was coming on fast. "You hang tight while I look around. Then we'll get somebody back here to take care of you."

Theodosia threw a leg over the window ledge, realizing she was shivering uncontrollably now.

Oh, man, if ever I needed a cup of tea to soothe my frazzled nerves . . .

Clambering out of the building, Theodosia drew a deep breath, let it out slowly.

Relax, she willed herself. *Calm down. We're not finished here yet.*

There were two other small buildings to explore. But now the dark of the evening had settled in, so Theodosia could hurry over to these buildings undetected. And even luckier for her, there still didn't seem to be any lights on at the house.

In the first of the smaller sheds Theodosia found a pair of strange-looking goats. The word "ibex" popped into her mind, but she wasn't completely sure what these creatures really were. Just strange-looking critters with backward-curling horns. Realizing she'd probably stumbled into some sort of illegal animal procurement ring made Theodosia's heart heavy. Poor caged animals and no sign of Earl Grey.

The second shed was located closer to the house, so Theodosia tiptoed up to it, careful not to disturb whatever was inside. The door to this shed had some sort of tricky latch, and she fumbled with it for a couple minutes, trying to get it undone.

"Maybe I should just smash it open," she muttered.

"Woof," came a sound from inside.

Woof? Could it be? Could I have really found him?

"Earl Grey?" Theodosia called anxiously. "Are you in there?

"Woof, woof, woof," came Earl Grey's shrill, excited bark as he immediately recognized Theodosia's voice.

That did it. Theodosia grabbed a board that was leaning against the side of the shed, swung it like a baseball bat with as much force as she could muster, and shattered the latch.

Then she ripped open the door and charged in. And saw . . . floor-to-ceiling cages!

"Good lord," said Theodosia, her heart sinking.

Amazon parrots, macaws, and toucans beat their wings in protest. All were confined to cages that were stacked atop the somewhat larger cage where Earl Grey was imprisoned.

Hot fury bubbled up inside Theodosia as she knelt down and yanked open the door to Earl Grey's cage. Excited beyond belief, he came barreling out, throwing his fifty-six pounds against her, sending her tumbling.

She didn't care. Gently grabbing Earl Grey's ears, Theodosia held his sweet face to hers and planted a dozen kisses on his furry snout. The dog's joyful yelps set off a further cacophony of chirps and shrieks from the feathered captives still in their cages. They beat their wings, chewed at the wire, all the while cawing and calling and making a terrible racket.

The captive birds confirmed it for Theodosia. Corky and Claudia were dealing in the exotic animal trade.

Of course, she thought. *Now it all makes sense! Corky used to fly to South America all the time on business. Plus he's got an import/export license so he knows a few tricks. And Corky and Claudia have some sort of warehouse facility somewhere. Perfect. An absolutely perfect setup.*

Theodosia bounded back into the building while Earl Grey hung back. She knew if she could find some sort of clue, some sort of useful information on the location of the warehouse, she could send Tidwell over there, lights flashing and sirens screaming, hopefully accompanied by a pack of federal agents.

Searching in her bag, Theodosia came up with the matches again. She took three matches, struck them all at once, then held her makeshift mini-torch up to the cages. The birds were furious with her. They pressed toward the back, cowering, yet scolding loudly.

"Sorry," she told the frightened birds. "I'm just trying to figure out where you guys got shipped to."

Luck was with her. There was a yellow tag wired to one of the cages. She grabbed it, flipped it over, saw immediately that it was a shipping label.

But was the address of Corky and Claudia's warehouse on it?

Yes, it was. *Terminal 47-D at Union Pier.*

Theodosia ripped the tag from the cage and flew out the door. Grabbing Earl Grey by the collar, she tugged him in the direction of her Jeep.

It was payback time.

26

❦

Driving back to Charleston, Theodosia hauled out her cell phone as Earl Grey snuggled next to her on the passenger seat. She was driving as fast as she dared at this evening hour, trying to remember numbers and dial them one-handed.

And wouldn't you know it, every number she called was either busy or not answering!

First Theodosia called Tidwell's private line. That was busy. Then she tried Drayton's home phone. That rang into oblivion. No answering machine, nothing. When Haley didn't answer either, Theodosia tried calling Parker Scully at Solstice. That was a major mistake since it was Saturday evening and the maître d' was frantically tending to customers. So of course he immediately put her on hold before she could spit out more than a couple words! Maddening!

Theodosia didn't get through to Burt Tidwell until she was within a few miles of the docks and warehouses. He listened to her abbreviated story, then quickly asked, "Where are you now?"

"Closing in on Union Pier," she told him. "Looking for Terminal forty-seven-D."

"No!" was his sharp retort. "Do *not* go there, Miss Browning. I'm ordering you to pull over to the side of the road, turn off your engine, and step away from the car. Let *me* handle this!"

"But I'm almost there," she protested.

"Theodosia . . . listen to me," began Tidwell.

"Sorry, Detective, you're breaking up," said Theodosia, tossing the phone on the floor of her Jeep. "I didn't catch what you said. Sorry," she called again for good measure.

From Interstate 26 Theodosia took U.S. 17 heading toward Mount Pleasant. Then, just before she hit the Cooper River Bridge, she exited at East Bay Street. She was close now, very close. Slowing her Jeep, Theodosia tried to figure out just how she was going to get into the dock and wharf complex that hugged the Cooper River.

In the end it wasn't all that tough. She followed a rumbling truck up to the chain link security gate, then tailed him through, throwing a friendly wave toward the gate attendant. The attendant waved back, assuming she was part of the truck driver's contingent. His wife, no doubt, following him in so she could ferry him home after he delivered his cargo-laden truck.

"Now all I have to do is find Terminal forty-seven-D," she told Earl Grey, who gazed at her with worried eyes and a furrowed brow. "But don't worry," she told him as they bumped along slowly, then pulled into a parking slot in front of a warehouse marked 47-A. "You're going to stay right here. Tucked safely in my Jeep." And this time she *did* lock it.

The Union Pier area was a jumble of warehouses and small buildings, an obstacle course of large wooden crates, containerized freight, fork lifts, and giant cranes. To Theodosia's right, large wooden piers jutted out into the darkness of the Cooper River and she could hear the mournful hoot of a foghorn off Patriots Point.

Stepping into a small spill of light from an overhead vapor lamp, Theodosia glanced at her watch. *Tidwell is probably . . . what? . . . five or ten minutes behind me?* she wondered. *There's still time to take a peek. See what, if anything, is going on here.*

Theodosia crept forward, trying to stay close to the buildings and remain hidden in the shadows.

Finally she got to the building marked 47-D. Lights were on and she could hear faint conversation.

Corky and Claudia? Must be. Has to be.

Pressing her body against the front of the building, Theodosia crept toward the door. She could still hear a low mumble of voices, but couldn't quite make out actual words.

Theodosia glanced about. The whole area was quiet, virtually deserted, with a little bit of evening fog beginning to roll in. Maybe if she could . . .

Tiptoeing around the side of the building, Theodosia spotted a window. But it was set high above her head. She scanned the ground, searching for something to stand on. A small wooden crate, a few feet away, caught her eye.

Slowly, quietly, Theodosia humped and bumped the wooden crate over so it sat beneath the window. Then, ever so gingerly, she boosted herself up onto it, grasping the window ledge for extra support.

The voices were louder now from this vantage point. In fact, Corky and Claudia sounded like they were arguing.

Pressing her cheek and eye against the window, Theodosia was able to peer into the front office of the Chait's warehouse. She didn't see anyone yet, so she tried to concentrate on what they were saying. After a few moments, she decided they were just talking loudly. Claudia could be heard a little more clearly, so Theodosia figured Claudia must be in the front part of the warehouse and Corky in back.

Maybe if I slid the window up a notch.

Theodosia reached up, grabbed the window frame and pushed. There was a tiny *creak* and the window eased up an inch.

Did anyone hear me? Lord, I hope not.

Theodosia craned her head and ventured another quick peek. Now she could see Claudia sitting at an old wooden desk, studying some sort of log book.

"How do our numbers look?" Corky's voice floated out of the back room.

"Much better than last time," Claudia told him. "Maybe forty percent on the birds."

Forty percent what? wondered Theodosia. *What are they talking about? Profit?*

"But we're still barely going to fill the order," said Claudia.

Shifting her weight, trying to get a better view, Theodosia hoisted herself higher until her elbows rested on the windowsill. But just as she shifted her weight, the weathered boards gave out a low creak.

"What was that?" asked Claudia, instantly alert, jumping up from her chair.

"What?" asked Corky.

"Someone was at the window," cried Claudia.

"Grab the gun!" ordered Corky.

That was all Theodosia need to hear. She jumped down off the crate and hit the ground running.

But where to go?

If she led them back to her Jeep, she would surely put Earl Grey in danger again! And if they somehow shot out her tires, neither of them would get away!

With darkness as her cover, Theodosia ran toward one of the piers and ducked down behind a large wooden crate. She held her breath as footsteps slowly approached.

"Who's there?" yelled Corky. "Come out and show your face!"

Theodosia shrank into the darkness as Corky's footsteps hesitated.

Maybe he doesn't know I'm here, she thought. *Maybe I was just quick enough.*

A loud metallic clatter filled the air, and then an engine roared to life.

What the . . . ?

Without warning, a forklift tractor smashed into the crate Theodosia was hiding behind. Wood shattered and screeched in protest as the crate was shoved back a good two feet and Theodosia had to scramble and backpedal to keep from being crushed.

Backed out onto the wooden pier now, Theodosia raised her head up and ventured a peak.

"You!" shouted Corky. "Get out here!"

Where to go? Where to go? Theodosia wondered. Glancing over her shoulder, she saw only the wooden pier leading to nowhere. *But this is a dead end,* she told herself, even as she continued to slowly back out onto the pier.

Corky gunned the engine and threw the forklift into reverse, pulling its giant metal tines out of the wooden crate. Then he pivoted slowly and headed directly toward Theodosia!

"Corky," pleaded Theodosia, who was now out in the open. She held her hands up in a gesture of surrender. "Can we please *talk* about this?"

"Use the gun!" came Claudia's shrill scream over the roar of the engine. "Shoot her!"

"No, *don't* use the gun," shouted Theodosia as she backed farther out onto the pier.

Now what?

Theodosia eased herself over toward the edge of the pier until the backs of her knees were pressed against a low, metal railing. She knew she could try to face down Corky and Claudia right here, unarmed as she was. Or, Theodosia glanced down at the muddy, oily water of the Cooper River, she could attempt a tricky dive into the black waters below.

What should I do? Neither are great choices.

There was a loud pop and a bullet snicked by Theodosia's head.

He's shooting at me!

It was an easy decision, Theodosia told herself, as she suddenly launched herself over the edge of the pier and plunged down into inky darkness.

Splash!

The river was shockingly cold. And, falling as she did, a good thirty feet, Theodosia slapped the water hard. Down through the murk she tumbled, until she was sure she'd free-fall all the way to the muddy, silty river bottom. But when her descent finally slowed, Theodosia's survival instincts suddenly grabbed hold and she began flutter-kicking hard with her feet, fighting to rise to the surface.

Opening her eyes, still under water, Theodosia saw nothing but inky blackness. She kicked harder, feeling a burning in her lungs as she extended her arms to manage a modified breast stroke as she slowly rose toward the surface.

Kick, stroke, kick, stroke . . . she fell into a frantic pattern. Every muscle felt like jelly now, her legs trembled from the exertion.

Is this what it's like to drown? Theodosia wondered. *Your legs stop pumping, your brain function slows to a crawl?*

And then thankfully, joyfully, she broke the surface of the water. Hungrily, Theodosia gasped in great gulps of air. Her head was reeling, her energy almost sapped. And then she heard a low-pitched *whoop, whoop.*

Don't tell me there's a freighter about to plow into me, thought Theodosia. *Out of the frying pan into the fire.* This was, after all, a busy pier where large ships docked at all hours of the day and night.

Scuttling like mad toward one of the wooden pilings, Theodosia forgot all her swimming know-how, reverted instead to a dog paddle. Then her fingertips touched slippery wood and she grabbed hold for dear life.

The sirens were from the police cruisers and U.S. customs agents' vehicles. One of the agents climbed down a ladder to help pull her out. Tidwell met her on the pier with a cold stare and a warm coat.

"You're shaking," Tidwell pointed out as he slung the coat around her shoulders.

"My adrenaline kicked in big time," Theodosia told him, still breathing heavily.

"Pity your common sense didn't," was his retort.

Theodosia wiped her face on her sleeve. "Where are they?" she demanded.

Tidwell jerked his head toward one of the police cruisers. "Apprehended," he told her. "So don't think you can . . ."

Ignoring his protests, Theodosia strode over to where a subdued Corky and Claudia were being read their rights while another officer secured them with handcuffs.

Theodosia got right in their faces. "You kidnapped my *dog*!" She said shrilly. "You killed poor Duke Wilkes because he was on to you. Then you panicked and murdered Sydney because she was poking around, too, with her investigative journalism show. You're both scum, murdering scum."

Corky immediately turned his back to her.

"Miss Browning!" called Tidwell. "Let the law deal with those two. And I assure you, the law shall be harsh."

"We didn't do anything!" cried Claudia.

"You murdered two people and imprisoned poor defenseless animals," shouted Theodosia. *Plus you wanted your idiot husband to shoot me.*

"It wasn't like that," protested Claudia.

"Shut up," Corky snapped. "Shut up until we talk to a lawyer."

Theodosia turned away from the two of them in disgust, thought for a moment, then turned back. "What was the forty percent?" she asked Claudia.

This time Claudia met her gaze with an insolent stare.

"The forty *percent*," thundered Theodosia. "I want to know!"

Claudia shrugged. "Mortality rate."

Mortality rate, thought Theodosia. *Forty percent of their birds died en route and that was just fine with them. What a couple of weasels.*

Theodosia locked eyes with Claudia. "I want you to know," she said, "that I intend to return those crappy tea towels you sold me."

"You wouldn't believe what they've got records on," said Tidwell. His bullet-shaped head bobbled atop his large body and he was looking more perturbed than usual.

"Try me," said Theodosia, as she stepped tiredly inside Corky and Claudia's warehouse.

"Lions," said Tidwell. He had dozens of papers spread out across the top of Claudia's desk. "They imported a pair of lions. As well as zebras, Russian wild boar, and something called an Axis Buck." He blew out a sigh. "To say nothing of the tiger and the rest of the poor creatures you found."

"Who were they selling them to?" asked Theodosia.

"Unsavory bird dealers," said Tidwell. "Lunatics who think it would be fun to own an exotic animal. Game preserves that offer canned hunts." Tidwell spat out his words with disdain.

"There's not much sport in shooting a lion or tiger that's enclosed on a few acres," said Theodosia bitterly.

"Not hardly," said Tidwell. He cleared his throat. "You should see the poor birds in the back room," he told her.

Theodosia made a motion to go back there.

"No, don't," said Tidwell, holding up a hand. "They came in wrapped like Egyptian mummies, just their heads sticking out. Then they were wrapped again in bundles of cloth."

"That was the percentage Claudia was taking about," said Theodosia. "Less than half of them lived."

"Yes," said Tidwell. "They were the lucky ones. I suppose."

"What about when they bring in big cats?" asked Theodosia.

"From what I understand, conditions are equally horrible," said Tidwell. "The cats are crated up, shipped over on freighters under the guise of some sort of legitimate cargo. They're down in a ship's hold for a week or so. Not much air, water supply running out . . . well, you get the picture."

"Can't this illegal importation be stopped?" asked Theodosia.

"It's difficult," replied Tidwell. "Every year close to fifteen million tons of cargo flow through this area alone. And to be honest, you could probably bring small cubs in on a commercial airliner. You walk in with a cat carrier and security would only take a quick peek."

Theodosia slipped by Tidwell into the back of the warehouse where two Customs Service officers were tending to the birds. What she found was not a pretty sight.

"So many dead ones," murmured Theodosia. She brushed away tears, found that new ones formed just as fast.

"The birds that manage to survive," said Tidwell, guiding her out, "we'll try to find homes for them in area zoos. Otherwise they'll have to be destroyed."

"And the animals I found out at Corky and Claudia's farm?" asked Theodosia.

"Same thing," said Tidwell. "Quarantine for six weeks if there's the possibility of a zoo taking them. That's providing space is even available."

Theodosia pulled the soggy shipping tag from her pocket. "According to this shipping tag, the birds at the Chait farm had already been there six weeks," she said. "So technically they've already been through a sort of quarantine."

Tidwell stared at her for a long thirty seconds. "I know what you're thinking," he said. "And it's highly illegal."

"I know where to take them," said Theodosia. "I know a place where they'd have a truly safe home." She swallowed hard. "Instead of being destroyed."

"Miss Browning . . ." said Tidwell, a cautionary note rising in his voice. "Best case scenario would be a zoo."

A zoo, thought Theodosia. *Though zoos have changed considerably over the years, there is still one constant. Cages. And I'm not a big fan of cages.*

"Please," said Theodosia.

Tidwell saw the longing in her face. "You're sure about this?" he asked. "The feds don't look kindly on this sort of thing."

Theodosia nodded, still fighting back tears. "The only way I'm going to get caught is if someone turns me in."

Tidwell stared at Theodosia as she stood there. Wet hair, wet clothes, oversized coat. He thought about how her dog had been kidnapped, she'd been shot at, and forced to make a perilous dive into the river.

"Move fast," Tidwell mumbled in a low tone. "Personnel from the Department of Agriculture will be heading out to the Chait's Edisto Island farm fairly soon to deal with the tiger and horned deer."

27

❧

"*My goodness, it's* early," said Drayton as he slid into the passenger seat of Theodosia's Jeep. "And you're being so secretive, too. I thought that after all your good work this murder mystery was tidily wrapped up, with Corky and Claudia apprehended and cooling their heels in jail." Drayton rubbed at his eyes tiredly.

"It is," said Theodosia. "And Earl Grey is safely and happily snoozing away on my bed."

"On top of the covers?" asked Drayton.

"Of course," replied Theodosia. "Now take a look behind you."

Drayton squirmed around in his seat. "What on earth?" he exclaimed. "Birds?"

"Aren't they gorgeous?" asked Theodosia, a broad grin lighting her face. Even though she was tired, exhausted really, she could barely control her excitement.

"Yes . . . spectacular," agreed Drayton. "The question is, what are you going to *do* with all your feathered passengers?"

"That, my dear Drayton, remains to be seen," chuckled Theodosia. She put the Jeep in gear and slowly pulled away from the curb. "Were you able to reach all the volunteers last night? Including Haley? Especially Haley."

"I did indeed," said Drayton. "And I'm happy to report they were delirious with joy upon hearing that Earl Grey had been safely recovered."

"Did you give them any details?" asked Theodosia.

"You asked me not to," said Drayton.

"You're a true friend, Drayton. A true friend."

The sun glinted pink on the horizon, the early morning sky was optimistic with streaks of blue and gold. Light clouds, like spun silk, would be just a memory by noon.

They'd been driving for approximately forty minutes and were out in the country now. Live oaks, dogwoods, hedges of azaleas closed in around the road in a comforting way. Theodosia slowed the Jeep to cross a rickety wooden bridge, caught a quick glimpse of the meandering stream below. Off in the distance was a vine-covered hump, probably a remnant of an old rice dike.

"This is the way to . . ." began Drayton.

"That's right," said Theodosia, smiling.

"So you're going to . . . ?"

"You'll see."

As they pulled into the driveway at Cane Ridge Plantation, Libby Revelle was sitting on the porch that stretched around her fanciful Gothic Revival cottage, waiting for them. Upon seeing Theodosia's Jeep roll in, Libby jumped to her feet and grabbed a silver tray that held a steaming pot of tea and three bone china teacups. Then she hurried down to greet them.

"How civilized," said Drayton. "And how very pleasant to see you, Miss Libby," he said, giving her a chaste peck on the cheek, then taking the tray and setting it on a large tree stump.

"So you're really going to do it," Libby said to Theodosia, once the greetings were said and the tea poured.

Theodosia put a hand on her aunt's thin shoulder. "If you'll have them."

Libby gave a casual wave. "Oh, I've always got room for a few more. In fact, I don't think the warblers and kites and painted buntings will mind one bit."

Working together, Theodosia and Drayton unloaded all the cages from the Jeep. When they finished, Drayton stood with a faint smile on his face.

"Well, it certainly seems like a perfect climate," he said. Indeed, the day was warming up beautifully.

"So you think they'll survive?" asked Theodosia. She stared down the hill toward the pond and off into the piney forests. Here were large tracts of privately owned wetlands and timberland as well as enormous plantations.

"They might even thrive," said Drayton. "This area is, after all, subtropical. If it can support a nearby tea plantation, it can probably support these birds as well. Plus there are plenty of inkberry and possumhaw bushes to feed on out here."

"Lots of food. And space," said Aunt Libby. "These creatures just need space. And a little care, as well."

Theodosia knew it was illegal to release birds such as these on public lands, but privately owned land . . . well, that was another story. She knew that exotic game farms existed all over the country, some licensed, some not. And scads of people had peacocks and other exotic birds strutting about their property. So . . . how was this any different?

"How many acres does your Aunt Libby have?" asked Drayton.

A look of satisfaction came across Theodosia's face as she opened the first cage and released a large Toucan. "Hundreds."

She pulled open a second cage and let a pair of scarlet macaws take flight. They circled around the pond, the red of their feathers jewel-like against golden leaves and the azure blue of the pond.

"Oh, my goodness," exclaimed Drayton. "Those creatures look like they actually *understand* what's going on. Like they know they just got the most wonderful reprieve."

"They know," said Libby. "And they are deliriously happy." Her eyes took on a satisfied, faraway look as she watched a bright blue Hyacinth Macaw flutter into a nearby tupelo tree, his long plumed feathers elegantly flowing behind.

Theodosia and Drayton continued opening cage doors and shooing out birds until, finally, all cages had been emptied, their feathered prisoners released into the green pine forests, rolling hills, and swampland that made up this southern region of South Carolina's low-country.

"God bless you," said Libby, kissing Theodosia on the cheek. "There's a special spot in heaven for people like you." Libby pulled her shawl around her slight shoulders, picked up a silver pail filled with cracklins, and headed down toward the pond. There, her local residents, wood ducks, herons, skimmers, and terns, fluttered eagerly about, awaiting their morning feeding.

Drayton gazed down at the dozen or so cages that were upended and scattered about on the ground. He kicked at one with his toe. "Lots of empty cages," he remarked.

Lifting her eyes, Theodosia smiled serenely. "But look how full the sky is."

Killer Blood Orange Scones

2 cups all purpose flour, sifted

½ cup sugar

1 Tbsp baking powder

1 tsp salt

¾ cup unsalted butter, chopped into pieces

2 eggs, beaten

½ cup whipping cream

2 Tbsp melted butter

1 Tbsp orange zest (blood orange or regular orange)

STIR together flour, sugar, baking powder, and salt. Cut pieces of butter into dry mixture until it is coarsely mixed.

In a separate bowl, combine beaten eggs and cream, then add to flour mixture. Blend together gently. Place batter on lightly floured surface and knead for one minute. Roll dough into a rectangle, about four by eight inches. Brush dough with melted butter and sprinkle on orange zest and a little additional sugar. Gently roll dough up so you have an eight-inch roll. Seal the seam by pressing and pinching with your fingers. Now cut your roll into eight one-inch slices. Lay slices on lightly greased baking sheet and bake in a 425 degree oven for 12 to 15 minutes.

Indigo Tea Shop Cucumber Soup

3 medium cucumbers
1 cup plain yogurt
1 loosely packed cup of fresh mint leaves
½ tsp salt
⅛ tsp black pepper
½ cup half-and-half
2 large ice cubes
sour cream for garnish
thin cucumber slices for garnish

PEEL, seed, and chop cucumbers, then put in food processor and puree. Add yogurt and mint leaves and cream together. Add salt, pepper, half-and-half, and ice cubes and mix well. Chill. When ready to serve, pour into small cups and garnish with a dollop of sour cream and thin slice of cucumber. Yields enough soup for four first-course servings.

Pineapple Cream Cheese Tea Sandwiches

ADD ¼ cup of milk (or cream) to a small package of softened cream cheese. Mix in 1 cup of finely chopped pineapple and spread the mixture on nut bread or Boston brown bread. Serve open-faced.

Apple-Raisin Soup

> 2 cups apple juice
> 2 large cooking apples, peeled and cubed
> ¼ cup raisins
> 2 sticks of cinnamon
> 2 Tbsp brown sugar
> 1 Tbsp brandy (optional)

COMBINE apple juice, cubed apples, raisins, and cinnamon in a large saucepan. Cover and simmer 15 to 20 minutes, until the apples are tender. Stir in brown sugar and brandy and simmer until sugar is dissolved. Remove cinnamon sticks before serving hot. Note: After cooking, you can puree this in a blender if you'd like a smoother consistency.

Haley's Almond Scones

    3 cups flour
    2½ tsp baking powder
    ½ cup sugar
    ½ tsp salt
    ½ cup butter
    1 Tbsp almond extract
    ½ cup half-and-half
    ¼ cup sliced almonds

MIX all dry ingredients, then cut in butter until coarse. Add almond extract, then mix in half-and-half. Form mixture into a round shape on floured surface and roll out to a thickness of about one-and-half inches. Use cutter to make eight to ten scones. Place on baking sheet, brush with milk, then sprinkle with sugar and top with sliced almonds. Bake for about 25 minutes at 350 degrees or until golden in color.

Charleston Cream Cheese Cookies

    ½ cup butter, softened
    3 oz. cream cheese, softened
    2 cups sugar
    2 eggs
    1 tsp vanilla extract
    ½ tsp lemon extract
    4 cups flour

1 tsp baking powder
½ tsp salt
½ cup marmalade or apricot preserves
¼ cup powdered sugar

CREAM butter, cream cheese, and sugar until light and fluffy. Add eggs, one at a time, and beat well. Stir in vanilla and lemon. Sift together flour, baking powder, and salt, then add to cream cheese mixture. Roll dough into a log, sixteen to eighteen inches long. Place on aluminum foil, roll up, and seal. Chill for three hours. Slice dough into ⅜-inch rounds and place on baking sheet. Spoon ½-tsp. jam into center of each cookie. Bake 8 to 10 minutes at 350 degrees. Remove from baking sheet to rack and dust with powdered sugar.

Drayton's Favorite White Fudge

2¼ cups sugar
2 tsp butter
½ cup sour cream
¼ cup milk
¼ tsp salt
1 tsp light corn syrup
2 tsp vanilla
1 cup chopped walnuts or pecans

COMBINE sugar, butter, sour cream, milk, salt, and corn syrup in a saucepan. Cook over medium to high heat until mixture boils. Remove from heat and let mixture set for about an hour. Add vanilla and beat until candy becomes non-glossy and begins to hold its shape. Add chopped nuts and pour into a well-greased, square pan. Allow to cool.

Chocolate Leaves

GATHER up some small, interesting leaves from your yard, then gently wash and dry them. Melt some of your favorite chocolate (like Hershey's or Ghirardelli) in a double boiler. Carefully brush chocolate onto back side of leaves with a craft paintbrush, then place on flat surface. Once chocolate has hardened, gently peel leaf away.

Sweet Potato Muffins

1 cup butter
1 cup sugar
6 eggs
1 tsp vanilla
2 cups buttermilk
1½ cups flour
2 Tbsp baking powder
1 lb. sweet potatoes (peeled, cooked, and mashed - or use canned)

BLEND butter and sugar together. Add eggs, vanilla, buttermilk, flour, baking powder, and sweet potatoes. Mix thoroughly. Pour the batter into greased muffin tins (about two-third full) and bake at 350 degrees for 20 to 30 minutes.

Low-country Black Bean Soup

2 cups dried black beans
4 Tbsp olive oil
1 cup onion, chopped
1 cup green pepper, chopped
1 cup carrots, chopped
Celery, 3 or 4 stalks, diced
¼ lb. diced ham
2 qts. chicken broth
Salt and pepper
½ cup dry sherry
Lime, sliced

COVER beans with water and let soak overnight. Then rinse, drain, and set aside. Heat oil in large soup pot, then add onion, green pepper, carrots, and celery. Simmer until golden brown, then add diced ham. Add beans and chicken broth, season with salt and pepper. Cover pot and bring to a boil, then reduce heat and simmer for 2 to 2½ hours. Add sherry and a little water (if needed). Heat. Serve garnished with a slice of lime. (You can also top with a small mound of sour cream).

Angel Biscuits

5 cups flour
½ cup oil
1 tsp baking soda
1 tsp salt
2 tsp baking powder
¼ cup sugar
1 pkg. dry yeast
½ cup warm water
1¾ cups buttermilk

SIFT flour, baking soda, salt, baking powder, and sugar into a large bowl. Add oil and stir to a coarse consistency. Dissolve yeast in warm water and stir in. Add buttermilk and mix well. Roll on floured surface to ½-inch thickness and cut into square using sharp knife. Place biscuits on greased baking sheet and bake at 400 degrees for about twelve minutes or until lightly browned.

Southern Cuppa Cuppa Cake

1 cup self rising flour
1 cup sugar
1 cup fruit cocktail with syrup
1 tsp baking powder
2 Tbsp melted butter
Pinch of salt

MIX all ingredients together by hand in an eight-inch square baking pan. Bake at 350 degrees for 40 to 50 minutes or until brown and bubbly. Serve with vanilla ice cream.

TEA TIME TIPS

from Laura Childs

Asian Delight Tea

Celebrate Chinese New Year, spring cherry blossom time, or the August moon with an Asian Delight Tea. Buy inexpensive paper umbrellas for decor as well as tiny Japanese or Chinese teacups from an Asian market. Serve egg rolls, spring rolls, steamed dumplings, tea marbled eggs, or even teriyaki chicken breasts. Chinese peonies or Asian lilies would make an elegant centerpiece and there are literally hundreds of teas for you to choose from.

Book Club Tea

Use bookmark-style invitations to invite your friends in for tea and a book discussion—or even a book exchange. Set the stage by piling stacks of books down the center of your table and top them with candlesticks or small floral bouquets. Make place cards with visuals of your favorite authors. Serve tea sandwiches, nut bread with cream cheese, and chocolate truffles. Individual slices of cake can be decorated to look like books. Sip Dragonwell (also known as Dragon's Well), the tea of Chinese scholars. Favors for your guests might include book review magazines rolled up and tied with ribbon.

Tea Party at the Office

Who says you can't have a tea party at the office? Celebrate a coworker's birthday, a special event, or just kick back and have a relaxing tea party in the conference room or cafeteria. Portability is the key here. Prepare chicken salad sandwiches, cucumber sandwiches, and tiny roast beef with pimento sandwiches in the morning. Then wrap them tightly in cellophane and don't slice into quarters or fingers until you're ready to lay them out on small plates or trays. Cookies or biscotti from a nearby bakery will make a perfect dessert. And don't worry if you have to rely on tea bags!

Pearl Tea

Invite your guests to wear their pearl jewelry! Then decorate your tea table with garlands of pearl strands from a craft shop and your favorite gleaming, pearlized china. Inexpensive stretchy pearl bracelets make great napkin rings and can go home on your guests' wrists. Serve cream cheese and cucumber sandwiches, but use a small, round cookie cutter to cut them into rounds.

White chocolate truffles and Russian tea cakes all evoke the color and shape of pearls and larger cakes can be decorated with shiny pearlized candies. Serve gunpowder tea, which is shaped in tiny pellets like pearls!

Cupcake Tea

Cupcakes are all the rage these days, so why not have a cupcake tea? Buy them from your favorite bakery or make your own miniatures so guests can sample several different flavors. Serve them stacked on three-tiered trays for maximum effect! Assam and English Breakfast are two teas that go well with sweets.

Tea Tasting Tea

This is a fun way to experience and learn about new teas. Brew three or four different pots of teas, then conduct your tea much like a wine tasting. Serve scones, nut breads, and small tea sandwiches such as chutney and cream cheese and hot crab fingers. Desserts might include spice cake or chocolate dipped strawberries. Serve three or four different Chinese teas—or mix it up and serve teas from China, Japan, Ceylon, and India.

Lemon Tea

Celebrate the cheery lemon with a bowl of lemons as your centerpiece or a showy bouquet of yellow roses. Use yellow-colored place mats, tea ware, and napkins. Start with lemon scones, then move on to tiny shrimp salad sandwiches garnished with thin slices of lemon. Desserts could include lemon bars, lemon tarts, lemon sorbet, or lemon meringue pie. There are plenty of lovely teas infused with hints of lemon as well as lemon verbena herbal teas. For tea-totalers, serve lemonade!

Peter Rabbit Tea

Treat your children and their friends to a Peter Rabbit Tea. Make large color copies of Peter Rabbit and his friends, mount them on cardboard, then cut out and use for table decor. Serve finger sandwiches of turkey and Swiss cheese, sliced strawberries and cream cheese, and peanut butter and jelly. Serve apple juice or lemonade in a teapot. Serve carrot cake or a sheet cake artfully carved into the shape of a teapot. Pin the tail on the bunny, anyone?

DEATH SWATCH

A Scrapbooking Mystery
Scrapbooking Tips and Recipes Included!

by

Laura Childs

New Orleans knows how to party,
and Mardi Gras is living proof—until
someone throws murder into the mix, leaving
scrapbook shop owner Carmela Bertrand
fearing for her own life…

penguin.com